CHASING THE AMERICAN DREAM

www.mascotbooks.com

Chasing the American Dream

©2020 Lorelei Brush. All Rights Reserved. No part of this publication may be reproduced, stored in a retrieval system or transmitted in any form by any means electronic, mechanical, or photocopying, recording or otherwise without the permission of the author.

For more information, please contact:
Mascot Books
620 Herndon Parkway, Suite 320
Herndon, VA 20170
info@mascotbooks.com

Library of Congress Control Number: 2020909879

CPSIA Code: PRFRE01020A
ISBN-13: 978-1-64543-498-6

Printed in Canada

In memory of my father, Edwin Franklyn Brush,
an OSS officer who craved risk and was assigned
the microfilming of documents.

CHASING THE AMERICAN
DREAM

A NOVEL BY
LORELEI BRUSH

PROLOGUE

MARCH 1945

"What is that stench?" Jim Atkins asked, wrinkling up his nose.

Mac McKenzie cleared his throat and glanced over at Jim from the driver's seat. From Jim's face, Mac's eyes drifted up to meet David's. "Dead bodies, son."

Now, Atkins was a good photographer. David had read his paperwork. The kid had learned from his father and worked in the family's studio all through high school. But naïve, he still believed people were basically good, that you should always obey the law—all baby-blue eyes and eager curiosity.

David thanked God for Mac, technical sergeant extraordinaire. Steady as a rock, six feet tall, and solid muscle. Could fix any engine and often had to scavenge or jerry-rig parts for their aging equipment truck. He watched over Jim like a dad.

The truck's windshield wipers scraped the glass. David pulled his pistol from his pack and touched his lower leg to make sure his knife was in its sheath. It was just possible a German regiment would meet them around the bend, rifles ready. He kept his eyes moving, watching the curve of the road ahead and scanning the sides of the hill. Nothing out of the ordinary that he could see, nothing poking up from the ground or down from above.

Their truck was third in the line of vehicles, behind a Jeep and a canvas-topped personnel carrier. Those guys ahead must be wet and freezing by now in addition to being scared. At least his truck cab got some heat from its own engine and had windows that closed. Its metal sides would do a lot better than the leading vehicles at deflecting bullets.

To the right and left were plowed fields, the crops having been harvested months ago and it being too early in the year to plant. The truck crawled up the incline, Mac downshifting, and stopped just before the road turned. The men in the forward vehicles unloaded and fanned out, rifles at the ready. As they squatted into place, several of them tied handkerchiefs over their noses and mouths. David climbed out, consciously breathing through parted lips, tucked his pistol in his waistband and went up to see why they'd stopped. In theory, the unit was under the command of a first lieutenant in the Army Group, but David Svehla, a captain in the Office of Strategic Services, held a higher rank and was prepared to take control.

David sidled up to the lieutenant, Edwin Tippet, who had his binoculars raking a seemingly empty compound. Big area surrounded by high wire fencing, electrified. Had a sort of parade ground near the entrance and rows of one-story wooden barracks. At the corners of the fencing and next to the gate were guard posts, now empty, and the front gates hung open. An ambush? Or had the guards fled?

Tippet let the binoculars fall to his chest. He signaled for two squads, now out of their trucks, to move in. "Don't shoot, if you can help it. Flush out whoever's in there. Bring 'em into this empty space."

The squads moved inside the gates—one to the row of wooden barracks on the left, one to the right. Tippet's binoculars went to his eyes again, and he settled on a single-story brick building up a hill. "What the hell is that?"

David squinted. "Separated from the other buildings. Lots of stuff stacked around it. Probably not headquarters."

"No movement there either."

David tapped Tippet's shoulder. "White flag at eleven o'clock." He pointed to a group of five skeletal specters staggering toward them, holding each other up. The one front and center brandished a stick with a rag attached and fluttering in the driving rain. He glanced at Tippet's horrified expression and said, "It's one of those camps. I'm goin' up there; see what we can do." David tasted acid and swallowed hard. Those poor bastards.

The Lieutenant threw out his arm to block David's path. "Could be a trap. Wait for the men to check it out."

Mac and Jim joined them, Jim with his nose stuck in his elbow and his voice wobbling. "Look at their clothes. They're in pajamas. They convicts?"

Mac jerked his chin toward the group. "I heard about these places. Not sure I want to go in, though."

David nodded and took a closer look at Jim. His face was white, like he was about to lose his lunch. David laid a hand on the boy's shoulder to steady him. "Get your camera, Jim; mine, too. And, no, they're not convicts—at least not the sort we're used to."

David watched the slow procession make its way across the muddy ground. Each step looked like it might be their last. How did they have enough strength to walk? He closed his gaping mouth, worried it would appear insulting to these staggering men, or at least make him look stupid.

Every few minutes, one of the regular Army guys called out, "Building's clear," and the squad moved on to the next.

The oncoming procession of stick men stalled as one of them sank to his knees, and the others hoisted him back up. They were all shivering as though made of skin-colored jello. Their black-and-white striped uniforms stuck to their emaciated frames, their eyes had receded into dark hollows, and only wisps of hair stuck out from under their caps.

Jim pulled on David's arm and handed over his camera. The kid was still breathing sketchily, using his free hand to cover his mouth and nose. "What's wrong with them, Captain? What are we doing here? I'm supposed to microfilm documents. I'm no medic."

David lifted the camera's strap over his head, determined not to show his uneasiness to this youngster. "We'll get this story, Jim, and it's not going to be pretty."

"That's for sure. Here, extra film. Do . . . do I have to go in there? I'll . . . I'll puke."

David stuffed the handful of film into his jacket pocket, checked the number of pictures left in the camera—ten—and let it fall against his chest. He was in charge of this team. They would do their duty, above and beyond, if that was called for. "Jim, you're going to show the Army brass what this place is like. Show them what these people have paid for Germany's rockets. And you're going to be strong. Got it?"

He turned back to scan the compound. Maybe ordering Jim to stand up and take it would work for both of them. It wasn't that David was afraid of what he'd see. No, he was appalled at the cruelty perpetrated in these camps. OSS had sent a memo to its officers about them, but it hadn't occurred to him he'd see one. What smacked him in the face was his total lack of preparedness to deal with such a travesty. Like Jim, he was no doctor. And taking snaps wouldn't touch the weakness and pain these scrawny men must be experiencing.

Jim swallowed several times.

The head of the procession planted his white flag maybe fifty yards from Tippet and David. The other walking corpses stood behind it, swaying slightly, as though they understood waiting and planned to hold their position as long as was needed. Unfurling himself to his full height, the procession's leader spoke, "Guten Morgan, meine Herren."

It was an educated voice, a pure Hochdeutsch that sent a shiver through David. He took a deep breath, gearing himself up to enter the compound. With a nod from the lieutenant, he called out in his less-educated soldier's German. "What is this place?" Silently, he thanked his OSS trainers for insisting they all speak only German for the months before he was sent abroad. His German might not be pretty or fluent, but he'd find out what was needed.

"This is Dora," the man replied in German, "the labor camp for the V-2 rocket facility. We are the labor that is left. The S.S. and the able-bodied prisoners marched off several days ago, leaving the sick and the dead, as I am sure your searchers will tell you. Have you food? Medicine? We have typhus and diphtheria and who knows what else. We need help."

The poor man shook, and it seemed at any moment that he could fall. Only determination must have kept him erect.

David turned to the lieutenant and translated. As he waited for the orders to move in, he ran his teeth over his lower lip.

Mac whispered in his ear. "'Scuse me, Cap'n, but we passed a small woods not too far back. How about—"

The lieutenant turned, though Mac had been addressing David, and answered. "Yes, yes, take a squad, Sergeant. Collect whatever dead wood you can find. We'll need fires. And get the medic up here. On the double."

Mac saluted. "Yes, sir. Right away."

Tippet's walkie-talkie squawked. "Yes, Corporal. Over."

David could just make out the squad leader, walkie-talkie to his ear, calling from the edge of the last barracks. "All barracks clear, sir. Guards have gone. The hospital's back here—if you dare call these pathetic filthy shacks a hospital."

Tippet thrust his lips out and in as he processed the words. "Medic's on his way. Is there a doctor?"

"A very sick one, sir."

"Right. Can we use a barracks for our men?"

"Negative, sir. The mattresses are crawling with vermin, and the smell is, well, pretty damn awful. Most of the men have lost their cookies."

"Okay, Corporal. You got some German?"

"No, sir. But the doc speaks some English."

"Good. Tell him help is coming and report back here. Over and out."

David liked Tippet's quick assessment of the situation and trusted him to get his men organized. "Permission to approach our welcoming committee, Lieutenant?"

Tippet eyed David, doing his own assessment. "Yes, take a couple of my men and find out as much as you can about the situation—what's on their minds, if all the guards are gone, you know. I'll get camp set up in the field across the road, see what we've got that can help."

David sent Jim off on a photographic mission. He'd figure out the best images to capture, if he didn't get too sick. Then David pointed at two of Tippet's soldiers to join him and headed for the white flag. The smell of sick and unwashed bodies made David rub his nose, but seeing the leader flinch, he put his arm down. "May I introduce myself? Captain David Svehla,

United States Army." They didn't need to know about the OSS connection. "Who might you be?"

The leader lifted one edge of his lips into a strained smile. "I am the shadow of Herbert Landau, violinist emeritus of the Berlin Philharmonic and now specializing in keeping inventories of rocket parts." He put out his hand, and David gently shook it, afraid that the sticks of bone would crack if he squeezed.

"Please, we need food, medicine . . ." The man's voice dwindled to silence.

"We'll do all we can. That's a promise. But—you sure all the guards have gone?" David looked around, suddenly feeling vulnerable.

Landau waved a dismissive hand. "Three days ago, they marched off. They heard you were coming."

One of the men behind Landau slipped to his knees, his yellowed face a mass of pained wrinkles. A soldier caught him, laid him shivering on the ground, and covered him with his thick U.S. Army jacket.

"Food, please," the prostrate man said. His pleading voice was a mere feather in the wind.

David pulled a candy bar from his pocket, one of those that came with their emergency D-rations, and stared at it. The bar was supposed to have enough nutrients to keep a soldier going for hours. But he had no idea how it would affect a starving man. Still, it was all he had, and he couldn't hold on to it in the face of such need. "Eat it slowly, okay?" He put it into the outstretched hand.

The man struggled to sit up, ripped off the foil cover, and took an eager bite. As he chewed, pain crossed his face—and then a broad smile. "Chocolate." It was an exhale of wonder, the sound of a happy remembrance.

David was surprised. GIs only ate these bars out of necessity, as they were tough enough to crack your teeth, crammed with oat flour, and the chocolate taste was barely strong enough to come through all that pastiness.

The prisoner took a second bite, and David watched him fight to bring his jaws together. His teeth seemed to slip off the chunk, refusing to mash it down. Then he looked greedily at the remainder of the bar and tried to swallow the mass he had in his mouth. He choked, tried to cough, and stuck a finger in his mouth.

David slid down to his knees, forced the man's jaw open, and searched for purchase on the slippery candy bar. It was jammed in the guy's throat. He turned him over and hit his back between the shoulder blades, desperate to get the food unstuck. At the same time, he worried he'd break the man's back with the force of his blows.

The body lost its tension, withering in David's arms.

One of Tippet's soldiers who had watched the whole thing squatted down and held his hand over the man's mouth. "No breath, Captain." Then he pressed the side of his neck. "Can't find a pulse either, sir. Sorry."

"Medic, medic!" David yelled. His hands were shaking, and he broke out in a cold sweat.

A young GI stepped out of the hospital door, a ratty towel in his hands already stained with blood or something dark.

David waved him over, still cradling the limp prisoner.

It took only a minute for the medic to verify that the chocolate eater was dead. He pointed to the remains of the candy bar. "Don't give 'em that stuff, sir. Their bodies can't take it." He dropped the corpse's wrist and stood. "Excuse me, sir, I got a lot of patients back there." He gestured toward the hospital.

David stared at the man he'd just killed and threw up. Here he was, trying to do something good, save a life, and he'd taken it instead. What kind of a hero was he turning out to be?

Landau leaned on his staff and closed his eyes for a moment. "We called him Samson, but his real name was Isaac, Isaac Chornyei. He had thick, black hair once and blew a powerful trumpet."

David laid Isaac's body out on the ground, gently straightening out the jacket that still covered his chest. He pushed some frizzled hair off the dead man's face. "I'm sorry, so sorry."

Landau sighed. "Have you, perhaps, more gentle food?"

After the chocolate incident, David retreated from Dora's welcoming committee, chastened, and reported to Lieutenant Tippet. The young man ran an annoyed hand over his hair on hearing of Isaac's death and admonished David to hold on to his rations. Then he released David to search out the targets he'd been assigned to find.

At the camp gate, David shook off a vision of the dead Isaac and scanned the countryside. He couldn't face following his orders: to interview the scientists working on rockets and confiscate their papers. No, he needed to do something to help these invalids, something to try to make up for killing that poor sod. So, he turned around and traipsed across the parade ground to see the place for himself. If anyone asked, he was looking for Mac and Jim.

He stuck his head in one of the barracks and jerked back into the rain. It took several gulps of air and a number of swallows to keep from throwing up. The place stank of unwashed bodies and excrement, and he could see the mattresses rising slightly and drifting downward as the armies of bugs conducted their maneuvers. The sight made him scratch his stomach at what he hoped was an imaginary insect bite.

The hospital was no better: each ward had three rows of three-tiered bunk beds close together. There were three or four patients per bed, maybe thirty to a room. Once again, his innards tossed and turned at the stench of the unwashed bodies and the filth of their surroundings. Some of the men shared beds with corpses. It'd take squads of soldiers to clean the place and remove the dead, dig pits, and bury the bodies. And he knew most of the men in those rags had contagious diseases. Still, someone had to sort out food, clothing, and blankets. Bloody laundry lay crushed into corners, and the walls were spotted with dark stains. How were they going to manage the medical care? The medications?

Mac was in the diphtheria ward, bent over a stove, trying to get a fire started with wet, smoking wood.

David picked his way over, avoiding the worst of the filthy floor. "That going to work?"

Mac fanned the small flame. "Got to. These poor lads are shivering, and it ain't just their fevers." When he glanced up at David and paused at the shaking hands, he cleared his throat. "What's going on? You look awful."

"Yeah, I feel awful. I tried to help one of these men, gave him a D-ration, and he choked on it. God, Mac, I killed the man with chocolate."

"Jesus, Mary, and Joseph. You okay?"

Mac stared up at David, sympathy in his eyes. Then he threw more kindling into the stove. "This stuff's too damn wet. Hell, Cap'n, those barracks are useless for sleeping. Could we get clearance to burn the bunk beds? We'll never use them, and the dry wood would keep these poor guys warm."

"Good idea." Nice of Mac to change the subject, send him in a positive direction.

With the Lieutenant's permission, David took a team of four to rip apart a row of tall bunk beds, smash the boards against the floor to push out the nails, and carry the stacks of wood into the hospital. Satisfied he'd done some good, he located Mac and Jim in the kitchen. "Let's get ourselves an armed escort and head over to this production facility, see what we can find."

With three Army guards, David led his team along the zigzags of a well-worn trail from the camp to a pair of parallel railroad tracks that led into a tunnel at the base of Kohnstein Mountain. They could see a second tunnel about a hundred yards away. Large blocks of concrete and a lot of camouflage netting blocked their tunnel's entrance, and a pillbox stood at the side to house guards. Next to the opening, out of the way of the tracks, was a pile of enormous silver half-pipes—the skins of the rockets. "Pay dirt, gentlemen." Excitement pumped through his body.

When they were about a hundred feet from the tunnel, David dispatched two of their Army guards to check the pillbox and make sure no booby traps would greet them as they entered the tunnel. While the third guard stood watch over David's team, Jim nervously glanced around as though expecting a bogeyman to jump from behind a tree or boulder.

David clapped a hand on his shoulder, covering his own nervousness with bravado. "HQ told us that the German military's gone."

"Yeah. But I'd feel a lot better if we weren't so exposed." He held his camera with both hands as if it were a safety shield.

David smiled and swatted him twice on the back. "Kid, we're about to learn more about rocket science than anyone in the U.S. knows. This is the big time. Swallow that fear and move your feet forward."

Mac stood, hands on his hips, and stared at the rocket shells. "They must be fifty to sixty feet long. Like the fuselage of a huge plane."

One of the advance guards waved them forward and indicated they were going through the barricade. Jim and David snapped several pictures of the silver rocket skins, and David walked to the shadow of the tunnel's entrance to change rolls of film. Tentatively, he raised the edge of the camouflage. "Hear that? Sounds like good news. They've left the exhaust fans on."

Mac held up the netting for Jim to go through. "Jeez, the lights are blazing and it's warm in here. You want me to take point?"

"Yeah, go ahead. Jim and I'll do some early documenting of this place. We'll keep Private—Bennett, isn't it?—with us."

The private nodded.

Looking up, David could see the marks of pickaxes and the blasts of dynamite that chipped away at the gypsum and anhydrite to create this twenty-foot-high tunnel. V-2 rocket parts lined the walls, and right down the middle, on the tracks, were two boxcars. To get by, David had to suck in his stomach and search for empty space with his foot. He stopped about halfway down the boxcar to snap a picture of the sign on its side: "Achtung Sprengstoff," beware of explosives. A few feet later, he got another nose full of death and stepped around a man slumped against the wall, quite dead, looking like a tossed-out sack of garbage in striped cloth. David swallowed hard. "Look at that. Damn Germans. That man deserves to be buried."

Beyond the boxcars were a series of flatcars holding fully assembled rockets. He whistled. "Check those out."

Jim's jaw dropped, and he started snapping pictures from below, from atop a ladder, from the front, and the rear of the rockets.

David heard footsteps approaching and pulled Jim behind a tail assembly standing against the wall. They lowered themselves so they couldn't be seen above the fins. David stuck a finger to his lips and peeked through the indentation on the fin's side. Bennett lowered himself behind a second fin, rifle at the ready.

U.S. Army pants came into view under the rocket's cone. It was Mac. "McKenzie reporting in, Cap'n."

David popped up. "Jeez, you asshole. You gave us a scare."

Mac grinned, clearly unrepentant. "Sorry, Cap'n. The place is huge. The tunnel we're in is S-shaped, must go on for about a mile. There are maybe forty side tunnels, probably connecting to that other main tunnel we saw. Looks like they use those alleys for assembling subparts, testing—that sort of thing. We could be here for days."

"And people?"

"None so far. I caught up with the other guards. They're gonna keep going to the end of this tunnel and check out as many of the cross-tunnels as they can. You know, it's like a school bell rang for vacation, and the kids and teachers took off."

"I suppose we ought to thank them for leaving the place intact. Except, I'm not in the mood to thank them for anything, the bastards." David stopped for a moment, focusing on the vastness of this job. Lots of material to photograph. And all the documentation to find and film. But where were the scientists? "Jim, you stay with Private Bennett and continue taking pictures. Mac, let's short-circuit this search and get the prisoners to tell us where the scientists are likely to be, where they keep the paperwork, you know."

It was late afternoon by the time David sought out Landau, who was slumped on a bunk sipping watered-down powdered milk. David asked, in German, "Does that go down all right?"

Landau smiled, showing a blackened front tooth. "Captain, nice of you to inquire. And the answer is that it stays down, which is just what I want."

David considered joining him on the bunk but was afraid of what would crawl into his pants. He found a wooden stool and dragged it over. "Mind if I ask you a few questions?"

"Go right ahead; ask what you need to. I haven't anywhere to go."

"I've been in the tunnels—very impressive set-up."

"Oh, yes. Quite a place. Especially Hall forty-one." Landau bowed his head and sipped again.

"Is that the big room with the crane for lifting rockets?"

"That's the one."

"It had a rocket in it pointed to the sky, like something out of science fiction. A behemoth surrounded by inspection scaffolds. I imagined teams of men pouring over it, checking its readiness to fire."

"And do you know what that crane was used for, besides moving rockets?"

David hesitated, not sure he wanted to hear the answer. "No."

"It was a favorite of the guards and one particular scientist, an S.S. man with a virulent streak of sadism."

"Who was that?"

"S.S. Sturmbannführer Dr. Gerhardt Adler. You see, many of us tried to sabotage these rockets, for obvious reasons, and sometimes we succeeded. Once, Adler discovered a partial arc weld on a fin, which would likely fall apart when the rocket was launched. He was so angry, he couldn't wait for his minions to identify the perpetrator. He hanged all fifty men who worked in that Kommando, suspended them from the crane, and left them there, not two meters from the floor. We had to watch as he ordered the guards to hoist the crane, and then keep staring until the last man stopped kicking. It took a half-hour. You see, we don't weigh enough to break our own necks. Of course, he left those corpses for days, as a warning. We had to walk under their dangling legs and look up at their purple faces and bulging eyes. We couldn't pull up the pants that had fallen from their insignificant waists, and we certainly weren't allowed to bury them."

"My God." David rubbed his hands down his cheeks and then either side of his nose. "I can't even imagine the horror that you've seen."

"You may thank your God for that, if you believe in one."

"How can you tell such a story so . . . so clinically?"

"It is how we survive. Emotions take too much energy. I hope, one day, to lose myself again in Mozart, in Beethoven, but today I must only focus on gaining strength."

"Yes. Well . . ." David paused, feeling queasy from the image of swinging bodies and yet respectful of the energy it took for these men to get through the day. He forced himself to focus on his work. "We'd like to talk to the scientists and find their documents: technical drawings, specs, research findings, cost estimates. Can you help us out?"

Landau sipped and rested the empty cup on the mattress beside him. "Sorry, but no. You'll need to talk to the men who worked directly with the scientists. Me, I played the Beer Barrel Polka each morning and then kept inventories of supplies. I handed them to an S.S. guard each night. I'm afraid I don't know what happened from there. Try Jacob Strauss, two bunks over, middle tier."

"Thank you, I will." David laid a hand on Landau's shoulder, not wanting to shake hands again and wary that saluting would remind the ailing man he was once more under the command of soldiers. David refused to worry about catching their diseases. Like all U.S. soldiers, he had his shots.

With stool in hand, he stepped over his pile of boards near the stove to get to Jacob, who lay on his side, head cradled in his right arm. David estimated his weight at eighty to ninety pounds. The man's thin, black hair clung to his scalp, making curls like a Negro's. Other than the slow movement of his chest and the sweat on his brow, it was hard to tell he was alive.

"Jacob?"

His eyes opened to slits. "What?" It was a soft growl.

"I'm David Svehla. Herbert Landau said you might be able to help me."

"Help you? As long as I don't have to move." He had an accent to his German, maybe French.

"Can I get you something? Water? A little milk? Looks like that's all we have that won't make you guys sicker."

Jacob's mouth opened like a dead man in rictus. "Some milk."

David held Jacob's head up a bit to allow him to sip from a metal cup. Then he lowered his head back to the crooked arm. After moving the stool even with Jacob's eyes, David leaned over to speak quietly. "Landau said you might be able to point me in the right direction. I'm trying to find the scientists and their documents for the rockets. You know, technical drawings, research reports, pictures, that kind of thing. Any idea where they are?"

"I am electrician."

"And I'll bet you're a good one. Landau said you worked directly with several scientists."

"Bah. Only as slave who shows no emotion, has no ideas."

"What happened to them all?"

"They disappeared a couple of days ago."

"You know where they lived?"

Jacob smiled, his lips so dry David could see little cracks. "For some reason, I was never invited chez eux."

"Right. And their documents. Where were those kept?"

Jacob sighed, rolled onto his back, and took a slow breath. "In the scientists' offices, in our desks. But you will not find them. Before the scientists left, they boxed up every paper, filled three trucks. Someone said the vehicles went north. I do not know where."

"Would you like a little more milk?"

"Bitte."

As David helped him sip, he said, "May I come back if I have more questions?"

"Always. If you bring food."

David's next stop was questioning the Army guards who'd been through the whole production facility. They reported no people anywhere, but it turned out they'd been stopped by a locked gate. That was the next order of business, so he took his team back to the tunnels and penetrated the halls to the gate. Since OSS had provided him with basic lock-picking skills, he had his tools attached to his belt. It took only a few minutes to get the gate open.

Behind the bars was a different kind of factory, not dealing with rockets but Junkers aircraft engines. And there were plenty of offices for managers of rockets and aircraft engines and their secretaries. However, as Jacob had said, the file cabinets held only scraps of paper—the desk drawers, basic supplies. Desperate to uncover something important, David pulled out the extra shelf that extended the work surface on a secretary's desk and murmured, "Eureka." He used his knife to release the paper taped to the surface—a list of the names, addresses, and telephone numbers of the scientists and senior managers of Mittelwerk, the entire rocket complex. Adler was at the top of the sheet. David poked his finger at the name. "We've got a place to start—the guy who took great joy in killing his workers."

Mac looked over his shoulder. "Not likely he's still here."

"Yeah. But we have the scientists' addresses now. Looks like all our human targets. We'll take it from the top: Gerhardt Adler. I'd sure like to give him a dose of his own medicine."

By the time they hiked to their truck, picked up Private Bennett to serve as a guard, and checked their map, it was dark. David's quartet headed east on the way to Nordhausen, and located Adler's hunting lodge tucked back into woods. It was locked up tight. No lights. No smoke from the chimney. "Come on, we'll give it a proper search. Might be somethin' left."

With Bennett on guard at the front door, David did another round of breaking and entering. This was a comfortable home but empty of most personal possessions like books, clothing, and toys. No papers at all. The men gathered in the front hall. "Find anything?"

Jim shook his head.

Mac said, "Ashes haven't been cleaned from the fireplace. Blankets are still on the beds. Those old swords crossed on the wall look valuable. Looks like they left quickly, traveling light."

David nodded. "Makes sense. Let's try a couple of other addresses and ask some neighbors if they know where these guys went. If any of 'em are still here, we'll find them. We've got to."

The next house they approached was also shuttered and locked. When the team entered, they found it stripped of personal items and anything professional. But at the third scientist's house, they discovered a woman scavenging in the kitchen. Several cupboard doors hung open. A few packets of flour, some wrinkled potatoes and turnips, and a small jar of jam sat on the square table.

She shrieked when David came through the door. "Don't hurt me! They said I could take what was left. I am housekeeper, not thief. Please, my children are hungry. Please, don't hurt me."

Mac and Jim drifted over to the two other doorways in the room, one to the back yard, one probably to the basement.

David ordered her, in German, to calm down. They just wanted information. "What is your name, please?"

"Frau Koehler."

"I'm Captain Svehla. We won't hurt you if you tell us the truth. When did the Schaefers leave?" He made his voice threaten the frightened woman.

"Yesterday, early morning. They knew you were close." Her words ran together as she hurried to explain what had happened.

"Uh huh. And where were they going?"

She clutched the collar of her dress, drawing its edges together under her chin. "I . . . I think Frau Schaefer said Oberammargau. Herr Schaefer shushed her."

He looked at Mac, who was good at sussing out lies. Mac mouthed, "Okay." So David went on, "Did they go alone?"

"No, no. They took the children." The poor woman was shivering all over.

David instinctively smiled. "Of course, I meant did other families travel with them?"

"Oh, yes, many. Three families came here. Well, most of three . . ."

"Most?"

She wrung her hands. "Professor Adler, he brought his family but would not go with them. The men argued. Dr. Schaefer said he must stay with the group. Adler said no, he was going to his family's old home. His wife pleaded with him, but he left anyway."

"Did you hear the name of the town Adler was heading for?"

She wrinkled her brow. "Dresden? Yes, I think so. Near Dresden."

David smiled, more in the delight of this new clue about Adler than pleasure in talking with her, but she could take the expression any way she wished. "Thank you, Frau Koehler. We'll leave you to your searching." He

Lorelei Brush

waved Jim and Mac to their truck and then turned back to her. She had slumped against the table and now leaned heavily on both arms.

"What kind of car does Adler drive?"

She pushed herself back to standing. "An Opel Olympia. Black, always polished. They used to come here often,"

But David didn't wait to hear about the social life of the Adlers. He zipped out the front door, climbed into the truck, and told Mac to step on it. "So, you believe her?"

Mac nodded. "I do. She was too scared to lie. No looking away to suggest inventing answers. No odd pauses. Yes."

"I thought so, too. We'll go with her info." Since no scientists or documents were around, he and Mac'd go after Adler, leaving Jim to finish the picture-taking.

David reported in to Tippet and asked for a Jeep with a detail of guards to accompany them to Dresden. As he explained to the lieutenant, the majority of scientists had a day and a half's head start, and another OSS team could search for them in Oberammargau. But David's team might be able to catch up with Adler. Given the volume of refugees on the road fleeing the Russians, he could not be moving with any speed.

And it turned out, David was right. Their two-vehicle caravan came upon the Opel about midnight. Deep holes in the ground at the back and side of its tires spoke to numerous attempts to get the vehicle back onto the road. Adler stomped about, yelling at the families camped in the field to come and help move his car.

David eased out of the truck.

Adler froze, his face infused with anger, and yelled in German. "What do you want?" He sounded dismissive, as if ordering the Americans to get out of his sight.

David itched to give the German a taste of his fists, but kept his orders well in mind: he could interrogate a scientist to make sure he had the right man, but they were to be treated with respect, asked courteously to open their files, and if they were valuable resources for the Allies, turned over to HQ for in-depth interrogation. No rough stuff.

"Herr Adler, please come with me. The U.S. Army will be your host for awhile."

"I am with von Braun, and I am going first to Dresden."

"No, sir, you are coming with us."

"This is outrageous. I will not be treated like a common felon, dragged from my car."

"There will be no dragging. We invite you to join these gentlemen in the Jeep."

"I will not." His chest rose and his face reddened.

David pointed to the soldiers in the second Jeep. "Escort Dr. Adler to the back of your vehicle."

Adler made fists as though willing to take on all comers and socked the first man who approached. It was a strong right to the jaw. But the next two guards, with Mac and David as backup, got handcuffs on him and frog-marched him to the car.

"You'll hear about this infamy," Adler said. "I'll have you court-martialed."

David followed Adler to the Jeep, enjoyed his prisoner's struggle to climb into the back seat without his hands to help with balance, and followed behind as the men went in slow convoy to Twelfth Army Headquarters.

CHAPTER 1

MARCH 1955

David paused on the courthouse steps to button his overcoat against the cold wind off Lake Erie. He hefted his bulging briefcase and was trotting down the steps when he noticed the long, rhythmic stride of a tall man in a well-cut black overcoat. It made him think of the final parade of Nazis in Berlin after the surrender: that heavy clomp of boots and the metronomic regularity of swinging arms and legs. But this was downtown Cleveland, and the war'd been over for nearly ten years.

He inspected the man's face and froze. That straight jaw, dark blond hair parted and combed to the side, squared shoulders. And, under that muffler, David suspected, on the left side of his neck, a jagged scar. That damned S.S. Sturmbannführer, right here on Lakeside Avenue. The last time David had seen Major Gerhardt Adler, he'd been in handcuffs, head held high, bouncing in the back of an Army Jeep on his way to an interrogation. A trial in Nuremberg. The bastard should be behind bars—or dead. David stared at Adler's back, his anger boiling with increasing certainty this was his man. Had to be, and yet . . .

Glancing to his right and left, David saw no one interested in himself or Adler, so he fell into step behind him, keeping several people between them. After Adler's brutality to prisoners in the labor camp, how could the Allies have let the bastard go? Had he escaped? Snuck into the U.S.? Was he a wanted man? God, he could be sabotaging the country's rocket research. Spying for the Germans—or worse, the Russians. He had to be stopped.

David's war-honed skills tumbled back into place. He dragged his hat down to cover more of his face and followed Adler toward Public Square, into the Rapid Transit station under the Terminal Tower. He hovered behind one person, and then another, in the crowd on the platform. Several carried boxes and shopping bags, which broadened their bodies into good cover.

When the eastbound train pulled up, David slipped in behind Adler and stood, swaying from an overhead handle with his back to the man. He pretended to read the ads around the top of the car while checking that Adler stayed in his seat. The German pulled a newspaper from his pocket, opened it, apparently found something of interest, and folded the paper into quarters, flattening the folds into solid creases.

What happened back in '45? David got a nice pat on the back for bringing Adler in. Must have been a fuck-up somewhere along the line for him to be here now. Whatever it was, this time David'd make sure Adler was adequately punished for his crimes against humanity.

He swayed with the movement of the train car like any average Joe on his way home from a long day at work. Adler didn't seem to notice him. The man relaxed into his seat, slowly turned, and folded the next page to meet his rigid requirements. He looked absorbed by some story.

David had the urge to haul him out of the train's seat and break his teeth. How arrogant and insulting Adler had been on that road to Dresden. Covered in mud from trying to dig his car out, he'd dared to boast to David of his genius in rocket fuels, how every country in the world wanted his talent. It hadn't occurred to David to check on Adler's sentence after the trials. Maybe he should have.

David felt cheated by his war. He'd pictured so much more: days full of risk, of excitement, of daring. He'd enlisted the morning after Pearl Harbor was attacked, eager to get into the fight, be an officer, lead his men to victory. But the Army had other plans. Oh, he'd been through officers' training, but the Army picked up on his background in chemistry and physics, put him in the Chemical Warfare Service, and gave him a stateside assignment at the Sun Rubber Company in Akron. Instead of heroic combat, he helped design gas masks for children with the rubber face of Mickey Mouse or

Donald Duck. It was humiliating. He was ashamed to tell the guys shipping out about his cushy assignment.

It wasn't until 1944 that he made it overseas. He'd thought OSS was his ticket to a real fight. And his spy training was superb: he proved to be an expert in stripping down weapons and reassembling them in the dark, excelled in the Fairbairn techniques of dirty fighting, and managed to be halfway fluent in German. But the job he got assigned? An *administrative assistant* for Secret Intelligence in London. He'd argued with his supervisor to send him to the continent and to let him work with the Resistance in France. He lost. Next assignment: a *photographer*, microfilming documents. No chance to show off his physical strength and mental acuity. Damn it, nor his bravery, loyalty, or commitment to human rights.

The Sturmbannführer rustled his paper and stuffed it in his briefcase. He left the train car at Shaker Square with David on his tail. Adler hurried across Shaker Boulevard, just making the light, but David got caught behind a mother, her children, and her shopping bags. One of the children, a girl about three, launched herself into the street, and David lunged forward to scoop her up.

The mom thanked him profusely, but by that time, Adler had disappeared in the vicinity of Halle's Department Store. David hurried around the building to its parking lot. No Adler. He ducked through the store's back door on the off-chance his quarry had gone inside. He hadn't.

David wanted to kick something. Here was a chance to prove himself by ridding the world of a man who committed crimes against humanity. He refused to let this opportunity slip away. Debating his options, he retraced his steps to the Rapid station and strode down the bank of pay phones to the one at the end. He needed to thrash this out with someone, but who'd believe him and understand the need to go after Adler? Not the police. Adler couldn't be tried in the U.S. for crimes committed in Germany. David's law training made that clear. The FBI? Maybe they could check on how Adler got to the U.S. and what he was up to—if they believed David. What reason could he give them? Pretty flimsy to say he saw a guy he'd arrested in the war. He'd call Mac, his OSS sergeant, the one who always had his back.

Sliding his dime into the slot, David eased his body around to check that no one was in listening distance and dialed. "You're not gonna believe this."

"What is it, Cap'n?"

David heard footsteps approaching him from behind. This conversation was top secret, by God. He swiveled to see a middle-aged businessman. Loudly, he said into the phone, "Yeah, David here, haven't talked to you in too long." He paused, as though listening to an answer.

"You want me to ask yes-or-no questions?"

David smiled, visualizing his tall, unflappable friend standing at the kitchen wall phone. He cut his voice to a whisper. "I just saw Gerhardt Adler."

"That sadist from Dora? I haven't thought about him in years. Wasn't he tried in Germany? I thought they had a special trial for the men in charge of that camp. What the hell's he doing here in Cleveland? I don't like the sound of that at all."

"Yeah. Worse, he got away from me in Shaker Square."

"Jesus H. Christ. You sure it's him?"

"Pretty sure. Something's wrong here. I gotta find out for sure it's him and what he's up to. If I can, how he got here. Maybe he escaped. Got off on some technicality?"

"I . . . I can't believe it. You 'member the smell? That hospital—more like a morgue?"

David swallowed as they'd all done back then to keep down the vomit. "Oh, God, I sure don't want to break this to Jacob."

"No, no. You got a plan? About Adler?"

"I'm thinkin' I'll hang around Shaker Square. I bet this trip wasn't a fluke. He's probably a commuter. I'll follow him home, see where he lives. Then follow him to work, see if he's using an alias. Maybe talk to neighbors, work colleagues." David stared up and down the street, checking the face of each tall man.

"You planning to pull in any OSS contacts?"

"Just you, so far. I need some context, more facts."

"You want backup?"

Good, dependable Mac. "Gimme a week, maybe ten days. I got vacation from the high school the week before Easter, and my legal work's still pretty thin. I may need you after that."

"Situation Normal—All Fucked Up."

"Amen."

All the way back downtown to pick up his car, David savored the thrill of a chase, anticipating his success and the thanks he'd get for bringing in this criminal. But the logistics. It'd be tough. There was that oath he swore at the end of the war never to discuss with outsiders his activities with the Office of Strategic Services.

Better keep this on a need-to-know basis, no family involved. He'd leave for school at his usual time, 0700. No sense hovering around Shaker Square before then, as it was a rare man dressed as formally as Adler who left for work at such an early hour. He'd hang around the square after his school day ended and follow Adler home. Of course, that would mean moving a few client appointments, shifting them to the evenings or weekend. Jeez, this mix of teaching and legal work didn't leave much time free for extracurricular adventures.

David pulled his black Studebaker Commander into the driveway on East Scarborough, threw the car into neutral, and yanked up the emergency brake. The white paint on the wooden garage doors was peeling badly. Worse, though, the doors scraped on the uneven asphalt, a sound as annoying as the scratching of fingernails along a blackboard. He ought to take them off their hinges and plane them down. Not going to happen anytime soon, not with this new complication in his life.

David pushed a lock of graying hair out of his eyes. In a few minutes, he'd have to make up a tale for Grace. God, he loved that woman. Resting his eyes on her through the kitchen window, he smiled. Her back was toward him, showing off her soft, brown hair and the perfect hourglass figure that lit him up. Maybe tonight?

He set his briefcase down on the kitchen floor and hung up his coat before bending to kiss her. It was impossible to miss the open checkbook on the table. "Sorry I'm late, hon. Had to file some papers down at the courthouse."

She looked up at him over the tops of her glasses. "I've saved your dinner in the oven."

"Thanks. How are we on the financial front?"

"Not good. I don't know how we're going to manage."

With a gleam in his eye, he said, "I could take up poker again. It did pay for this house."

"Oh, please. I hated that—lying awake, scared that you'd lose everything we had. I can't go through that again. It's not just us now; we have children to think of."

"I know, I know. Just tryin' to lighten the mood. What's today's crisis?" He pulled his dinner plate out of the oven and set it across from her, checking that his face and body masked the exhilaration he'd been feeling.

"That Studebaker you bought. We can't pay your mom anything this month, and that makes three in a row. Davy's pushing through the toes of his shoes, and I don't know how long the washer's going to last. Is there any chance you'll be getting some of those outstanding client checks soon?"

David grimaced. He loved that car. The first one he'd ever bought new. His Ma never let him forget she'd paid half. "I'll do a little pushing." But most of his clients were poor. And desperate.

"Doesn't Gladys Thompson owe you a decent sum? She's called here often enough that the time you spent on the phone with her ought to pay for new shoes for all of us."

"Yeah, maybe. But her husband's in jail. She doesn't have any income."

Grace flipped the last couple of pages of the check register and looked up at her husband. "Maybe I should get a job."

"We haven't come to that yet."

"It's not the end of the world. I worked during the war."

"That was a different time."

She rose and faced him. "I'd like to work. The kids are in school all day. It'd help us out."

David heard his Ma's voice echoing in his head as she derided a couple in the old neighborhood. *The only reason a woman works is that her husband is incapable of supporting her.* If Grace worked, it wouldn't only be his Ma saying that. He believed it. The humiliation.

"Let's give my law practice more time. It's coming along."

Grace sighed. "I know you're busy, but so much is pro bono."

"It's how I build up experience, how I become known. I have to be seen in court, be recognized by the judges." They'd talked about this numerous times. The friction increased with each repetition.

She spoke through gritted teeth. "So you've said. But when are you going to get any big cases? Paying clients?"

"When they hear about me and seek me out." He realized he was shouting.

"And how long will that take? I want a time limit." She matched his volume.

"Aw, hon, I promised I'd stay on at the high school until the law work was steady. We aren't going to starve." A glance at his briefcase reminded him of the stack of science quizzes he had to grade.

"What does 'steady' even mean? You're always working now, just earning next to nothing."

David sucked in breath through his teeth. "A time limit feels like a ticking bomb. What happens if that date goes by, and my docket's still filled with small fry? Do I give up the law? Teach forever? That won't help our finances. And Grace, honey, I'll dry up if I have to keep teaching."

Heck, she knew he loved risk. Not just betting on cards, but taking the Studebaker to max speed, and, God, he'd love to fly.

"David, I want stability. I've taken enough risks. I left for Chicago with you after our wedding with less than ten dollars between us. I agreed you should enlist the day after Pearl Harbor. I sat here for months not knowing if you were alive over in Europe. I'm done with all that. We have children, a house, a car. I don't want to have to decide each month what bills to skip." She jerked open her purse and jammed the checkbook inside.

He reached for her hand. "We'll work this out. Just have a little more patience. Okay?"

"I don't have much choice."

David asked, "Where are the kids?"

"Hildie's over at Karen's house. Davy's in the attic, I think." The lines etched in her forehead smoothed out. "He does like his trains. You hit a home run on that gift."

"Yeah. It turned out good. I'll go up in a minute and see how he's doing."

"He'll like that."

During the next five school days, David grew intimately familiar with the benches in the Rapid Transit shelter at Shaker Square. From 1530 to 1800 hours, he patrolled the area, watching for Adler—or the man he thought was Adler. Over the days, he eased his growing frustration by memorizing the hype for *On the Waterfront*, the movie showing at the Shaker Theater, thoroughly evaluating the fashions in Halle's big windows (none of which would suit Grace), and sheltering in the doorways of every store. He'd even caught up on his grading and those stupid lesson plans, in case he needed a substitute. So far, no policeman had accused him of loitering, but he worried that one would if his vigil went on much longer. At least there were decent afternoon crowds, what with Easter approaching.

On day five, a Thursday, David spotted Adler getting off the train. David was hanging out in the drugstore and drifted into step behind Adler as they all crossed Shaker Boulevard. The German set a punishing pace down North Moreland, eyes forward. David kept a half a block behind. Instead of stopping to pick up a car at one of the lots behind the stores, he kept walking, looking neither right nor left. As they passed Doan Brook, the stream that bisected the park, David and Adler were the only pedestrians in sight. David matched his pace to Adler's, hoping to muffle the sound of his footsteps. With luck, if the man looked back, he'd see a nondescript gray-haired guy with a paunch—instead of an ex-spy tamping down his elation at bagging his quarry. If Adler looked twice, David would turn off at a cross street.

And so they marched in step for perhaps a mile, at which point Adler took a sharp right onto Fairmount Boulevard, a divided road with a wide, grassy strip down the middle covered with half-melted snow, sand, and salt. The houses on either side sprawled on big lots with hundred-year-old trees. One long block later, the man he thought was Adler crossed the street and headed up the driveway of number 2905, on the left. He picked up a newspaper on his way to the house.

David stopped a couple of houses earlier and catalogued the details. The man who might be Adler lived in a red-brick Georgian on a corner lot, set back from the road on maybe an acre of land with three high chimneys, white trim, black shutters, and neatly-shoveled driveways—one opening on Fairmount, the other on the side street. Tucked behind the house was a matching garage with stairs leading to rooms above—servants' quarters? Any way you looked at it, the place cost more than David could hope to afford. His anger ate at him. How did this barbarian rate a cozy mansion in a ritzy part of town when David was struggling to make ends meet?

He scanned the yard. The house had a full hedge around the perimeter and so much shrubbery that a lot of the first floor was hidden from street view, even without the leaves.

A man in a well-cut suit emerged from the house on David's right and eyed him as he stooped to pick up his copy of the *Press*. "You looking for someone?"

David absorbed the insulting tone: this man didn't think his worn overcoat and well-used briefcase belonged in the neighborhood. But, not wanting to be remembered, David responded politely. "Been admirin' that house. You know if the owner is thinking of selling?"

The man, beating the newspaper against his other hand, turned cordial. "Don't think so. I think he's here for the long haul."

"Oh, well, thanks." David waved and turned back the way he'd come, his excitement at finding Adler's home tempered only a little by this man's suspicion.

So, Adler (and he still needed proof this man was Gerhardt Adler) had a comfortable mansion set back among the trees, the home of a well-to-do family living the American Dream. Solid brick, no doubt well insulated, well protected, safe. An eternity from the housing of Dora's inmates, a lifetime from the squalor in which they lived—and died.

CHAPTER 2
APRIL 1955

On the Friday before Easter vacation, David gave all the required mid-term exams, assigned homework he was sure few would complete, and worried that he was missing Adler. On Monday morning, he was on duty at the Shaker Square Rapid station by 0730, determined to follow Adler to his place of work. As he paced the sidewalks, he asked himself if it was time to use his old OSS contacts still in the government. They had some clout, whereas he was just a working stiff who used to be somebody with national security responsibilities. The problem was what to tell them. Saying he had suspicions was pretty weak stuff. No, he needed concrete evidence that this man was Adler, the German rocket scientist. That might well come when he found out about the man's job.

The Nazi showed at 0930, marching across the square and mounting the stairs of the train heading downtown. David settled in several seats behind. When Adler emerged from the Terminal Tower, he strode down Euclid Avenue to an optician's. David refused to believe the man worked there—not only because it was far below Adler's skill level, but also because, if he did, he was flagrantly late for work. Didn't fit the Adler personality. From a doorway across the street, David watched through the optician's front window as Adler was fitted for new glasses and completed his purchase. After leaving that store, he loitered at a couple of other shop windows, entered Higbee's and interrogated a saleswoman about gloves, and returned to the Rapid platform. David followed, grinding his teeth at the waste of his time, and got off at Shaker Square to watch Adler head back toward home.

For the rest of the week, David wandered the square each morning and late afternoon, feeling his frustration rising, along with his desire to hit someone—preferably Adler. Time for reinforcements. He'd be back at school next week, could probably organize his legal work to get to Shaker Square by 1600 hours, but he couldn't do mornings or he'd piss off his principal. So, after a fruitless Friday afternoon vigil, he drove down Miles Avenue toward the VFW, shaking his head at the litter on the street. Definitely the working-class neighborhood of his youth: lots of asphalt and concrete, small stores opening onto the sidewalks, not much color. The single-story red VFW hall squatted on the corner of East 119th, showing no windows on the Miles side, like it had something to hide. Whatever its warts, it was their place—somewhere vets could come to unwind at the end of a week, remember where they came from, where they'd been. Mac had made it a habit.

David's eyes skipped across the mirror above the VFW's mahogany bar, then flicked across the faces of his listeners. All WWII vets he'd met in past visits. Mostly Mac's friends. In the dim light, he watched Bill's thick eyebrows drawing together, his mouth hung open like a panting dog. The man was a short-order cook; he needed to keep it simple. Mac, at David's right, shifted in his chair, attentive, waiting.

David leaned toward his audience, his belly inching the table forward. He brushed the straggling gray hair off his forehead. "The Russians said they wanted to negotiate. They'd send a senior officer and a few men to talk, but I was suspicious." He sat back for a moment to add an aura of excitement to the story.

"What'd ya do, huh?" Bill asked. "Betcha fooled 'em."

With a glance toward Mac, who shrugged a shoulder, David went on. "I positioned my men on the hills on either side of the narrow valley, watched four Russkies on horseback ride toward us. Must have been a platoon of their men on foot chewin' the horses' dust. I'd given orders no one was to shoot unless some Russkies started something, so the hills were quiet. No birds—just thought of that now, how odd it was, like they knew to get the hell out of there. Anyway, the Russkies held their horses to a walk. They just kept on coming, nice and slow." David sipped his beer.

"So, did they attack? C'mon, Dave, tell us!" Bill bounced his head up and down.

David winced. He'd told Bill not to call him Dave, oh, three-four times anyway. "What do you think, Bill?"

"It was a trap. I'll betcha it was a trap."

David made his hand into a pistol and shot at Bill. "Right you are. See, my lieutenant and Mac here watched with me." He jerked his thumb toward Mac. "You know Mac was my sergeant, right?"

Bill thrust out his chin and nodded.

"Well, there we were, standing at ease, until the senior officer dismounted, maybe fifteen, twenty feet away. Looked like he was going to extend his hand to me, but he raised it above his head and waved side to side." David demonstrated. "His platoon fanned out and aimed their rifles straight into our eyes. Just as you suspected, it was all a trick." Another sip of beer.

Bill reached over the table and pushed at David's hand. "So, what'd you do? How'd you not get killed?"

After checking to his right and left, David whispered, "I lifted my hands slowly, like I was surrendering. The three of us dove to the ground, and all hell broke loose. Not a Russki standing when my men were done."

"How 'bout the horses? You kill them, too?"

"They sort of got caught in the crossfire."

"Too bad. We wasn't over there to kill horses."

David looked at Mac, rolled his eyes, and grinned.

Mac cleared his throat. "Cap'n, you make OSS sound like one of those westerns on TV. White hats, black hats, dry gulches, ambushes." He tipped his chair back, balancing it on two legs.

"Yeah, well, it was—sometimes. Lots of boredom, and then utter terror." David turned to Bill. "That little ambush of ours got some important press. Stalin was so mad, he wrote a letter to FDR asking him to discipline me. Wanted a presidential apology for massacring his men."

"What'd FDR do?" Bill swiped beer drops off his chin.

"Didn't do a thing, 'cept maybe celebrate. We should've turned right around and attacked those Russkies when Germany surrendered. We wouldn't be in this mess now if we'd stood up to Stalin back in '45." David paused, pissed again at the brass and politicians afraid to step on Russian toes. Should've stomped on them with steel-shanked boots. "You know, they asked me to stay on in Paris after Germany surrendered, help with the negotiations, but I told 'em no, I wanted to get home."

Bill nodded. "They sure needed you. Wouldn't be no Iron Curtain if you'd a been there."

Mac grinned and took a slug of beer. "And here I thought you turned it down because the idea of sitting at a table in a confined space talking nice to assholes was your worst nightmare."

David shook his head at Mac and upended his mug into his mouth. "Sorry to break up the party, boys, but I need to get home to the wife and kids. Mac, how about walkin' me to my car?"

Mac's eyes widened just a touch. "Sure."

When the two shut the VFW's side door and got a few steps across the parking lot, David stuck his hands into his pockets. "I tracked my Adler look-alike home, a mansion right on the border of Cleveland Heights and Shaker Heights. But last week, he only showed up once at the Rapid, and that was to get some glasses downtown. Could be he was on vacation for the week, like I was. You know, because the man's a teacher." They walked a few more steps, and David got out his keys. "Or maybe his use of the Rapid that first day was a fluke. I thought about staking out his house, but his neighbors seem vigilant, so I'm figuring another week at the square."

"Want me to do some of the watching?"

David grinned. "Sure do. I can do Tuesday, maybe a day later in the week, if I can find coverage for my early classes. Could you do Monday?"

Mac thought for a moment. "I need to be at the shop by 0900, but I could do 0700 to 0830." He raised his eyebrows.

"That's great. We'll check in each night. We'll get him, Mac. I know we will. When we know where he works, we'll find out the name he's using and whether this guy's a rocket expert. Then I'll have to figure out how he got away from the brass and into the U.S., whether he's up to something bad."

"Yeah. Good luck on that."

David leaned back against his car; his body relaxed like he and Mac were talking about football or the weather. He waved to an old man as he crossed the parking lot toward the entry door. He'd seen him from time to time on Friday nights—didn't know his name. With a wave in return, the guy went in, showing no more than a passing interest in two men swapping stories. The jukebox blared for a moment, and then silence returned. David focused again on Mac. "You suppose he got here through South America? Lied about his past?"

"Could be."

David jingled the keys in his pocket and heard the dissonance of their clanking. "I promise you one thing, Mac. He's not going to get away a second time. Not on my watch."

"Nor mine. What did we fight the goddamn war for, anyway?"

Dinner on Easter Sunday was set for 1500 hours. A cleaned-up David set his shoulders, tamping down thoughts of cruising Adler's neighborhood to see how he dealt with the holiday and bracing for the onslaught of the Svehla family. He opened his front door to the two cars' worth of guests. Ma puckered up, forcing him to bow down and deliver a mouth-to-mouth kiss. Only four-feet-ten, she commanded the troops. Her figure had squared off with age but stood solid, an immoveable object.

"Jak se máš?" she asked in greeting.

He answered he was fine, as he was supposed to, in Czech. "Dobře, jak vy?"

His father came in behind Ma. David saw the liver-spotted top of his barely five-feet-five dad. Its small fringe of hair above the ears made him look like a monk—a kind, hard working one. They shook hands, a moment of sanity and mutual appreciation. Then David clapped the shoulders of his older brother, Chet, and his younger brother, George. Chet looked like him:

a little broad in the beam, round face, high cheekbones. Smaller, thin, and already losing his hair at thirty-five, George took after their father. George's Polish wife, Stella, came in last. Petite and pregnant, she shepherded their two children and offered her cheek to David. He kissed her, taking in her heavy perfume, and sent the kids upstairs to play.

Ma, before she even reached the couch, shot her first verbal salvo. Bragging as usual about her oldest son, she said, "Chet's been promoted to purchasing agent for the Cuyahoga County Commissioners, did you know that? Pretty soon he's going to be mayor. You know, Chet can find anything the city needs. He knows everyone. Gets the best prices." Her chest poked out with pride.

David busied himself pulling a couple of dining room chairs into the living room, smoldering with resentment at being the "lesser" brother. He glanced at Chet, who shrugged a shoulder.

"Ma, Dad, Chet, George—highballs?" David asked.

As he yanked the Seagram's out of the bottom cupboard, he heard his mother start on his younger brother. "You know, George, you have a lot to live up to. You should follow in Chet's footsteps. Your insurance job is a dead end. You'll never earn good money there."

In the short silence that followed, David imagined George working through possible responses.

Stella spoke up first. "George likes his job and the people he works with."

"Yeah, Ma, I like Ohio Casualty."

It was quiet when David distributed the drinks. "How are things down at Stone Shoes, Dad?"

"Good, good." The man's serene voice smoothed the ruffled edges of the earlier conversation. There he sat: legs stretched out, arm across the back of the couch, not a worry line in sight. Here was his wife, demeaning work in an insurance company when her husband sold shoes. Didn't it bother him?

David put the empty tray on the coffee table and sat down in the room's most comfortable chair, *his* chair. "So, any new customers?"

"Oh, sure, nearly every day."

Ma interrupted. "How is that law practice of yours going? You can't be making much money because you haven't paid me back for that car loan." She continued speaking to his father in Czech, which David had worked hard to ignore as a child and now didn't understand—except for a few choice words.

"It takes time to build up a practice, Ma." He probably shouldn't have borrowed the money from her. He knew this would happen, this carping on his failures. But, God, he loved that car.

"How much time do you need?"

"I don't know. I'm real busy just now."

"Doing what?"

David looked at both of his brothers, who had also served in the war—Chet in counterintelligence in Australia, and George as an air traffic controller in Greenland. Did he want to bring up the war? Hell, why not? "You guys noticed the number of Germans we seem to have in Cleveland?"

Chet harrumphed. "Jeez. What do you care? We finished that war. You hauling it back up again?"

"Just curious."

"You looking for a fight?"

David gritted his teeth. He'd fought battles for Chet and George back in junior high and high school. Neither of them stood up to bullies; they left it to David. This was the thanks he got. "No. It just seems like there are a lot of folks with German names around here. I'm wondering if they're all loyal to U.S., or if some are—I don't know—spying for Germany? Or Russia?"

"Jeez, David. Cleveland's been a melting pot for years. Of course there are Germans. And Bohemians, and Poles, and Hungarians. Look at this family."

Before David could form a reply, Ma shook her index finger at him. "You stop this nonsense of looking for a fight, trying to be a hero."

David caught Grace pulling on her ear. They'd worked out this signal to get him out of confrontations with his mother. He swallowed a gulp of his drink, gave up having a sane discussion with his family, and let her take over.

"I've been trying out your recipe for kolaches, Momma Svehla, but mine aren't nearly as flaky as yours. Would you try one and let me know what I'm doing wrong?"

Good old Grace. His mother passed him on the way to the kitchen, already lecturing.

The atmosphere around the dining table was subdued, even courteous, as everyone passed the roast beef, mashed potatoes, gravy, peas, and green Jell-O salad. When the family finished their second and third helpings, Grace asked the children to help clear the table. She brought in a multi-layered Lady Baltimore cake with lots of icing, just as David liked it, along with the box of Fanny Farmer candies that Ma and Dad had brought.

Ma scrutinized David's plate. "I don't understand you. You love sweets, and you haven't taken one of the candies. You loved chocolate as a boy."

David stared at the square, chocolate-covered caramels and the round candies with cream fillings, feeling slightly nauseous. The chocolate glistened; small tendrils of the decorations reached out toward him. And all he could see was that poor sod Isaac laid out on the parade ground. David swallowed, twice. "I lost my taste for it in the war."

Chet, picking another candy from the box, pushed the topic. "But these ain't rations. They're A-1 pure chocolate."

"Shut up about it already."

The table was quiet with everyone looking at him.

Chet threw up his hands. "All right, all right. Calm down."

Easter Monday at school was like a zoo: the kids behaved like animals who had been free and now fought the rules that bound them, turning up late to class and creating mayhem as they greeted each other in the corridor. David became a policeman, directing traffic and sounding off at slackers. He had a full schedule of classes and not a free moment until lunch, when he tracked down Newton Rider—a fellow physics teacher—to cover his first- and second-period classes on Tuesday and give them quizzes.

Mac didn't see Adler on Monday, so David was on duty Tuesday morning. He made sure to leave his house at his usual time so as not to raise suspicions in Grace. She'd quizzed him on his Easter comment about Germans, and he'd sidestepped with his answer. One of those "I was just curious" comments. And he knew her limited flexibility about rules wouldn't allow for his handing over of two classes to someone else. She'd see it as a clear case of shirking his responsibilities. He missed the OSS sense that rules were made to be bent, if not broken.

Keeping near the Rapid platform, he could smell the coffee and pastries in the café and worked hard not to succumb to their temptation. He imagined his mouth open for a bite of a Danish, spotting Adler, and having to slap down money and run. No, he'd brave the light rain and ignore the warm room and tasty food.

He checked his watch at 0746 and almost immediately thereafter saw Adler striding toward the oncoming train heading downtown. David followed his quarry up the steps, into the car, and sat at the opposite end of the carriage. Through most of the journey, he stared out the window, still able to catch Adler in his peripheral vision. The major seemed fully engaged in the *Cleveland Plain Dealer*.

The rocking of the car made David sleepy. As he shook his head for about the third time, he saw Adler get up, paper folded under his arm. With a surge of excitement held carefully inside, David glanced at the station's sign: University Circle. The big employers near here were Case Institute of Technology and Western Reserve University. God, could the Nazi be a professor? That would fit with the training of the Adler he knew. But that also meant the man was reaping rewards for the work he'd done in the war, the talents he used to try to destroy the Allies. David ground his teeth at the thought, the unfairness of it all. He'd double majored in physics and chemistry at Adelbert and had the talent to get a Ph.D. but not the money. Yeah, the GI Bill paid for his law degree, but to get it, he worked full-time during the day and studied at night. He sacrificed while Adler got a free ride. Another reason to bring this guy to book.

With a yawn and a stretch, purely for the effect as he was wide awake now, David made his way slowly down the aisle and followed Adler out the door, across the street, and up the steps toward Case. David knew the place well, as Adelbert was right next door, having been absorbed by Western Reserve, and David had taken courses here. Adler crossed the grassy area of the quadrangle, bypassing the admin building. With no place to hide, David lingered at the top of the steps, pretending to look for a pack of cigarettes in his pockets. Adler didn't turn around, but simply made a beeline for the Albert W. Smith Building. David checked his watch. He only had a few minutes to spare if he was going to make it back to the high school for his third period class. In a half-run, he crossed the quad, took the steps, and followed a student into the building. No Adler in site, so he took a few breaths and looked around. A directory just inside the entrance showed a list of faculty names and room numbers. Dr. Gerhardt Adler was boldly displayed as a member of the chemistry and chemical engineering faculty with an office on the third floor. Bingo. Same Adler as in Germany.

Hours later, exhausted from his early morning exercise, exasperated by students who were more interested in their upcoming dates than physics, and angered by Adler's apparently successful career, he let the back door slam behind him and dropped his briefcase on the kitchen floor.

Grace took a quick look at him and smiled. "What's going on?"

"I'm done in."

"I'll make us some coffee." She plugged in the percolator. "Get the milk out of the fridge, would you?"

David registered how perfectly her gray, straight skirt outlined her hips and backside, showing off her well-contoured calves. He felt a stirring in his groin. Maybe the day was going to turn around. Maybe he'd even strike it rich with a quick trip to the bedroom. "We have any cream left from this morning?" That was a gift of winter: the milkman came early to the back door and, when David got up, the cream sat at the top of the bottles.

Grace laughed at him. "You finished that up at breakfast, you glutton."

"Don't laugh at me. It's good, and you like it, too." David pulled the milk bottle out and filled the pitcher that the kids liked—a cow that poured milk from its mouth. With his assignment completed, he sank into his chair and extended his legs.

Grace sat down across from him. "So, what's soured your mood?"

Maybe it was time to bring her into his search—a little. "I saw a German scientist, and I found out he's a professor at Case. I can't understand how that happened. He's not one of the good guys." He drummed his fingers on the table, trying to decide if he could get the man fired.

She cocked her head, her eyes squinting. "I don't like the sound of that."

"Me either." His voice came out as a growl.

"Let me be clear. I don't like that there's a Nazi around here. But I hate my certainty that you're going to do something about him. Right?"

David nodded slowly. "You remember my exam in OSS, the final test?" They'd been married five years by then, and he'd been away for most of that last year in OSS training.

"Wasn't that something about a bank?"

"Yeah. Wild Bill Donovan himself told me to break into the First National Bank of Washington. Its president had boasted to Donovan that no one—no one—could pull off a successful heist with the brand-new locking mechanism on his vault. The two of them were going to play golf at some country club, and Donovan wanted to show off what his outfit could do. I had two guys with me—a safecracker out of jail to fight in the war and a man without fear. We deactivated the alarm system, got through the state-of-the-art lock, took one bill from a packet with successive numbers, and I put it into Donovan's hand." David felt again that wild excitement and the heady pleasure of that coup.

Grace's coffee cup clattered into its saucer. "All that story does is make me nervous about the risks you're going to take. They make me scared for you—and for me. I don't want to worry about where you are and what you're up to—the way I did in the war—and whether you'll come home."

He rubbed her hand. "I like coming home. But I miss the risks. And I like the hunt."

"Why can't you let him get on with his life?"

"What he did . . . I can't let it slide."

"But it's not your job. The government let him in the country, and you know how tough the visa process was after the war. Case hired him. They must think he's okay."

David stirred his coffee, wondering how to put into words the horror Adler had perpetrated. He didn't want to give her the story of that time because it was just too damn gruesome—and maybe still secret. "He was cruel, Grace. Depraved. And he hurt Jacob, so it's personal, too. I want justice for this Adler."

"Are you going to get Jacob involved in this?"

Jacob's wife, Rebecca, was Grace's good friend. His daughter, Karen, was in and out of their house daily, as they lived only a couple of blocks away. "Hon, I don't know if I can—or should—keep this from Jacob. But, believe me, I have no desire to see him hurt, not again."

She played with her spoon, turning it over a couple of times before laying it down next to her cup. "You've never told me exactly what happened, only that you met in a camp, but my imagination has conjured up some horrible visions. I don't want him thrust back there."

"Me either."

"Please, try not to stir up his bad memories. I wish you wouldn't do this, but if you've got to, please keep him out of it as much as you can. Promise?"

"I'll try."

March 1945

At Dora, David had been ruthless in tracking down information on German rocketry. Having sent Adler for interrogation, he returned to the camp and set up a second round of questioning of every man in the hospital. He developed as complete descriptions as he could of each scientist's expertise, job skills, and responsibilities. While not searching for personalities, he also recorded a lot about their characters. Jacob had been his best source and assistant, as he spoke seven or eight languages and could translate for the others. David found himself returning to Jacob's bed each night, sharing what he'd heard and absorbing Jacob's thoughtful reactions. As Jacob started to recover from his diphtheria, he felt more like talking.

Propped up by a blanket rolled to resemble a pillow, Jacob added stories from his life in Dora. "I remember one night of desperate hunger worse than usual because I had to work through breakfast and no lunch was offered. When I picked up my supper bowl to lick every drop of soup, an old man reached for my bread. Without a thought, I hit him across the mouth. He fell off his bench, and I didn't care. I was animal, baring my teeth."

David shook his head, finding it difficult to imagine this gentle man as a wolf. "Were the scientists involved in starving you and working you to death? Or just the S.S. guards?"

"Everyone. Even our own Kapos, the ones in charge of each Kommando."

"I'm having trouble connecting scientists with savagery. I studied the sciences in college, and I thought my teachers lived in their heads, the world of ideas. Sure, your rocket scientists needed help to get their plans into production, but the scientists I've known would assign that to some minion, not involve themselves. Hell, many of my professors didn't want to bother with undergraduates and focused on their graduate students. I suppose they drove the lab assistants pretty hard, but nothing like in the camp."

"Some scientists ignored us. They did not speak to us directly. Perhaps they did not like how we were treated, but they did nothing about it. A few were friendly from time to time when no one was looking and gave us food or learned our names. Some, like Adler, relished their absolute control over us."

"Tell me more about this Adler." David had to write a report about each of his "target" scientists. This man, this Adler, seemed like a particularly sadistic officer, someone the brass would like to know more about. David, too. What motivated a scientist to starve and demean others?

Jacob played with the edge of the blanket pulled over his legs. "One day, a fourteen-year-old boy, weak from dysentery, sat on the board over the hole that passed as our latrine. It broke. He went into the shit, yelling for us to pull him out. Adler ordered the guards to shoot. They played with the boy, firing into the muck so it splashed his face, shooting his hand as he reached for the edge, and yelling foul names. He cried, pleaded for help. Adler laughed, and when he finally turned away, ordered his men to finish the job and us to take the body to the crematorium. They forbid us from washing him and made us carry his slick, stinking body. It was . . . evil."

David winced. That moment with Isaac came rushing back: the candy bar, his cruelty in killing a man who was starving. He felt droplets of sweat forming under his arms.

The men sat silent for a few moments. "So, Adler had a big role with the labor?"

Jacob sliced his finger across his throat. "I'd like to kill that Hurensohn!" The scum of the earth. "You saw the scar on his neck?"

"No. How'd he get it?"

"From a pick-ax in the hand of a Jewish prisoner. Adler whipped the man's son for stumbling under the weight of a rail car full of rocks. We were hacking out the tunnels then. The father turned from the wall when he heard his son's scream and lashed out at Adler. That salaud ordered father and son beaten to death—and left to rot."

Not sure what a "salaud" was, David got the gist from Jacob's growl and nodded. There seemed no end to Adler's cruelty.

"I think he likes to blow things up."

David smiled. "I'd like to blow this place up."

Jacob's mouth split into an enormous grin. "Better than fireworks, when the fuel tanks go."

They'd laughed together that night.

CHAPTER 3

APRIL 1955

A little after one o'clock in the morning, David jerked awake to the piercing jangle of the downstairs phone. He groaned and rolled off the bed. "I'll get it."

Grace burrowed under the covers. "Who calls at this hour?" Then her head poked out. "You don't think it's one of my sisters? An accident? Maybe I ought to get it."

He waved her back to bed. "No, don't get up. I'll call if it's for you." He thrust his feet into his leather slippers and grabbed his robe off the chair.

He recognized the hysterical voice on the phone from its "hello."

"David, he's pounding on the door. He's going to get in. This time he'll kill me. Help me, David. You've got to come."

So much for the temporary restraining order on her shit of a husband.

"Okay, okay, Gladys. I'm on my way. Call the police right when we hang up. Get the baby locked into the closet; lock yourself in the bedroom. Got it? Just like we discussed."

David took the stairs two at a time.

Grace met him at the bedroom door. "Is it Lydia? Helen?"

Brushing past her, David made for the closet and pulled out an old pair of pants and a work shirt. "No, it's Gladys. Her husband's back."

"Why do *you* have to go? You're her lawyer, not the police."

"I can't go back to bed and let her get beat up." David pecked Grace's cheek. "Be back as soon as I can."

When David pulled up, the porch light was on at the Thompsons'. The white paint was peeling, but the house looked like all the others on the block, the ticky-tack built after the war. Except that the front door of this one hung open, its glass broken. David pocketed his car keys and checked the street. No people out; no sign of the police.

As he approached the house, David heard the keening and the pleading voice. "Not the baby. Please, Joe, please leave the baby alone. Please."

He raced up the stairs and saw Gladys lying on the hall floor, her right leg sticking out at an odd angle and her face scraped and bleeding. She pointed to the bedroom at the front of the house.

David knelt for a moment and hissed, "You call the police?"

She nodded, too upset to talk.

He scanned her body, saw nothing that suggested she'd die if he left her, so he squeezed her arm and headed down the hall toward the sounds of splintering wood and a baby screaming.

Joe was a steelworker, and when he wasn't drunk, he seemed like a nice enough guy. Been a Seabee in the war, somewhere in the Pacific. David had seen him a couple of times at the VFW, downing beer. Tonight, Joe's body swayed as he aimed his foot at the closet door. He was sloshed.

David seized the man by his shoulders, got an arm around his neck, and kneed him to collapse his legs. He had him on the floor in no time. Those OSS trainers would be proud. He'd been a damned good fighter before the war, but the OSS had honed his skills to perfection. He might be a little out of shape these days, but really, taking down a drunk was no big thing.

Joe struggled. "Get off me. Lemme go. It's my kid in there. You're hurting me."

David had Joe's wrist up as close to his shoulder as it would go, wrenching the man's arm until it was ready to break. "You keep movin' like that and this arm of yours is a goner. Your choice. I'm not letting you go anywhere, except jail."

A police siren sounded, its rising Doppler effect a giveaway it was closing in on the house.

When David heard boots on the porch, he yelled down. "Up on the second floor. Get an ambulance. I got the husband on the floor."

It took a couple of hours to get Gladys' mother over to take the baby, see Gladys off to the hospital, show the police the temporary restraining order—which David kept in the car for just this sort of occasion—and file the complaint down at the station. By about 0400, he knew Gladys would be okay physically. The leg would take some time to heal, of course, but that inner turmoil, her fear that Joe would be back next time he drank . . . that was going to take much longer. Maybe she needed the certainty that her husband was behind bars.

On his way home, his headlights piercing a gentle rain, David mused on the odd parallel of tonight's situation and his conflict with Adler. Not that David was scared of Adler in the same way Gladys was of her husband, but David was wary. He'd gotten soft these past few years while Adler looked in good shape. If the man commuted each day via the Rapid, he got in quite a distance of fast walking. David sat in a car. And he was pretty sure he'd lose a face-to-face fight. Adler was taller, leaner, and had a furious temper. In fact, David would be stupid to try anything physical. No, he needed a smarter strategy.

With only an hour's sleep, David rose to face another day of teaching. His body felt heavy. He barked at a couple of kids talking in class more harshly than was warranted. He didn't want to be here; he wanted to chase down how that bastard Adler worked his way into Case. As a compromise, during his break, David called for an appointment to see a Case admissions officer. He'd be a perfectly credible applicant posing as himself—a veteran considering graduate school—and he thought an hour spent unearthing scuttlebutt about Adler would get him closer to figuring out what he could do about the situation.

The very next afternoon, he parked near the University Circle Rapid stop and headed up the hill to Case. A rush of adrenaline made him take the steps two at a time. He'd been told on the phone that the Admissions Office was in Main Building, like the old days; he knew where it was.

Arriving ten minutes early, he had time to pick up a course catalogue, find a seat, and rifle through the pages. Not only was Adler named as faculty in the Department of Chemistry and Chemical Engineering, he was also in charge of the Fuels, Water, and Lubricants Laboratory. As David had assumed, the major was continuing the work he'd been doing in Germany. And, apparently, whoever decided to bring the man to the U.S. didn't think it necessary to change his name. That suggested some pretty powerful supporters.

Just as David finished flipping through the list of courses offered by Adler's department, he looked up to see a well-dressed man coming toward him. Louis Price met him with a firm handshake and led him to a smallish office with a tall window, secretary's desk, and straight-backed guest chairs. David wondered if the wooden seats had been chosen to make applicants squirm.

"As I said on the phone, I'm now teachin' high school physics and chemistry at John Adams here in town and am interested in graduate work."

Price leaned forward onto his elbows, nodding. "Um hmm."

"I've been intrigued by aeronautics and rocketry since the war when I heard the rockets over London and saw the destruction they caused."

Price responded with an introductory spiel on the university's programs, ending with, "This is a good place to bring those interests, Mr. Svehla."

David nodded back. So far, so good, like reeling in a fish. Time to use the net. "I've read about your programs and professors. I think I'd like working with Dr. Adler in chemistry and chemical engineering. Is he taking on students?"

"Adler, Adler," murmured Price. He pulled out a file labeled "C&CE Faculty" from his desk drawer and turned over several typed pages. "Oh, yes." He stopped at a paragraph and ran his finger down its lines of text. "I see Dr. Adler is a chemical engineer, an expert in fuels. He's been pushing for more graduate students." Price read more and turned a page, his hand sheltering the text. Itching to read the file, David inched his chair forward, but Price closed the file and tucked it back in its drawer. David thought the last section was headed "Evaluations." He'd have liked to read those.

Knowing that was a pipe dream, David asked if he could sit in on a class and was granted permission. He rose, thanked Price, and decided there was no time like the present. Crossing the quadrangle, he was tempted to head straight for Adler's office for a confrontation. An impulsive thing to do but not smart. What could it achieve? Adler was not going to say *mea culpa*, take me away. He was more likely to throw David out. Besides, knowing someone was after him meant that Adler could prepare, taking away that element of surprise from David's side. Better to start with the department office, see what he could find out from a chatty secretary.

Sure enough, a girl in her twenties, her light hair in a pageboy, sat behind a secretary's desk. She had an inviting smile and asked what he wanted. David repeated his story about becoming a graduate student and wanting to see the labs and attend a class of Dr. Adler's. The girl beamed. "What a distinguished man he is."

With considerable surprise, David detected a wistful note in her voice. Reading the small sign on her desk, he addressed her by name. "And a kind man, Miss Langer?"

The side of her mouth slid up a fraction. "Well, yes." Red blotches crept up her neck. "You know, not all the professors understand that I'm just one person and can't always respond immediately when they need something typed. Dr. Adler is very understanding." She straightened a stack of papers next to her typewriter, an action that allowed time for the redness to recede. Then, nodding at the chair in front of her desk, she suggested David sit.

"Am I right, he's German?"

"Yes, and, you know, I don't think of Germans as having a sense of humor, but his is downright wicked. Just the other day, he told this joke . . . Oh, I probably shouldn't be repeating things he said. What is it you wanted to know?"

David offered his most understanding smile. "Since I'm thinking of working with him, I'd sure like to know more about what he's like. Sort of forewarned and forearmed, you know."

"Let me see," She stopped and folded her hands on her desk. "His students are impressed by how much he knows about petroleum derivatives, lubrication, surface films—that sort of thing. They really respect his depth of experience. There isn't anyone else on the faculty like him. He's so clear and well organized; his fluency in German and English is impressive, not like some of our immigrant faculty; and he gives me plenty of time to do his typing." She paused, probably debating if she had said too much. "Do you speak German?"

"Yes, pretty well, though I haven't had the chance to pick up the vocabulary of rocketry and fuels."

She sat back. "He likes that. Especially when it comes to jokes. I think he saves his best for his German-speaking students. I have a little German, but not enough to get the punch lines."

David nodded. "I can see that you're the person to come to when I'm having trouble with a professor. You've got 'em all pegged, don't you?"

And what happened to the gruff autocrat he had met in Germany? This Adler sounded like a different person altogether. Better poke at this personality issue a bit more.

He rubbed his forehead to look concerned and maybe ashamed.

She rolled her chair closer to the desk and tilted her head in an inviting way.

David said, "Um, I have a, well, a personal question. It's sort of hard to ask, but you've been so helpful, I'd like to give it a try."

"What is it?"

"Well, how does he feel about having a Jewish graduate student? You know, in the war . . ."

She reached out toward him, not quite able to touch his arm. "Don't you worry about that. I know a couple of Jewish students who've been in his classes, and neither of them has had any problem with him. He's a good man, really. You have nothing to be concerned about."

She smiled, pulling herself back into her official role. "Anything else I can help you with?"

"Now that the tough question is settled, I gotta couple of easy ones. Which courses is Dr. Adler teaching this term, and when and where are they offered?" He opened the small notebook he carried, pen in hand.

"This term he's teaching Chemistry 250, the chemistry of petroleum derivatives." She consulted a schedule pinned above her typewriter. "It's Monday-Wednesday-Friday at 10 a.m., third floor, in the recitation room at the other end of the hall."

David rose and offered his hand. "Thank you. I look forward to seeing you again."

As he touched the doorknob, he turned back. "Oh, one more thing, if you don't mind. I don't remember seeing Dr. Adler's name on the faculty list when I checked a couple of years ago. How long has he been here?"

"This is his second year."

"Where did he come from?"

"That's an interesting question. I don't really know. I'm afraid you'll have to ask him."

"I'll do that. Thank you again for all your help." David saluted.

After softly closing the office door behind him, he prowled the halls and found Adler's office on the third floor unoccupied. Through the glass in the door, he saw that not a paperclip was out of place. The desk stood in the middle of the room, squared off against all walls, its surface cleared except for a desk calendar and an ink well. Its chair was pushed under the desk, wooden slats in its back standing at rigid attention. Even the books in the bookcase looked as if they dared not slouch. No chair invited a student to sit and chat. No personal items softened the austerity. This was more the Adler he knew. How odd that the secretary had a different impression of the man. Her picture offered David a veteran with whom he could exchange jokes—and throw in his extensive knowledge of a Kraut's colorful vocabulary. Only, he didn't want to like the man, didn't want to be a "fellow veteran."

So, what next? David checked his watch. Plenty of time to see if he could find an Adler student or two. He'd try the Fuels Lab down in the basement.

The back of a tall, slender man was visible through the glass in the door of the lab. David knocked and walked in. The young man slewed around, startled, a look of fear crossing his pockmarked face as though he'd been caught doing something wrong. Poor guy wasn't long out of an acne-filled adolescence.

David waved and introduced himself. "Sorry to disturb you. I'm thinking about graduate school here, working with Dr. Adler, and was curious about this lab."

The student's shoulders relaxed, and he exhaled audibly. "I was afraid you were Dr. Adler checking up on me. He's not happy with me right now."

David slid onto a lab stool a few feet from his "source." "What's the problem?"

The young man bit his lower lip. "I suppose it's not a secret. I'm working on a design for a solar-powered rocket."

"Wow, sounds fascinating. This isn't a fantasy, a Buck Rogers story?" He grinned to show the joke.

"No, not at all. Our rockets have to carry so much fuel, it's just not efficient." He closed the journal he was reading and leaned over to shake David's hand. "I'm Charlie Miller."

"So, rocket fuels are a special interest here?"

"Yeah. There're lots of problems to solve. You have any idea how much liquid and solid fuel a rocket has to carry? The stuff weighs so much, it'd be a boon to use solar power once these babies are in the air."

"You sound pretty excited about the prospect."

"For sure. If I can figure this out, it'll be a real breakthrough, and I'll get a good job out of it."

"Hope it works out for you. If you don't mind, could we talk a little about Adler? Like, does he know his stuff?"

Charlie stared out one of the windows, which featured gray snow and slush being splashed by student shoes and boots. "Yeah, he does."

David was afraid he was pushing the kid too hard. He looked to be avoiding this subject. Well, he'd take a couple more small steps, see where they got him. "Seems like you don't like him much."

"No, I don't. He really puts us all down: students, the lab, the university."

"Boy, that's got to be annoying. How'd he get here anyway? Sounds like he ought to have stayed in Germany."

"I don't know. I heard he was at Wright Field in Dayton doing something hush-hush."

"That's an Air Force base, isn't it?"

"Something like that." His hand wandered over to the journal he'd been reading. "I've really got to finish this article. Nice to meet you."

"Just one more thing. What keeps you here?"

The worry lines on Charlie's face disappeared, and his eyes glowed. "You hit it on the head when you mentioned Buck Rogers."

"Really?"

"I want to be a part of getting a man on the moon. I wouldn't mind being that man."

David rose and extended his hand, a sympathetic smile on his face. "Well, good luck with that, and thanks for being so honest. Sounds like I've got a lot to think about. And I'll be sure to watch for your name when we make it to the moon."

As David strode across the campus and jogged down the steps to his car, he reviewed what he knew: Adler had a legitimate job using his own name. He had a light and likeable side, especially with young ladies, and was respected. He was still doing research on rocketry. Apparently, he wasn't broadcasting his past, as Miss Langer, that delightful girl, was ignorant about it. Not a whole lot of new information. True, Charlie had said Adler had been at Wright Field. That was a puzzle piece to fit in along with the missing bits of how Adler got out of being tried for his crimes and into the U.S.

It was when David fired up his Studebaker's powerful V-8 engine that he decided it was time to call in the big guns. He needed to use his OSS contacts to check in with someone who'd hung around for the trials and was likely to know about Adler. He tapped his fingers rhythmically on the steering wheel. The only logical choice for who to contact was the man who had been in charge of London's Office of Secret Intelligence, Bruce Williams. David had heard through his Army Reserve unit that Williams was back from his stint as U.S. ambassador to France and living in D.C. That was his man. He'd track him down tonight.

Grace met him at the door. "David, something's going on with Davy. He's too quiet, and he won't tell me what it's about. Would you talk to him?"

Contacting Williams was a matter of national security, surely more important than an eight-year-old's issues. He grimaced at the delay this would mean. Adler could be involved in critical work for the Soviets, feeding them information about secret research going on in the U.S. He had to be stopped before he did any real damage. "Can it wait until after dinner?"

"If it has to." She gave him that stare-over-the-glasses look. "It'd make me feel better to find out what happened with his friends or at school. He says it's nothing, but I don't believe it. He's willing to say more to you, man to man."

Jeez, he wanted to write the letter. But okay, ten years had gone by since the war. The letter could probably wait a couple hours.

David chugged up to the steps to the third floor. It comprised two unheated rooms: a large, almost-square space at the top of the stairs and a storage closet under the eaves at the far end. He'd built a big table to hold the Lionel train set, attached an oval track, and tinkered with the electrical system until the train ran smoothly.

Davy ran over and pulled him toward the table. "Daddy, Daddy, come look. Mommy let me cut bits from the tree out back so I could make pine trees on the mountain. See?" He pointed at the sawmill.

David looked at the blobs of white paste with twigs sticking out in odd directions. "Yes. But trees grow upward, Davy, not sideways." He straightened up several twigs.

The room was very quiet. David glanced down at his son and was surprised to see tears in his eyes. "Davy, I'm just fixing them. Don't make a big deal out of it."

Davy turned and raced down the stairs. David followed slowly, torn between irritation and sympathy. He followed the sobs into Davy's bedroom and pulled the desk chair up to the bed. "How 'bout you tell me what's going on?"

Davy lay on his side facing the wall. "I can't."

"Nothin's so bad you can't tell your dad. Nothing." Well, he hoped that was true.

Slowly, Davy rolled onto his back, eyes fixed on the ceiling. The wetness on his face reflected the overhead light. "I don't want to go to school. The kids are mean to me."

"What are they doing?"

For a full minute, Davy kept silent, as though working out what to say. "They call me havey-cavey Davy."

David wiped an incipient smile off his face. "I see what you mean. Why that?"

Davy's eyes scanned David's face. The kid looked scared. "Promise you won't be mad?"

"Okay, I promise."

"I don't fight."

Hookay, his son wouldn't fight. Seven-year-old Hildie, on the other hand, thought nothing of wrestling friends to the floor. Just the other day she'd taken down a neighbor's son. The poor boy had hit his head on the coffee table and needed stitches. David's genes must have gotten screwed up somewhere along the way. "Did you walk away from a fight?"

Davy nodded his head slowly, studying his dad's face.

"Tell me about it." David kept his tone conversational, wiping it of any shaming or blaming. Whatever the challenge he'd faced as a kid, he'd answered with his fists. Ma might have whipped him for it later, but every kid in the neighborhood knew who was in charge.

"Mommy told me fighting wasn't the way to solve a problem. She said I should talk to the boys."

David kept his body relaxed. That sounded like Grace. They'd agreed to support each other in child-rearing, but this was too much to let go by. "You know, moms and dads sometimes look at things differently."

Davy nodded again.

"This here's one of those times. I think, sometimes, a punch is the right thing to do. You gotta stand up for what you believe in, not let other kids walk all over you."

"But what if they hit back?"

David pushed his chair back. "Come on, you need a few tips. Stand up here, facing me."

Davy jumped down from the bed and put up his fists.

David took in the fists at chest level, leaving his son's face open to blows, and the right leg in front of the left, putting him off balance. He tapped Davy's right foot with the tip of his shoe. "This foot goes back, the other one forward. That's better."

Davy shifted his feet and hit David's arm with his right fist. "I got you, Daddy. I got you." He jumped up and down.

"Yeah, but if you let go of your stance like that, I can hit you. You gotta hold your arms up, protect your face."

Just as they were trying out jabs, Hildie bounced into the room. "Whatcha doing?"

"Daddy's teaching me to fight." He threw two jabs and actually connected with David's stomach on one of them.

"Oof. Hey there, hold up for a minute."

Hildie ran over to them. "Teach me, too."

"Hildie, girls don't fight."

"I do, Daddy, when Jack makes me mad."

"We've talked about that. He had to get stitches last time." He knew he should order her out, but she had the fire to wade in and quash an opponent. She might, just might, put some of that fire into Davy. "Okay, but don't tell your mother."

Hildie nodded and jumped into the proper stance, fists ready to punch.

David held up his hands, palms toward Davy. "Punch my hand. First jab with your right—the one with more power—then follow up with your left."

Davy only missed his hand once in a series of jabs. Hildie actually caused him to move backward. Jeez, you can't fight genetics.

After dinner, David sequestered himself in his office, pleased by the deepening silence of the house. He pulled out his desk chair, turned on the lamp, drew his yellow legal pad toward him, and sat down to write. Then he lifted the phone's receiver and dialed zero. A friendly operator, probably bored at this hour, found Williams' number and threw in his address so David could "check it" against the one he said he already had. Job number one complete.

David sat, staring at the information. Should he call or write? OSS training made him wonder if the phone could be tapped. Williams could have stepped on important toes. With the Red Scare going on, there had to be tight reins on people like him with political jobs. Safer to write. Surely he opened his own mail, or he would if David wrote "confidential" on the envelope. If he sent it airmail, he'd have an answer in three or four days. It was worth the wait.

Now the issue was what to say? A problem before he put down the first words: How should he address Williams? He could use his rank, Colonel, since that was how David knew him, or Ambassador, the last role the man held, or Mister. David decided on Colonel. It was his OSS rank, and this was going to be an OSS job.

April 22, 1955
Dear Colonel Williams:

I served under you in the OSS in '44 and '45 in Secret Intelligence, attached to the Target Forces on the continent and the Field Photographic Unit in Paris. At the end of the war, I came back to Cleveland, where I remain in the Army Reserves. I resumed my job as a high school science teacher, completed my law degree using the GI bill, and have opened a small law practice.

Did he need that last sentence? He was proud of his accomplishments, but was this the time to push them? He didn't intend to enter a competition with Williams. He'd lose, as he had so often to the OSS' East Coast elite. No, he'd stick to the relevant facts. He crossed out the sentence.

I am writing to you—confidentially—because I recently saw Dr. Gerhardt Adler on a downtown street and found out he is a professor at the Case Institute of Technology. This man was a particularly vicious S.S. Sturmbannführer, a rocket specialist at Nordhausen, and the liaison with the concentration camp that supplied workers for the V-2 production facility. I arrested him under the instructions of the T-Forces in April 1945 and watched as he was taken away in a U.S. Army Jeep. I expected, from the information I collected, that he would be convicted at the war crimes trials for crimes against humanity. I do not understand why he is free and employed in the U.S.

Please let me know if this man is still a wanted criminal and if I can contribute in any way to his recapture. If he is here legally and it's possible to satisfy my curiosity, I'd like to know what happened that he was not convicted.

Yours truly,

Captain David Svehla (USA Reserves)

It was nearly midnight when David finished typing the letter, burned the draft, and filed the carbon deep in his old file cabinet. No one would mess with all those hundreds of pieces of paper—at least in the foreseeable future. He had enough trouble finding the papers he wanted when he'd done the filing. The letter could be seen as a breach of his oath never to discuss anything he'd done in OSS, but only if it was found and the finder made the right connections. Still, he vowed to put the carbon in the safety deposit box when he next went to the bank.

David sat down once more at the desk, ran his hands over the polished walnut, admiring the intricate decoration on its drawers. It was a gift from his father-in-law who had sold lumber and appreciated the craftsmanship of hand carving. Some poor sod had given it up during the Depression to pay a bill. David hoped the man had recovered his fortunes, maybe during the war, like so many others. Most people were better off now—even those who shouldn't be. Like Adler. He might be a nice guy at Case, but he used to be a scum of a Nazi.

Grace wandered in wearing her nightgown and robe. "You're working late."

"Just coming up now."

"What's keeping you up 'til midnight?"

Not wanting to worry her, he said, "A couple of wills. I kept making typos and having to start the page over again."

"You need a secretary."

"You volunteering?"

"No. I can't type and intend to keep it that way. I know what would happen if I learned."

He snorted. "Yeah, I'd overwork you."

CHAPTER 4
APRIL 1955

For the next few days, David managed a drive-by of Adler's house once or twice each day, scoping it out. A real quiet neighborhood. Few pedestrians. Not much activity. The street boasted one large house after another, no parking lot where he could hide among other cars to watch the place, no park with a bench. Too bad he didn't have a dog he could walk.

Finally, he could stand it no longer. On Tuesday, he left home before his usual early hour and drove to Adler's neighborhood to take a closer look. Leaving the car around the corner, he strolled past Adler's house, crossed Fairmount, and strode back. No hint that the place housed a German. On the second pass, he saw Adler come out the front door with a blond young man, likely his son—who was maybe sixteen or seventeen—wearing high-tops and carrying a tennis racket. They walked toward the black Mercedes in the driveway. David memorized the license number—GA 45. Probably Adler's initials plus a meaningful number. His age? The year he made some discovery or Hitler gave him an award? The year the war ended? When Adler reached for the door handle, David hurried back to his car, determined to follow them. His heart pounded as he turned the ignition key. He'd be late for school. Shit, this was more important.

As he sat at the corner, the Mercedes shot past on its way southeast on Fairmount. David accelerated into place about fifty feet behind. There was not much traffic in these residential areas, so he increased his distance, looking like he was hunting for a house number. The traffic circle at Warrensville Center was busy, giving him the cover of more cars. He slipped into the flow four cars behind the Mercedes and followed it onto University Boulevard. Again, not much traffic, but David had figured out where Adler was going: University School, a private boys' school for the well-to-do of Shaker Heights. David drove on by, turned around, and stopped at the curb maybe fifty feet from the school's entrance.

He stared at the divided entry road. Was there a theme here? Did ritzy areas have to define themselves by lawn strips in the middle of the road? Only a few minutes later, he saw Adler's car leave the school and turn back the way they had come. The German was headed for Case, most likely. Glad to be dressed in his newer suit, David pulled into the school's entrance. Nice place. A big, circular drive connecting a series of brick buildings. Very Ivy League, especially with that white tower over the main entrance. Must employ a team of gardeners to keep the extensive lawns mowed. He parked the car near the door under the tower.

In the main office, a motherly dark-haired woman sat behind a desk and looked disapproving about the idea of dropping in rather than having an appointment. Or perhaps her disdain was for his baggy pants. "I'd like to speak to the principal about enrollin' my son."

The woman's eyebrows went up. "The headmaster, Dr. Cruikshank, is busy right now. Would you care to make an appointment?"

Well, well, this was not a welcome like the one from that nice girl at Case. And was the hint of a British accent in this martinet's voice real or put on? "I'd rather see him this morning. I'm in town with my wife for a short time, looking for houses. Perhaps I could walk around the campus until he's free?"

She turned the pages of an appointment calendar and ran her finger down the day's schedule. "If you return at eleven o'clock, the headmaster should be able to see you."

David checked his watch. "I'm due to meet the realtor in about an hour. Could I set a time to call the headmaster . . ." He paused for an extra second. ". . . maybe this afternoon?"

"He should be free about three. You could try then."

"Thank you."

"And your name, sir?" The questioning tone might have been an honest one or expressing an opinion that "sir" was stretching the concept. David gave his name and left the office, feeling virtuous. He had a little time to find the Adler boy, and then he'd speed to school. Newton Rider would take care of his first classes. He should make it by third period with none the wiser if the traffic cooperated.

So, David headed for the gym hoping Adler's son was still there. A couple of boys with white high-tops were walking toward the end of a building that had the height of a gymnasium, and David followed, cataloguing their shared characteristics: clean-cut, slender, and well cared for. Not a rip in any clothing, no stains on their clothes, no holes in the shoes. Nothing like the rag-tag group he grew up with. Oh, it's not that his friends started the day in dirty clothes. Their mothers wouldn't have permitted that. But the boys always ended up covered in grime. Healthy boy stuff did that to you—sliding along the dirt into third base, hunting through the trash for treasure, shinnying up a tree to get a trapped kite. Idly, he wondered if these "model" students ever did that stuff. Jeez, did Davy?

With his hand on the door handle, David spotted a dozen or so boys at the outdoor tennis courts, including young Adler, who had three laughing high schoolers around him. A few feet away, two dark-haired boys stood taking periodic glances at Adler's group. They looked younger and a lot like Jacob Strauss must have as a teenager. David leaned against the doorjamb. This should be interesting.

After a few minutes of shared laughter in Adler's group, during which David pegged him as the ringleader, the Adler boy clapped a henchman on the shoulder and waved to the Jewish boys. "Hey, Friedberg, you want to play against me?" His crisp consonants and the slight sing-song of a German accent sent David right back to wartime Germany. God, the kid must be around seventeen now, so he would have been born about 1938. He'd surely heard the bombast. Given his father's position, he'd probably swallowed it all.

One of the dark-haired boys, apparently Friedberg, replied quietly. "I'm not in your league, Rudolf."

So the arrogant upstart had a name: Rudolf. David wondered if it had started off as Adolf and changed with immigration to the U.S.

"You never will be. Kikes don't make good tennis players." Rudolf's gang laughed.

Shaking his head, David wandered back to his car. Cliques who kept to their own, and the Adler boy carrying on that Nazi legacy. Did Jacob get this kind of insult thrown at him these days? Or were people generous? David tried to be. When Jacob had written him that he'd met a young, American woman in the DP camp and wanted to marry her, David had done all he could, though it took more than a year for all the permissions to come through. In early '47, Jacob had made it to Cleveland, a happily married man. His daughter, Karen, had been born in 1948, a month before Hildie. Funny, he and Jacob only saw each other once in a while. David felt he reminded Jacob of bad times, and their relationship had become superficial. Grace seemed to know Rebecca better, and Hildie was thick as thieves with Karen.

Unfortunately, his high school principal, Paul Broz, was standing in the doorway of the administration's office when David walked in, watching the streams of students change classes. A balding man with gold-rimmed spectacles, he looked David up and down. "Where have you been? You're late."

"I'm so sorry. I had an early appointment and got Newton to give assignments to my first classes."

"That's not Newton's job. It's yours. You're pushing your luck, David, and I don't take kindly to your behavior. You better know that I'm watching you. I want no more of these unplanned absences the rest of this term."

"Yes, sir, message received. Now, I'll be off to class."

On the phone later with Harold Cruikshank, he got his head filled with statistics about University School, including its fees—which were far beyond his means—and finally had a chance to ask questions. "Are there many Jewish students in the school?"

Cruikshank cleared his throat. "As I'm sure you know, the public high schools in Shaker Heights and Cleveland Heights are excellent and have many Jewish students. We, of course, accept students of all religions, but our boys are mostly Christian."

It was a political answer probably required in Shaker Heights since a good deal of the suburb still had covenants on house deeds that prohibited selling to Jews. Having gained more than sufficient insight into the school, David thanked the man and hung up.

After his final period, David drove back to Adler's house, left the car around the corner, and strode up the street. It was 1600 hours, so the professor was probably still at Case and his son practicing with the tennis team at school. Younger children, though, would be getting home soon, and perhaps he'd catch a glimpse of Adler's wife. The boulevard was empty of life—well, except the birds and squirrels—and its residents had done well at cleaning out the fall leaves and trimming the hedges. He marked out a route of about a half-mile in his head and set off.

On the third pass by Adler's residence, he spotted a woman with a blond pageboy walking to the garage and then backing out a tan Volkswagen Beetle. The family was certainly loyal to German-made cars. She drove it a few feet down the driveway and stopped. David halted, too, hidden from her by the hedge, and gently shifted a branch to improve his line of sight. He saw the house's front door open and a girl emerge, slam the door, and run to the car. She was maybe twelve or thirteen, with light brown hair in a ponytail and slim legs sticking out of the bottom of her coat. As she reached for the car door, David dropped the branch and ran for his car.

The VW headed northwest on Fairmount, made a series of turns, and ended on Shaker Boulevard, leading into the posh shopping area of Shaker Square. With little time left for observation, David followed their car into a parking lot behind one section of stores and then trailed his quarry on foot as mother and daughter walked around the front of the stores, entered Marshall Drugs, and walked straight to the Hough Bakery counter.

Adler's wife asked for streusel coffee cake in a thick, German accent. David could tell what she said, but the woman behind the counter looked confused.

Adler's daughter repeated the order with a pure American accent. She smiled across the counter. "My mother's still learning English."

The mother whispered to her daughter, "Greta, shh."

"Mom," the girl said in an annoyed teenager voice, "there's nothing wrong with telling the truth."

Another whisper was lost to David, but Greta's face drooped. Too bad. David liked her spunk.

When the two women left the store, David trailed behind. The Adler women headed toward Halle's department store, probably planning an afternoon of shopping. He didn't need to watch them try on clothes, so he walked back to his car. He'd learned what he could. Two children. One thoroughly open and Americanized, the other more closed, more bigoted. How about Adler himself? Was he hanging on to his S.S. fervor? Was his house filled with relics? Did he plan to advance his Nazi ideas here in the U.S. of A? David needed to pass his thoughts through Mac.

That evening, with the double doors of his sunroom office closed, he called Mac and reported what he'd done, what he'd seen. "Besides Williams, I've been trying to think of others to ask. How big is this scientist thing? Who authorized it? How could they have let in a murderer like Adler? How many others like him got admitted? You think Major Fleming, in the Reserves, might know about this?" He listened in the silence on Mac's end.

Finally, Mac cleared his throat. "I been out on Lake Erie in his speedboat, you know, listening to a noise that worried him. Gotta say, he came off as a straightforward infantry guy. Revealed too much to have been in intelligence."

David grunted. "Like I thought. Not G-2. You got any ideas on who else to probe?"

"I'll ask around, but I ain't got much hope. You know how it is. Everybody's concerned about the Cold War heating up, rooting Reds out of our forces. Seems like we've shut the door on Nazis like they was ancient history. You think there's any chance the police can help?"

That was a stretch, and they both knew it. "We haven't got any evidence he's broken any laws here. Or even that he got here illegally." They didn't have access to the right kind of government paperwork.

Mac chuckled. "I suppose we could take him out ourselves. Make it look like an accident. Say, get him out on my boat, let a good wave wash him overboard halfway to Canada?"

David laughed outright. "I wish, but no. Not that the guy doesn't deserve it. The problem is he may be part of a bigger scheme. Taking down one Nazi wouldn't stop the rest."

Mac said, "Yeah, true. I was just kidding. You got something in mind?"

"Well, my brother, Chet, knows a lot of reporters. Maybe one of them follows science and has been following the German rocket team. Von Braun made the cover of *Time* not so long ago."

"Worth a try, I guess."

"And I've been thinking about visiting his house, not just driving by. Casing the joint, you know? I can't get it out of my mind that we'll find something we could take back to Williams." David held his breath, knowing Mac was a straight shooter.

"You want to break in?"

David swallowed hard. "Yeah, I do."

"Cap'n . . ." Mac paused, as though choosing the right words. "You don't really think that's a good idea."

"I can't think of a better one."

"Yeah, well, this ain't the war. You can't just break into somebody's house. You'd get in big trouble."

"So, you won't back me up?"

"That's not what I said. If this is on the up and up, I will, but no funny business."

David pushed his hair out of his face. "Okay, okay. I get it. I'll just look in the windows."

"And after that, no surprises. You let me in on the plans, and I get veto power."

The determination in Mac's voice came through loud and clear. He was dead serious. "I got it. And you don't need to tell me again this ain't the war."

Two days later, David got home about 2000 with a nice client check in his pocket. They'd even fed him. He called "hello" inside the kitchen door, picked up the mail—nothing from Williams—and returned it to the table. Grace came down the stairs, looking frazzled, like she'd been out in the wind without a hat. He kissed her cheek and handed her the flowers he'd bought. An apology for being away so much and a thank you for being understanding. "Everything okay?" Silly question.

"It's—ah—been a long day. Can you read to the children?" Her eyes pleaded.

"Sure." He didn't want to ask for details. Grace'd tell him eventually.

When David walked through Hildie's bedroom door, he startled. It happened a lot. At her request, he'd painted the room a bright yellow, which was definitely eye-catching—sort of like being hit with a burst of sunlight. She was sitting back against her pillow, the ends of her fine brown hair still wet from the bath. She moved her gray stuffed rabbit to the other side of the bed to make room for David and handed him a copy of *Charlotte's Web*. "Mommy always reads two chapters, but you'll read three, won't you, Daddy? Please?"

God, she was a born negotiator. He raised his eyebrows. "Let's see how long these chapters are." He flipped pages to the table of contents and estimated eight to ten pages a chapter. Not particularly large print, either. "I think two will do. I need to read to Davy, too, you know."

"But if we're at a really important part, you'll want to go on. Just like me."

"We'll see."

About halfway through chapter six, which was only six pages long, Davy padded down the hall and stuck his head into the room. He'd buttoned his PJ top incorrectly, making him look a little off kilter. The boy was on the stocky side, more like a tackle than an end, and not as coordinated as David had been. A bit of toothpaste stuck to his cheek.

"Daddy, I'm ready. You'll tell me a war story, won't you?" Davy hung on the doorjamb and swung his body forward into the room.

David smiled. "Yeah, okay. But not until you're in bed. And I need to finish this chapter first."

A few minutes later, with Hildie already half asleep, David kissed her forehead and turned out her bedside light. No need to negotiate about that extra chapter. He'd made his voice get quieter and quieter and watched her slide down under the covers.

He rubbed his hands together as he traversed the short hall to Davy's room. He pulled his son's desk chair over to the bed, sat down, and rested his forearms on his thighs. "How about the story of Karl Ludwig Fischer?"

Davy shifted onto his side with his hand propping up his closely cropped head. "I like that one." His eyes sparkled.

Knitting his brows, David started, "Sometimes we were asked to take on the identity of a captured German, and my assignment was a major named—"

"Karl Ludwig Fischer."

"Right." He nodded. "I learned every detail about him: his wife's name was Helga, he had three children—Max, Hans, and Gertrude. I even knew how many teeth his grandmother had when she died because she was very proud of only losing two." A pause for effect.

"Karl was a liaison officer who traveled from unit to unit carrying messages, the perfect assignment for an Allied spy. I could pick up lots of important information and transmit it back."

"And you had to visit the family, and they could have told on you, but they believed Karl would be killed if they turned you in, so nobody talked." Davy pulled the blanket up over his shoulder. "They could've killed you, Daddy. I'd have been so scared I couldn't sleep."

"Well, to tell the truth, I was scared. But that was my job." He shifted positions to relieve the tingling in his left leg. "And remember, my code name was Brunhilde, who's a powerful mythic figure. I had to be strong like her. I think that name kept me safe all those months behind enemy lines, like I was protected by a ring of fire. That's why I gave that name to Hildie, to keep her safe."

"You were a hero, Daddy."

David ruffled his son's hair. "How are you doing with those boys who were calling you names?"

"They're fifth graders. Big and mean." He turned his face to the wall.

"Humph. I'll bet they're a lot bigger than you are."

"For sure. They scare me."

"Maybe I need to get involved. Sounds like that jab I taught you won't be a winner on its own."

Davy's voice sounded small. "Would you, Daddy?"

"Sure. What are their names?"

"Bobby Westhaven and Tim Donley. Tim's the ringleader."

"Okay. Now you get some sleep."

He rolled back to face his dad. "What are you gonna do?"

"I'll give their dads a call, see if we can't resolve this. Don't you worry."

Once downstairs, it only took a minute for David to find "Westhaven" in the kitchen phone book. There was only one in the neighborhood. A woman answered and David asked for Rusty Westhaven, which was the name listed. A friendly voice got on the line.

"Rusty, there seems to be a problem between our sons. My Davy's in third grade, and your son, Bobby, and a friend of his, Tim Donley, are picking on him. I'm hoping we can do something to stop that. You agree?"

"Oh, my. This doesn't sound like my son. Let me get to the bottom of it."

"I'd appreciate that. Best to stop it before it gets into violence."

That was easy; now for the father of the boy who seemed to be the ringleader.

"Mr. Donley?"

"Yeah, who's this?"

"I'm David Svehla, father of a third grader, Davy, who's being bullied by your son. I'd like it to stop."

"Huh. So, he's going after little kids, is he?" His voice was deep and a little aggressive.

"Seems like it."

"Well, we'll see about that."

When he hung up, David saw that Grace had come into the kitchen and listened to his last exchange. She raised her eyebrows. "Trouble?"

"Name-calling by some older boys. I think I've got it taken care of."

"I hope so. He's moped around all afternoon, and Hildie's teased him."

"Ah. No wonder you've had enough." He hugged her for a long time.

Pleased Davy's issue was resolved, David strolled into his office to call his brother to see about a journalist who could do some digging for him. He sat back in his desk chair and tried his parents' number. "Is Chet home?"

"David. You could at least ask how I am."

It was never easy. It was never going to be easy. "How are you, Ma?"

"My arthritis has kicked up in all this rain. And your father has a cold, probably from walking in wet shoes and socks."

"I'm sorry to hear that." David drummed his fingers on the desk and told himself he had to hold on to his temper. She was expert at getting him riled up.

"Your Aunt Nette and Aunt Edna, your father's sisters, are moving to Florida next month. It's very sad. Why they feel they have to move, I don't know. Our families have been in Cleveland since we came from Bohemia. I've told them they should stay, but they're very stubborn and insist they're going."

"I'm sure you'll miss them." Did she think he didn't remember his aunts' names? Did she keep talking just to annoy him? How did Chet stand living with her? Except, David knew the answer to that one. Chet spent most of his evenings with girlfriends, and it was convenient to have Ma do his laundry and clear up after him. "Is Chet home?"

The receiver clunked onto the table, and David heard his Ma yell for his brother, followed by heavy footsteps on the stairs.

Chet chuckled as he picked up the phone. "What did you say to her?"

"Nothing. Listen. Do you know a journalist who covers science and can do some checking for me?"

"Let me think . . . Try Ted Hessoun. I've known him forever, and he owes me a favor. I think I got his number around here." After a moment of rustling papers, he gave it to David.

During a free period the next day, David used one of the school phones to reach Hessoun. Their exchange was brisk and efficient. Hessoun would see what he could find out about the German scientists doing rocket work and see if Adler's name came up. And he'd keep it quiet.

When David got home that evening, Grace handed him a message: "Called Huntsville about rocket work. Got lecture on rocket development. No Adler. Tell Chet we're even." David laughed.

"Was that what you wanted?"

He kissed her. "What I asked for, not what I hoped for."

"It means you're still after that German scientist, doesn't it? Is that...is that why you've been leaving early, even during vacation?"

"Ah, yes."

"Is he becoming an obsession, David? Do I need to start worrying in earnest?"

"Naw. I'm just following up a couple of leads, that's all."

CHAPTER 5

APRIL 1955

By the time David got home from his Saturday legal appointments, his coat was soaking, and his hat dripped rainwater from the many trips he'd made between his car and client houses. He shuffled through the mail Grace had left on the kitchen table, dropping all but the white business-sized envelope with the Washington, D.C./April 20 postmark. Barely registering his wife's cheery comment about dinner, he took his long-anticipated response past the children to the sunroom. It had been nine days since he had written to Williams. He wanted the man's backing, wanted the force of the U.S. government behind him as he went after Adler.

With excitement electrifying his body, he shut the double doors behind him and searched for his letter opener. Too many damn stacks of paper on the desk. His fingers hit the sharp edge wedged under the calendar, and he made a neat slit in the envelope. There it was, his answer typed on a single page of standard white bond. The e's sat a little above the line of other letters, so it was probably typed at home rather than in an office.

Dear David:

His first name, but a colon afterwards. Friendly, maybe, but mostly business.

Certainly I remember you, though it's been almost 10 years. We did good work for our country back then, and I can see from your letter that the old habits have stayed with you.

Hmm. Was that a compliment to ease what was coming? Would Williams be telling him to mind his own business? If the colonel truly remembered him, wouldn't he cite some fact about him—the men ribbed him a lot about being thirty and already turning gray—or the code name of one of his assignments?

I checked into your sighting of Dr. Gerhardt Adler and believe I can clear up your confusion about why he is in Cleveland. As you know, at the end of the war, the U.S. military and scientific communities were very concerned about how far advanced Germany was in the areas of aviation and rocketry. We didn't want their knowledge to go to Russia, so we brought many of them to the U.S. to work alongside our scientists.

What you may not know is that their immigration was accomplished under the War Department's Operation Paperclip, which made sure their visas were properly provided by the State Department. Everyone seems pleased with the results, and you may be interested to know that 100 of the rocket scientists will become U.S. citizens soon. Dr. Adler is one of those 100. He worked at Wright Field in Dayton (now Wright-Patterson Air Force Base) until 1953 when he took the position at Case Institute of Technology.

I thank you for your letter and commend your patriotism. I trust that this information satisfies your curiosity and that the matter is now closed.

David sat down hard on his desk chair, not liking the contents of the letter. He read it again. The rockets at Nordhausen had seemed so far ahead of the Allies in weaponry that, like Williams, David firmly believed it had been critical for the country to take advantage of German knowledge and keep it from the Russians. That was doubly true now, since the Russians had tested an H-bomb. Damn Russkies. His thoughts shifted back to Berlin, May 1945. He'd watched the Russians enter the city, their cannons pulled by horses. He'd thought it a travesty at the time to hold up Germany's surrender for them, to let U.S. soldiers die while the Russian army trudged alongside horses to get to the capital. Yeah. And the worst tragedy was not to turn on the Russians right then and beat the crap out of them.

But those rocket scientists. Sure, it was good the U.S. got them, and yet, shouldn't the brass have eliminated the rabid Nazis, the ones who savaged the prisoners? David ground his teeth at the notion that Adler had a cushy job at a U.S. university. The son of a bitch should have been behind bars. David read the letter a third time. *Operation Paperclip. Visas were properly provided.*

Grace appeared at his office door. "Your dinner's getting cold."

He waved his hand and said, "I'm coming," but when she left, he sat for several minutes. Those careful words told him Williams was warning him to lay off Adler. That reference to "patriotism" could be a reminder of his oath of silence. He folded the letter and tucked it back in its envelope. Well, he preferred to have Williams on his side, but the man wasn't his commander anymore, and David couldn't let this go.

His mind churned with possibilities. Adler might carry his Nazi zeal. Maybe he was plotting against the U.S. If David could find evidence of treason, the U.S. government would have to move against Adler.

He remembered Grace's word: "obsession." Maybe Adler was becoming an obsession. So be it.

When the rest of the family was in church on Sunday, David called Mac to see if the following Thursday would work for their look-see at Adler's. Mac reiterated he wouldn't have a part in anything illegal. David said, "Yeah, yeah, I heard you the first time." They agreed to meet early to be sure the house would be empty.

On Monday, he approached his principal to negotiate a day off for "important legal work." Broz grumbled but eventually agreed as David did have another vacation day coming. On the next two days, David drove by Adler's house each afternoon, checking on when each of the family members got home. The ground looked reasonably hard and the grass thick enough to camouflage footprints if it didn't rain. The hedges, though precisely trimmed, would hide him pretty well. God, he wanted inside. The mechanics would be no problem. He still had the keys he'd used to pick German locks. They'd come in useful several times since the war as word had got around the neighbors: anyone who locked himself out just had to ask David for help.

Thursday dawned crisp and bright. Without rain for a three-day stretch, he wouldn't have to worry about leaving footprints. David and Mac drove in separate cars to the parking lot of the Presbyterian church a couple of blocks from the Adler house. David suggested they take Mac's car because his might be known from the number of times he'd driven by. Together in the new Ford Fairlane, they sat a few doors down and across the street, hunkered down in the seat so they'd be hard to see. It was a risk, sitting still, but they wanted to be sure the house was empty. Slowly, over the hour between 0700 and 0800, the neighbors drove out from their garages. Rudolf got into a friend's car, which headed down Fairmount toward University School. Greta walked up Fairmount toward David and Mac, who slipped down below visibility while she passed.

"Cute girl," said Mac.

David watched her hiking away, books piled up in her arms. "I think she goes to Roxboro Junior High."

Then the Mercedes emerged from between the hedges, Adler at the wheel and his wife at his side.

"He's not going to work if she's with him," David muttered.

"Maybe dropping her somewhere?"

"Maybe. At least the house is empty. Let's go. Don't know when we'll next have a chance."

Mac dropped David a block down Fairmount from the house, then set off for the side street where he'd park and loiter as lookout. David strode purposefully, as a mailman would, though he wasn't in a uniform. A mild rush of energy lit up his body. He stopped a moment as if to admire Adler's yard with the grass neatly cut and edged and the flower garden showing new spring growth. No people moved on the street. You couldn't tell, of course, if the other houses had eyes looking out a window, so it was best if David walked onto the driveway with confidence. Only two or three steps along, he ducked behind the shrubbery lining the drive, pulled on a black, knit ski hat, and crept toward the house, bent over so his face with its pale skin stayed hidden. It was unlikely that neighbors would be watching or that a cleaning woman was inside, but he was taking no chances. The rotten smell of the mulch that covered the ground under the bushes made him curl up his nose.

He made it to the house with no alarm raised and eased up its side and around the back. A movement along the side street sent him into retreat. A streak of fear hit his stomach. He peeked around the corner of the house and blew a sigh of relief. It was just Mac, on duty. Hearing nothing from the Adlers' or neighbors' houses, he ducked low and ran for the garage, about twenty feet away. Since its large doors were visible from the house and road, he eased his way in the side door, puffing. Bless this neighborhood. Few people saw a need to lock their garages. The brick building had tall ceilings in its parking bay and one car, the VW Beetle. Frau Adler's. No visitors, most likely.

He jogged up the garage stairway to a room above, which might have housed a driver at one point but was now used for storage. No papers, though—just old furniture, a dusty bedstead, and old toys. Nothing of interest. He reversed his route, cracked the door, detected no whistle, and crept back to the house.

As he made his way slowly across the back of the structure, he stopped at each window to check the contents of the room for people and papers. The basement wasn't finished but had a nice washer and dryer, big, old, coal furnace no longer in use, and a solid cement floor. The kitchen looked well kept, the living room was downright elegant, and that dining room chandelier had to be fine crystal. Very neat, very clean, pretty darned expensive. Fit the man's pattern.

Before David rounded the corner, now almost certain the place was deserted, he looked back. Damn. If someone knew what to look for, he'd left a trail with a tramped-on plant, a couple of broken branches, a scrape along the ground. Oh, well, couldn't be helped. Besides, it looked like the first-floor window on the far side of the house wasn't locked. "Eureka," he whispered. It was the den with an oversized desk as neat as the man's Case office had been, and it called him to come in. He used both hands to push up the bottom of the window an inch, and then stuck his fingers in the opening and shoved the window upward. He'd have to hoist himself up and over the sill, and his bulk meant that was no small feat. He grinned—God, this was great, like those wild training exercises OSS had set for them.

And then he heard it: Mac's warning whistle announcing the caissons were rolling along. Only David didn't know from which direction. For a second, he wondered if Mac had whistled the tune just to stop his entry, but there wasn't a lot of cover on this side of the house, and he couldn't take the chance that someone was coming. He dove between a leafless bush and the house, hoping his dark trousers and army jacket would melt into the background if he stayed still, tucked in his chin so his dark hat faced the driveway, and took slow deep breaths. A few seconds later, the Mercedes pulled into the driveway from the side street and drove slowly past him, less than twenty feet away. Daring a slow turn of the head, he saw two occupants, with Adler staring forward as he drove up the drive and his wife looking away from David, toward her husband. Phew.

They made their way to the garage, and under cover of the noisy tires, David crawled up to the corner of the house to keep them in sight. He pulled his legs under his body, tearing his pant leg on a rock. In a crouch, he figured he could sprint down the drive to reach Mac and the car. Sprint, right—like that was likely with his paunch. Well, he'd run as fast as he could. After all, this secondary drive was pretty open with no hedge, and he could be seen from the house. There was nothing like fear for an incentive. He considered the alternatives and didn't like any other direction better.

At the garage, both car doors opened. Adler got out, walked toward the garage doors, and opened the bay that housed his Mercedes. His wife stood to the side, apparently waiting for him. In a few moments, they both walked up the brick path to the house. They spoke in German, distinctly using an educated Hochdeutsch. He listened hard, without moving.

"Gerhardt, will you talk with Rudy? Please? His physics teacher called. He failed his last test, and the man is worried."

Adler's voice came out gruff. "He's perfectly smart. Why is he doing this? To spite me?"

The light crunch of footsteps stopped. David imagined her turning to face her husband. "You know the answer to that. He wants to be a poet."

"The son of a professor of chemical engineering, a researcher revered on three continents, cannot be a poet. I won't allow it." David heard the S.S. officer issue an order.

It was deathly quiet in the yard. Even the birds seemed to be listening, and Mac had hunkered down. David imagined a glowering Adler, hovering like an angry vulture over his wife.

"He is his own person, Gerhardt. Is it so bad to have a Rilke in the family?"

Anger erupted in the man's deep voice. "He can't earn a living as a poet. What kind of father would I be if I told him poetry was an acceptable vocation?"

"I'm not asking you to do that. What I'm asking is that you let him figure that out for himself."

David envisioned generations of Prussian officers lined up behind Adler, urging him to push his son into the military or a competitive occupation.

Her voice was so quiet he almost missed it. "Rudy is not Johann. He'll be leaving soon for university. Give him time."

"That's if any university will take him." More quietly, he added, "And I don't need any reminding about Johann."

David wondered for a moment who Johann was, but heavy footsteps sounded inside the house, coming toward him. Frozen in place, his worries moved to whether Adler would spot the open window.

And then his wife's voice, stopping her husband, "Please. We are Americans now."

David shook his head in disbelief. He'd expected her to be a dyed-in-the-wool Nazi like her husband and son, not a budding American. First the daughter, now the wife.

David's left leg, the one that had been squeezed most by his crouch, had fallen asleep, so he shifted his weight. His foot snapped a stick. He froze, hardly breathing for several long minutes. Nobody inside spoke. No footsteps came his direction. Maybe they didn't hear it. They stood a room or two away from the window. If they did, perhaps they thought it was a small animal. Still, it was time to get out of Dodge, so David pushed himself to a standing position tight against the brick wall and tried out his leg. It needed another minute or two if he was going to trust it to hold his weight. And now he was sweating. He could be seen from the street, for sure, and as soon as he left the protection of the house, he could be seen from several of its windows.

He waited, massaging his leg, his senses on high alert. He caught a flicker of Mac's hand, signaling from the fence at the end of the driveway that the coast was clear. It was time. One more glance to his right showed an empty yard, a listen picked up his heart pounding but no noise from the house. That could be good or bad. Oh, well. He'd assume good. And he took off, more like a gimp than a track star.

Sticking to the lawn on the house side of the drive, he figured to cut the sound of his feet and use the house as a partial shield to roving eyes. Anyone looking out from the den or room above had him in their sights, but a person in the kitchen, living room, or dining room might not see him at all.

A shot rang out, coming from the house behind him. David automatically began to zigzag and picked up speed, repeating in his head "shit, shit, shit" with each footfall. As he rounded the iron post of the fence at the end of the drive, he heard a second shot ping on the metal close to his head. Jesus, Mary, and Joseph.

Mac, now squatting behind the stockade fence that marked the neighbor's property, hissed, "Pick it up, Captain. Twenty feet to go." And when David reached him, Mac grabbed his arm, pulled him toward the Ford, and threw him into the passenger seat. Then Mac sprinted around the front of the car, and they shot up the side street.

David, gasping for air, fumbled with the handle of the still-open car door. Sweat poured off him. God, he needed to get in shape if he was going on escapades like this one.

Mac sped around several corners, and with David's directions, eventually got them back to the church parking lot. Pulling up next to David's Studebaker, he switched off the engine, sat back, and ran his arm across his forehead. "What was that shit about, opening the window?"

"I saw it was unlocked and got carried away."

"Right. Well, you better know that I'm not risking my life for you. Not when you renege on your promises. This ain't the war. I'm a law-abiding citizen, and I've put my guns away."

David soaked his handkerchief with the sweat rolling off his head and then dropped his hand into his lap. "I'm sorry, Mac. I was out of line. The temptation was too much."

"I'll bet." He pushed a load of air out hard. "You okay?"

"Yeah, yeah. My heart hasn't had this kind of a workout in a long while." He made one last pass on his forehead and stuck the wet cloth in his back pocket. "Thanks for getting me out of there."

"Was it worth it?"

"Absolutely. I've missed the excitement. But did I learn anything? Not really. Adler's wealthy, but we knew that. His house is neat, but there's nothing particularly German about it. No S.S. medals on the wall. No papers visible." He paused. "This little episode, well, it reminded me of the last time we were shot at—in Neuss. Remember? Plenty of adrenaline flowing."

"And we didn't win there, either: no new information, no prisoners. Just crawling away with our tails between our legs. And our colonel missing one of his legs."

It had happened in the last month of the war. They'd drifted off to sleep in an empty apartment building. David had his arm across his face until he was blasted off his cot by a shell hitting the side of the building. Fear had torn through him then, too. His T-Force fired upon. The only weapon he had with him was a handgun because they'd been told the German army had evacuated the town. Underpowered and forced to run for shelter. Helpless. He hated being helpless.

There was plenty to think about on the short drive home that day. As he said goodbye to Mac and drove off, adrenaline ebbed from his body, and the thought grew that he was failing in his search for justice for Adler. Most likely, he'd blown any chance of getting into the man's house. The guy'd be on high alert and would probably increase his security. And David may well have blown his partnership with Mac, who'd never agree to another try. The more David tried to plot ways to get at Adler's paperwork, the more strongly he felt the project was futile. Even if he discovered proof that Adler had exceeded his orders and the law in Germany, it wouldn't be admissible in a U.S. court, and he sure didn't have the money or qualifications to take it to a German court—if they'd even accept such a case. And if something was wrong with Adler's immigration to the U.S., a possibility Williams denied, it was basically impossible for a small fry like David to find out. Frankly, that idea of Adler plotting to overthrow the government—pretty far-fetched. The guy was busy being a Goddamn scientist, teaching and doing research. Maybe a bit more inquiry about loyalty was merited. Or maybe David needed another strategy altogether. He'd let his mind chew on that for a while.

Meanwhile, time to decide what he was going to tell Grace about his torn and dirty trousers. If this were his lucky day, she'd be out, he'd hurry upstairs to change, make up some excuse for the clothes, and walk away scot-free. But Grace pulled open the kitchen door as he came across the concrete walkway.

"What happened to you? You're a mess."

David looked down and took in the dirt and mulch encrusting his outfit. "Oh, yeah. I was out with Mac. We were horsing around." His eyes swept her face to see if she was buying this.

She helped him peel off his jacket. "I can wash the jacket, but those trousers will have to go to the cleaners." She peered at him over her glasses. "And I'm not buying it." She let his filthy jacket brush the floor and put her free hand on her hip as she did when demanding a better explanation from the kids.

She didn't look angry, more annoyed. Perhaps he could get away with a carefully crafted story. After all, he'd spent years not talking about the details of war, the real war, until it had become a habit to invent. Except, he didn't want to lie to her. He wanted her on his side in this Adler business. "Mac and I went to Adler's house to have a look-around and got shot at."

She dropped his jacket as her hands flew to her cheeks. "He shot at you?"

"Well, I did get right up to the glass."

"I can't believe this." She took two steps to the sink and held on. "You're going crazy over this Adler. Can't you hand him over to the authorities? Let them take care of it?"

David's eye caught some mud sticking out from his cheek, and he brushed if off with his arm. "They aren't interested. I mean, Adler hasn't broken any U.S. law—that I know of, anyway. My OSS boss says he's here legally."

"You talked to him?" She sounded incredulous.

"His was that letter from Washington. But, Grace, what Adler did was horrific. It's not right him getting away with it. It's just not right."

"I'm lost—and scared. Why is it *your* job to punish Adler?"

"Hon, you know I can't tell you the details of what I saw. But use your imagination. You've heard about the camps, the organized killing, the slaughter of human beings. We can't condone that."

She blew air out in an audible sigh, leaning back against the sink. "All right, I agree in principle. But, I need a promise: no more physical attacks, no more heroic—and stupid—risks to bring him down. And please, no more guns! Okay?"

He wiped his hand across his pant leg to clean off the mud. "Yeah. I've figured out I can't beat him at that game."

"Oh, dear. Just what game are you going to play?"

"I don't know yet."

"That doesn't make me feel any more comfortable." Her hands framed her face as she shook her head.

David considered arguing further but gave up the idea. Not tonight, anyway. He'd let this rest until he had a firm plan. Then she'd be sure to want him to see it through. Well, she might be.

Later that evening, in the sanctuary of his office, David called Jacob and asked if they could take a walk together. He couldn't keep his friend out of this any longer. Adler was as much—or more—of an issue for Jacob than David. He had to warn his friend before he, too, encountered the German on the street. Jacob might even want to help; at least he wouldn't have a shock later and wonder why David had kept quiet.

David lifted his chin into the light breeze of the April night. Easter—and Passover—were over. The weather was mild: a good night for being outside. Even though it wasn't his usual habit, and he was sure Grace was wondering what he was up to. He'd tell her—soon.

It only took about seven minutes to walk the block and a half to Jacob's house. He knocked on the Strausses' front door, and Rebecca opened it. "I'm on a walk and called to see if Jacob might join me."

Rebecca nodded, invited David in, and called her husband, who emerged from the back kitchen and got his jacket.

Only a few steps down the driveway, Jacob said, "I do not know what you have in mind, but I am suspicious. Please go to point."

"I'm afraid I'm going to dig up old sores. This may be painful. I wouldn't do it if I didn't think it was necessary."

"Do what?"

David pulled Jacob to a stop. "Gerhardt Adler is here, in Cleveland Heights."

Jacob's face froze in horror. "What? You must joke."

"I wouldn't do that to you. Not about something this serious."

Jacob pulled his hair, mumbling, "Adler, Adler here."

David guided Jacob down the sidewalk, a hand under his elbow. Giving Jacob time to adjust to the bombshell, he described coming upon Adler and following him. "When I saw him that first time, I felt such rage. For what he did to you, because he wasn't punished. I can't let him go, let him glory in his wealth and privilege."

"He is wealthy?" The question came out quietly.

David responded equally gently, telling him about the Mercedes, the nice suits, and the son's attendance at University School.

They walked several yards without a word, Jacob with his limp more pronounced and David slowing his stride to accommodate his friend. "I have had too many dreams of Adler. Often, I see his whip come at me and I scream. Always, I awake myself in a sweat." He paused and glanced at David. "Sometimes I commit murder." He brought up a hand shaped into a gun.

David nodded. "Yeah, vigilante justice. We need that from time to time."

"What is that?"

"Oh." Of course, Jacob wouldn't automatically know cowboy slang. "Taking the law into your own hands, like forming a posse and making sure justice is done."

"Posse. Like the westerns on TV."

"Yeah, like that." David remembered a heady day in the T-Forces collaring a nasty target in Moers. It had taken all three men in his microfilming unit and the three guys on the safe-cracking team to chase the Nazi down and subdue him. They beat the crap out of the guy. Damn, but that posse was pleased with itself.

They strode on to the corner with Jacob's heels clacking an uneven beat on the slate sidewalks. Then he spoke, "Shooting is too fast for that bad man. Death must come slowly. He must feel the pain he gave to all of us." The dim streetlight showed Jacob's hands curling into fists, releasing, and curling again.

"The S.S. caught a couple of OSS guys and stuck splinters under their fingernails to make them talk. Their bodies didn't have any nails left when we got to them."

"Such pain. I do not understand why men like to demean others, to take away their joy, their loves, their humanity. I would like, for a time, for him to know such humiliation."

"Is that enough? That—humbling—for a time?"

Jacob turned toward him. "I do not know what is enough. I do not know if anything can take away the shame I feel at what he made of me in the camps, what I did to survive."

They rounded the corner onto Taylor Road, matching steps, and caught sight of a few children at play in the parking lot of the Evangelical United Brethren Church. David stopped and touched Jacob's sleeve. "If this were war, we could capture him, stick him in a room without any windows, and make him admit the horrors he perpetrated. That would humiliate him."

Jacob stuck his hands in his pockets. "I want that he suffers. I do."

David rubbed the back of his neck. Kidnapping was not a sane possibility. Humiliation, though—at Case, in front of his family?

Jacob patted his heart. "I want him to hurt here. It is not necessary to hurt his body. No, he must atone. You see, in my religion, one must repent for one's sins, with all the heart, and not only that. It must show in words and actions."

"I'm not sure what he'd have to do." Though unschooled in church matters himself, David had grown up in a Catholic neighborhood. "I mean, Catholics have gotta confess their sins, but I don't know how many people are honestly sorry for what they confess. Most of my friends confessed to touching themselves, but I can't say that the Hail Marys the priest assigned ever stopped them.

"Adler must atone," Jacob said.

"How? I mean, we might get him to say he was sorry, but I bet he'd just recite the words." He thought about the number of times he'd been forced to apologize by his mother and couldn't remember ever meaning it.

They walked on in silence for several minutes, until Jacob stopped at the end of David's driveway. "I will think about this—and you will, too. Perhaps I will talk to the rabbi."

"Okay. I'll think about it, see what makes sense." Right now, nothing did. Not even the thought that he'd keep this conversation to himself; no need yet to tell Grace.

Jacob pulled him from his reverie. "I may talk also to others at the synagogue. The rabbi will know the men I should see. We cannot forgive the Germans for what they did. It is not expected or desired. But how to react to this individual? Can I forgive him? Should I even try?"

David fussed with these notions of atoning and forgiving. They didn't have the satisfaction of wiping the ground with your opponent in a knock-down dragged-out fight. After that, you knew who won and who lost. This atonement business—was it enough?

At the VFW on Friday, David caught up with Mac at the bar getting a refill. "Am I forgiven for my stupidity yesterday?"

Mac raised an eyebrow. "Not yet." He pointed his finger at David. "Don't ever try that again."

"Got it . . . shall we join the boys? I'd like to hear what they think of the situation—well, in general. I'm not naming names."

Mac hesitated for a moment. "Sure. I was just on my way over."

As they walked toward a group of Mac's fellow enlisted men, Bill waved and shouted over the din, "Hey, Dave, over here!" David ground his teeth at the use of this shortened name and waved back. Out of the corner of his eye, he saw Mac grin. The other men around the table looked up.

Bill drew his brows together. "Haven't seen you in a while. Things okay?"

"Yeah. Been busy, that's all." He studied the three men he didn't know well. All had the look of non-coms: tough, a little grizzled. He introduced himself and shook hands all around. "So, what have I missed?"

He listened to hopes that the Indians were solid enough to make it to the pennant race this year, grousing about the cost of fixing a fifteen-year-old car, and one man's worry about the Russians and whether he should dig an air-raid shelter in his backyard. The consensus seemed to be it was too expensive, but for David, the topic made a smooth transition.

"All this stuff we hear about the Red Menace is bad. We could have finished them off, and we let 'em go." He paused, using his finger to connect the drips of condensation on his glass. "At least we got a bunch of German scientists to come over to our side." He scanned the men's faces.

The one everybody called Sarge spoke up. "Wasn't there an article in the *Plain Dealer* about how Russia's got monster rockets now because they got so many of Germany's scientists after the war?"

David waited for a reaction, willing the discussion forward.

Mac jumped in. "Yeah, I saw that article. And the picture." He leaned back and his eyes lost focus. "I wouldn't want one of those headed for me."

David nodded.

Bill cleared his throat and hawked into his handkerchief. "Wish we'd a gotten all them rocket scientists. We should've brought 'em home with us, so we'd 'ave beat out the Russians. Wouldn't be no more Red Menace." He nodded several times and reached for his beer.

"I'm glad we got some scientists. They're like reparations," David started. "But I wanna know who they're loyal to. Do they write to their colleagues in Russia and tell our secrets? Are they working as hard as they can for the U.S.? As hard as they would for Germany?"

Mac leaned forward, tapping his finger on the table. "Some vets at my shop were talking about Wernher von Braun and what he's doing for the army down in Huntsville, Alabama. They said we wouldn't even be in the race with Russia without von Braun and his team."

"You ever worry about their loyalty?" David repeated. All heads turned toward him. "Ever worry whether they've been held accountable for what they did?"

Bill piped up. "The war's over, Dave. Let it go. These scientists are doing good for us." He looked around the table. "Anyone else want another round? It's on me." He stood up, glass mug in hand.

Sarge picked up the topic after Bill headed to the bar with three empty glasses. "We had the Nuremburg trials. The Nazis got punished. I say we deal with today's problems, not go back there." Nods all around.

David shook his head slowly. "Yeah, but what if you found one of these guys and he was a criminal. Like, maybe he ran a camp and oversaw the deaths of thousands of Jews. And he's here, a free man. Would you let him be? Let him have a great job, earn U.S. money, buy a big house?"

"That's despicable," Mac said.

"True. But what should we do about it?"

Sarge narrowed his eyes and stared at David. "He ought to be hung."

"Yeah, well. We can't *legally* hang him for something happened in Germany."

Bill slapped the beers down on the table, twirled his chair around, and sat down with his arms on the chair back. "What's the problem?"

Sarge caught Bill up.

"That all happened ten, fifteen years ago," Bill said, reaching for his mug.

Mac said, "But the statute on murder doesn't have a deadline."

Bill sniffed hard. "Still, it was wartime. You oughta let it go."

David gave one more try. "Suppose it happened to your family, this putting people in a camp, letting them die."

Bill wriggled, as though in discomfort. "I don't know."

Sarge pushed his chair back and crossed his arms. "I'd be out for blood."

David stared at Sarge's determined stance. One of them on his side, anyway. The rest—and probably most of the American population—not so much. They wanted to move on, put the war in the past, enjoy the prosperity. He finished his drink and twirled the glass on the table.

Maybe he should move on, too. He wasn't going to change U.S. policy, reopen the Nuremburg trials, or reject the leaps forward by German scientists in the U.S. But, no, he wasn't going to put this aside, either. There wasn't going to be a kidnapping; that was a naïve idea. But there had to be something.

CHAPTER 6

MAY 1955

Sunday evening, David called Major Fleming, his senior officer in the Reserves, from his sunroom office. He didn't know the man well but couldn't think of another guy in the Reserves more likely to have info on what was going on at Wright-Patterson. He wasn't following this lead because he thought he'd get red-hot evidence against Adler down there, but because it was possible he'd find out something useful. And he couldn't stand to leave any stone unturned.

"Captain Svehla here, sir. Do you have a minute?"

"Just a sec." Sound got muffled, so Fleming had likely covered the phone's speaker. "What can I do for you?"

"I'm thinking about job options. You know, I teach high school physics and chemistry, and I've been exploring a graduate degree in chemical engineering. But I got a family now. Can't afford not to be earning money."

"So, how do I come in?"

"One of the graduate students I talked to at Case said there was interesting work going on at Wright-Patterson. I wondered if you knew about it, thought they might be hiring?" Not bad, clear, and to the point.

"I'm afraid I don't know a lot. I did hear they were doing flight testing, some jet engine work, something with a wind tunnel. I have no idea if they're hiring. I may have a name you can call, though. Hold on."

David tucked the receiver between his shoulder and ear and pulled a notepad out from a stack of papers. He rocked his pen back and forth, waiting for Fleming's return.

"Here it is. Man I fought with in Italy, Capt. Duncan. I think it's his office number."

David wrote it down. He'd get a lot of quarters together, use the pay phone near school during his free period.

When he tried the number the next morning, Duncan was out, but his secretary said he should be back in the afternoon. David tried again after school, reached the man and gave his spiel, this time saying he'd connected with Adler who'd suggested he might get some experience at Wright-Patterson.

"Adler, eh? Haven't heard his name in a couple of years. I think he left in '52, maybe '53. How's he doing?"

David tried to gauge the emotion in the voice and decided it was a polite inquiry not backed up with actual liking for Adler. "He's the head of the Fuels Lab at Case, teaches in the chemistry and chemical engineering department, and seems to have a lot of research going on."

"Glad to hear it. You think you'd like to work here?"

"It sounds interesting, and I'm afraid high school teaching is getting repetitive and losing its appeal for me. I'd like to be learning, moving science forward."

"You active duty Air Force?"

"No, sir, Army Reserves. I was in the Chemical Warfare Service, then OSS during the war."

"Well, I should warn you. We get most of our junior staff from the Air Force Institute of Technology here on the base. But you sound like you might be qualified. When could you come down for an interview?"

David looked at his schedule for the month of May. "Any chance for a Saturday time?"

Duncan chuckled. "We generally work Monday to Friday these days."

Knowing he was about to wave a red flag in front of his principal, David suggested the following Wednesday.

"Okay, we'll see you at 1000 hours."

David left the house at 0500 not knowing how bad the traffic would be. He told Grace it was research about Adler. She was skeptical but held her peace, only asking that he drive carefully. He figured, as the miles went by, that if he got to Dayton early, he could scope out the area around Wright-Patterson before his interview. And, oh, yes, he'd have to stop soon to call in sick.

The base was an impressive place. From a small airfield named for the Wright Brothers, it had grown and grown, especially during the war. Now the old Wright Field was a research and development center, Area A of the whole installation. Scores of buildings. The place was humming with uniformed soldiers and men in suits.

After showing his credentials, the soldiers at the gate directed David to one of the new buildings, and a receptionist led him to Capt. Duncan's office with its gray metal desk, chair, and file cabinets. Area B was clearly careful with security; no visitor roamed around without an escort.

When they were both seated, Duncan began the interview. "So, David, I did a little checking on your war record. Ambassador Williams recommends you highly and said your German was decent. Shall we switch languages? Around here, it's helpful to know both, though we do usually communicate in English."

It was a command rather than a request, and David immediately complied, commenting in German on his admiration for Williams and his gratitude for the recommendation. Feeling he had little to lose in being forthright, he asked, "How is the relationship working out between the German and American scientists?"

Duncan sat back in his chair, relaxed and confident. "We don't mix much. They've brought invaluable talent and experience to our team, they're pretty happy here, and the research is moving ahead nicely."

"I'm glad to hear that. How would I fit into the picture?"

"We have an opening in one of our testing sections. Until we renew your security clearances, I'm afraid I can't tell you many details. In general, though, we're working on some new aircraft, including an unmanned craft.

Sort of like the stuff of science fiction. You'd be under the direction of the scientists, keeping track of the data."

"Any chance for a more theoretical role, kind of like a research assistantship?"

Duncan smiled. "I'm afraid those positions go to the Air Force officers getting their master's degrees or post-doctoral fellows."

David forced a smile in return. "Too bad."

"Let's go through the basics of the science you need to know to work here."

For the next twenty minutes, Duncan threw questions at David—thankfully in English. He started with easy ones and transitioned to ones that challenged David to think through complex ideas he hadn't brought to mind for years. At the end, Duncan said, "Well, you're a little out-of-date, but I'd say you have a solid basis in theory. What other questions do you have?"

"Where would I live, if I moved down here with my family?"

"We all used to live on base, when the Germans first arrived, but over the past few years, we've spread our wings. There are a range of houses nearby. I'm sure you can find something satisfactory."

"When would you want me to start?"

"Say, in a month? That should give you time to make your living arrangements."

"How about at the end of this school year? It's a bit more than a month away, but I'd feel better if I could finish out the term." And so would his principal, Broz.

"Sounds possible. Now, would you like to talk with one of the younger men about what it's like to work here?"

"Oh, yes. Definitely."

"Good. There's one down the hall who can tell you what work and life are like here."

"Thank you, sir."

So, David walked behind the captain down the hall toward a lab and considered the option on offer. The trip had started out as a fact-finding mission, but now he felt flattered by the job possibility. At the same time, he was appalled at the thought of working for the same German scientists who had subjugated Jacob and so many others.

Johnny Frait, the chatty lieutenant down the hall, was effulgent in his praise of the facilities and the work being done. "We're at the forefront of aeronautical engineering here. I never thought I'd be working with the top men in the world. It's an incredible honor."

"Any friction between Germans and Americans? You know, because of the war?"

Johnny looked thoughtful. "Not really. The Germans were ten years ahead of us when they came over, and it was probably hard for some of our top guys to become students again. But now that problem's gone." He swiveled in his chair and pointed to a large building. "That's the new supersonic wind tunnel. State-of-the art. You won't find another one like it."

"Impressive. Can I see inside?"

"I'm afraid not—until you work here."

David hid his disappointment, glad from a security standpoint that they were careful to limit access to this classified work. "Looks like a big place. You seem to know your way around. You been here long?"

"Coming up to three years. Got my degree next door and moved right onto the staff here."

David nodded. "Congratulations. I do know a man who worked here, and I wonder if you knew him, Gerhardt Adler?"

"Adler? Yeah, I did. Very smart. A little stiff. And a little sad."

Surprised, David turned from the window to face Johnny. "What do you mean?"

"Well, the Germans brought their families, but no one had a child over the age of seven or eight. I suspect their older sons were Hitler youth and got killed. Don't know about the daughters, and I'd hate to guess. I overheard Adler say his oldest boy, Johann, I think—maybe ten or eleven?—was staying in Berlin with relatives and went to man the barricades. He was killed just days before the surrender."

"I didn't know."

"I'm afraid many of the German families have stories like that. The war wasn't easy on them, even when they had positions of respect."

"Yes, respect." David wondered, once again, if the other scientists at Middelwerk respected the role Adler assumed. Were they pleased to let him take charge of the labor force, leaving them out of it? Did they egg him on, participate with him, or pretend they were not aware of his activities? Sure, it was sad that Adler lost his son, but still, could one forgive him his reign of cruelty?

David got home late, missing dinner and the nightly ritual with the kids. Grace had saved a plate for him and sat down catty-corner to him at the kitchen table, a steaming cup of coffee in front of her. "How was this trip you *had* to make?"

David stopped his fork on the way to his mouth. "Exhausting." He put the fork down. "But I got a job offer."

Her cup clattered as it hit the saucer. "What?"

"They'd like me to help with the testing of systems for new aircraft. It's all hush-hush, but interesting, maybe exciting."

She pushed back in her chair, as though distancing herself from him. "You didn't tell me you were looking for a job. You said the trip was about the German. You thinking of taking this job?" Anxiety—and growing anger—was written on her face.

"I don't know." True, he'd been flattered to be asked, proud that his skills were recognized. But he'd had that visceral reaction to working under Germans—and the job would uproot the family. "It'd be a big change for all of us."

She leaned forward, elbows on the table, and scraped his face with her eyes. "This is a bombshell. Didn't it occur to you I should have a part of this right from the beginning? I thought we were partners in this marriage."

He fumbled with his words. "I didn't know I'd get an offer. I wasn't looking for one."

She jumped up from her chair, strode to the sink, and turned to face him. "Let me make myself clear. I'm not interested in leaving my sisters, my cousins, our friends. I like this house. I like the schools. The children have good friends."

He raised a hand. "Simmer down. It's okay. I don't really want the job. Sorry I dumped the idea on you. It was nice to be asked, that's all."

She returned to her chair and gripped its back. "Next time, talk to me first when you're thinking about moving across country. I'm the other half of this relationship. I get a say in these decisions."

"It's only Dayton!"

She looked at him over the top of her glasses as she sat back down. "This time."

After several bites of food when he was sure the air was clearing between them, David asked, "Any messages for me?"

Grace pointed to the address directory at his elbow.

He pulled a scrap of paper out from under its corner. Grace had written to call Jacob. "What's this about?"

"He didn't say, just asked for you to call. Is it likely to be something I should be warned about in advance?" Her eyebrows rose with the question.

David smiled. "I'll let you know when I know."

While Grace finished the dishes, David sequestered himself in his office to make the call.

"Jacob, I've been meaning to call you. You have any ideas about how to humiliate Adler?"

"Yes. I talked with the rabbi and some other men whom he suggested. We would like to meet at my house on Sunday to talk about what to do. Will you come?"

"You sure I'd be welcome?"

"Oh, yes. You saw Adler; you know about him."

"Well, all right. What time?"

"Three o'clock."

With no client appointments on the books, David got home early the next day. Broz had kept him for a few minutes, airing his worries about David's time off and ordering him to be in school for the remainder of the term. David humbly apologized, and the principal had gone away merely grumbling. Now, feeling freed of any repercussions from playing hooky, he flipped through the mail and thought he might head into his office and catch up on some legal correspondence. On his way to the sunroom, he spotted Davy limping up the driveway. Blood dripped from the boy's nose, one jacket sleeve hung half off his arm, and mud splotches covered his pants.

Grace met Davy at the back door with David close behind. "What happened to you?" She helped him out of his jacket, and he plopped onto a chair.

"I tried to talk to them, Mommy. I really did." Then his face screwed up and he started to cry.

Grace untied his filthy shoes and pulled both socks and shoes off.

David stared down at this son. "Who was it, Davy? Who did this to you?"

"Those fifth graders, Bobby and Tim. They said I had to fight or they'd beat up Hildie." He sniffed, ran his forearm across his nose, and cried out from the pain.

David held Davy's chin and turned his face from side to side. The blood was drying, and his nose wasn't off-kilter. "It's not broken."

Grace stood up. "Let's get your pants off and see what happened to your leg." She helped him stand and step out of his trousers. His thigh had a large bruise coming up, but the skin was intact. "It looks painful, but I don't think it's too serious. I'll get a washcloth and be back down in a minute." She patted Davy's knee.

"So, what happened?" David squatted beside his son, feeling his anger rise. No asshole was going to beat up his son and get away with it.

Davy bounced his leg a couple of times. He seemed mesmerized by a spot on the floor. "Bobby knocked me down, then Tim kicked my stomach and my leg."

"What did you do?"

"I didn't do anything. They started it."

"How did you respond?"

Davy glanced up at his father. "Daddy, I tried to punch and kick Bobby like you showed me, but he jumped away." He returned his gaze to the floor. "They laughed at me. Tim said I was a sissy. But I wasn't."

Grace breezed in, her hands full of washcloth, Mercurochrome, and bandages. She filled a basin, wet the cloth, and scrubbed the blood from Davy's face. Then she had him take off his shirt. Other than a bruise on his stomach, no injuries were obvious. Well, except his hands were pretty well scraped. "I don't understand why they want to fight—with you, with Hildie, with anyone. It's senseless." She pulled bits of grit from his palms using first her fingers and then a set of tweezers.

"Where were the teachers?"

Davy shrugged.

David glowered. This wasn't supposed to happen in nice, suburban neighborhoods. He'd talked to the fathers and thought the business was resolved. He sized up his kid. Still yelling "ouch" when the Mercurochrome hit. Not crying, but his lip quivered.

Grace patched Davy's hand wounds and sent him to get into clean clothes. "I'm going to put these clothes in the washer to soak."

David stood up to let her by and made up his mind to take care of this threat to his family once and for all. He dialed Rusty Westhaven. "David Svehla here. I'm coming over." He shrugged into his army jacket.

Grace came up the basement steps into the kitchen. "Where are you going?"

"To see Westhaven, then Donley."

She stuck her hands on her hips. "Are you going to beat them up this time? Violence on top of violence?"

"I'll talk, but if this needs to go beyond talk, it will." David hadn't been in a brawl in too long, and he was pissed enough to wipe up the floor with an asshole.

Grace stood her ground. "David, you're a horrible model for Davy."

He yanked the door open and strode out.

Rusty Westhaven hadn't changed out of his work clothes, which were only a little creased at the end of the workday. He invited David in.

David stood at the open door. "You talk to your son today?"

Westhaven shook his head.

"He and his pal Tim beat up Davy this afternoon. We talked about this before, and I thought you'd take care of it."

Westhaven drew himself up to his full height and held up a finger. "Just a minute, please. Let me get Bobby." He went into the kitchen, and David heard a door open, Westhaven yelling Bobby's name, and some murmuring. The two came back into the living room, Westhaven's hand on Bobby's back. "You tell Mr. Svehla what you told me, all of it."

Bobby mumbled. "It wasn't my idea. Tim said Davy was a sissy, and we needed to teach him a lesson."

"Apparently, you told Davy you'd beat up my daughter if he didn't fight. Is that right?"

Bobby nodded, glancing up at his dad's disapproving face.

His dad asked, "You always do what Tim wants?"

"He'll beat *me* up if I don't."

"Oh, Bobby, look at me, man to man. Giving in to a bully and helping him beat up other children isn't the right way to behave. It's not what your mother and I want from you. We'll talk about this more later. Now, you tell Mr. Svehla you're sorry, and you better mean it."

David glowered at the kid.

Bobby stared at the floor. "I'm sorry I hurt Davy. I won't do it again." He turned a scared face up to his dad.

Westhaven swatted the kid's behind. "I don't ever want a repeat of this, not a hint that you've bullied other boys or girls. You hear me?"

Bobby nodded and scampered back down to the basement.

"I'm very sorry this happened. I don't like his friendship with the Donley boy, and I'll see that it ends." The men shook hands.

David turned to leave, tamping down his anger. As he walked to his car, his frustration oozed out. His hands itched to throw a punch, but this Westhaven cut off that option. Damn. Well, at least he'd got one kid off Davy's back. One more stop should do it. He rubbed his hands together.

Donley lived across Lee Road on Meadowbrook in one of its two-family houses. The man who came to the door was square-built, and his suit coat looked like it would no longer button across his stomach. He had the neck of a tackle. And he wasn't pleased to see David. "Whaddaya want?"

"I'd like to come in. This won't take long. I've been at the Westhavens'. Your son, along with Bobby, beat up my kid today, my third grader."

"Yeah? Thought I'd put a stop to that." He shook his head. "Lemme get him." In his stentorian voice, he yelled, "Timmy!" Donley glared at the hallway door to the back bedrooms.

David, who'd been primed to fight, let his hands fall to his side. This guy looked like he knew his way around a boxing ring.

A kid built in his father's image appeared in the doorway: big shoulders, thick arms and legs. "What?"

"Get over here." Donley pointed at his feet.

Tim stuck his chin in the air and swaggered over.

Donley pulled out his belt, made the kid bend over and hold on to the end of the sofa, and beat his butt and legs. The kid's body swayed forward and back, and he murmured not a word, not a sound. He didn't even ask what the beating was for.

David winced a number of times, turned, and walked out. No wonder the kid was a bully.

On the way home, David chewed on this fighting business. He hadn't learned to fight from his parents or because of his parents' behavior. He'd figured it out for himself. Had he been a bully? Naw. He'd fought when challenged or insulted or to right a wrong done to him or his brothers. That was justified. This random picking on little kids came from someplace else, someplace more wicked—maybe the unfairness of the dad's punishments. Unfortunately, he'd bet this taunting of his son wasn't over. Timmy hadn't acted at all subdued by that beating. More likely, enflamed. Davy needed to be able to defend himself.

He'd have to give the kid more lessons. Grace, of course, would be up in arms. David smiled at his choice of words. In a half-assed sort of way, he agreed with her that times were changing and arguments between kids shouldn't be resolved with fists. Davy did need to be able to argue his way out of tough spots. However, if those arguments didn't succeed, David firmly believed that his kid needed to know how to use his fists. It was part of becoming a man. So, for the next few weeks, when Grace was out shopping, he'd take Davy into the backyard, behind the garage and into the weed-infested dirt that had been their Victory Garden, make it their own Madison Square Garden. The kid would learn; he had to.

On Saturday afternoon, feeling he'd done his duty as a fight trainer, David hiked over to Jacob's to find out more about the upcoming meeting. He spotted him in his side yard digging. "What are you planting?"

Jacob stood up and leaned on his shovel, easing up on his lame leg. "Rebecca has plan for a rose garden. I do not know why, but I do the manual labor."

"Yes, I know how that works."

"I—ah—heard you were teaching Davy and Hildie to fight."

Hoo boy. News traveled fast. That would be Hildie. Once again, she'd pushed herself into the lesson, and he hadn't been able to dissuade her from staying. "Has Hildie been over?"

"Yes, right after the lesson. She was very proud. She showed Karen how to jab and do an undercut. Do I have that right?" He smiled with the question.

"It's 'uppercut,' but you were close. I had hoped to keep that quiet."

"Rebecca was there, too, and we had a family discussion with strong feelings expressed. Rebecca did not approve."

David grumbled. "I meant it just for Davy, but you know Hildie. Hates to be left out. And Grace isn't going to like this."

Jacob's eyes glittered as he laughed.

"Well, I grew up fighting. That's how we settled things in my neighborhood."

"Not in mine. I was too busy working after school, with my father, learning the trade . . . and how to calm angry clients, how to compromise, how to bow to the power of others." Jacob jammed his spade into the soil and turned over a large clod of dirt and grass.

"I bet those skills came in handy in the war."

Jacob gave the spade an especially hard shove into the ground, sweat breaking out on his forehead. "Yes, I suppose they did." He jammed the shovel into the soil so it stood up straight. "Let us sit at the picnic table. We can talk better there in the shade."

When they were settled opposite each other, Jacob said, "Did you find out anything useful in Dayton?"

"Adler lost a son in the war, a Hitler youth."

"It is hard to lose a son."

David was startled that Jacob's reaction was one of sympathy. "Yeah. It makes him more sympathetic, and I don't want to like him."

Jacob picked up several blossoms that had fallen from the cherry tree onto the table and dropped them on the grass. "Yes, I know."

As Jacob said no more, David changed the subject. "What did you find out at the temple? I'm curious what to expect tomorrow at the meeting."

"I spoke first to Rabbi Meschen, a good man. He is attentive to the pain of the survivors in our community. He suggested others for me to talk to and warned me it would not be easy." David heard a softness in Jacob's voice—empathy, perhaps, but not sadness.

David wondered about this belongingness that seemed to go along with religion. He knew little of Judaism, even though the neighborhood had lots of Jewish families. He distrusted religion on principle, really. Too much bowing to authority, whether you were a Catholic at confession or a Jew or a Buddhist. He'd picked up some basics, like wearing a yarmulke at a Jewish wedding. And he knew the holy days came in September. There'd been discussion about closing the schools on those days for lack of attendance. But he had little experience of rabbis. "So, what did the men say?"

"They did not like to talk about the war. They hated to remember. Some refused, but I had good conversations with four, plus the rabbi. With patience, I listened to their stories, what it was possible for them to tell. Even then it is terrifying. Less they say, more you imagine." His voice died.

"Such loss, David, of persons cherished, of health, of dignity." He stopped, and David waited.

"No one wants confrontation. Nothing public to do with Adler or any other Nazi. We all boycott German companies. That is discreet, private. You must understand. Germany is not the only country to persecute Jews. We have experienced this many times. And I am sorry to say it, but many Jews believe we are feeling hatred now."

"How's that?"

"McCarthy has named many Jews. It is not good to express a liberal opinion, to have a cause."

"But McCarthy's been rooting out Communists."

"Ah, David. If it were only that."

"Well, he got censured by Congress. According to the paper, people aren't supporting him anymore."

"It is not over. There are others who believe as he does. The lawyers warn us to be careful."

David felt his optimism drain away. Maybe the survivor community, along with those veterans, wouldn't support a move against Adler. "So, did anyone agree to help deal with Adler?"

"It is strange coincidence, but one man I met knows the Adlers. He is tailor of Madame—Herr Klein."

"Yes? So, what's next? Can we up the ante on Adler?"

"What is this, 'up the ante?'"

"Oh, right, I forgot. It's from poker, the card game. Means to raise the amount of money you're risking, make the game more serious, play for higher stakes."

"I see." Jacob paused. "Well, Herr Klein said he will refuse to do work for the Adlers from now on."

"It's a start. Did the rabbi have some ideas about how to make Adler atone?"

"In fact, Rabbi Meschen was more concerned to heal the people who were hurt by the Nazis, but I think it is possible that he accept to do more."

Wow. Healing. David wanted to punish the bastard. "I'm no psychiatrist, Jacob. Sounds like the survivors need therapy. They don't need me."

"Perhaps both." He raised his eyebrows. "You have time for instruction in Judaism, no?"

David scratched the stubble on his cheek. "Sure."

"You see, David, we Jews have a way very particular to celebrate our New Year, Rosh Hashanah, and ten days later, the Yom Kippur, the day of atonement. In this time, God gives us the chance to repent of the sins that we have committed. We look back on the past year, and we ask people we have harmed for forgiveness."

"Yeah, you talked about forgiveness on our walk."

"Well, Rabbi Meschen thinks that it can be good for me to forgive Adler, that I have received an opportunity that not many men have in their life."

"I suppose." He pulled at his nose.

"I smile at your confusion. The men at the temple agree to meet with us and decide how we can face our anger and hurt. I cannot hide from them any more. You have them, too, David."

"But I'm not Jewish. I wasn't a prisoner in a camp. I don't know first-hand what it was like. I don't belong in the group." It was more than not belonging. David felt again the shame of killing Isaac Chornyei with that damned chocolate bar.

"We shall be in my house next Wednesday. That is comfortable for you, no?"

David blew out a gust of air. "I guess."

CHAPTER 7

MAY 1955

When the kids were in bed, Grace sat at her dressing table and brushed her hair, a nightly ritual that kept it soft to his touch. "Rebecca called this afternoon, probably when you and Jacob were talking."

David took his pants off and reached for a hanger. "Oh?"

Grace turned around to him slowly, her eyes narrowed. "She's worried. Jacob's been having nightmares this past week or so. Apparently you told him about Adler?"

Without meeting his wife's eyes, he hung up the pants and unbuttoned his shirt. "Yes, I did. I was afraid he'd run into the man. I thought the news would come better from me." He should have told Grace right away.

"Why didn't you tell me?"

"I guess it slipped my mind."

"When I asked explicitly that you not tell him? When we've discussed your keeping secrets from me?"

"I'm sorry. I didn't mean to leave you out."

She stared intently at him. "Well, last night he lashed out and hit Rebecca in the face. But the worst part, she said, was his screaming. He made those eerie dream screams and woke Karen, who came running into their room and huddled in Rebecca's arms. She was terrified of her father. He kept pulling at his hair, keening." She dropped her brush into her lap. "Oh, David, what have you started? He's a friend. You've brought up his worst memories. He's going through it all again. Why did you do it? How could you put him through this?"

David sat down hard on the bed and ran his hand through his hair. "Adler lives so close to us, hon. I didn't want Jacob to run into him on the street. That would have been worse."

"I don't know. He's holding on to so much sadness. Rebecca said his family almost got out before the Germans took over France. When Hitler announced he was moving into Alsace, they left Strasbourg for Paris, thinking they'd be safe, but the French police came and took them away."

"Sent them to the camps. Their own citizens." David reached out to take Grace's hand, suspecting that she was picturing her six siblings, nearly two dozen aunts and uncles, and too many cousins to count, the crowd at family reunions—a crowd she loved and Jacob didn't have.

"When he came here, I bet he thought he was through with all that. And now you've brought it back. It makes me worry, David, about how far you're going to go with this."

David let his hands slip between his knees. "Let me fill you in. I've talked with Jacob a lot the last few days. We're gonna meet again tomorrow with his rabbi and men from his temple to talk about what to do. It might make Jacob's nightmares go away."

"You're working with his temple?"

"Yeah. The group, especially the rabbi, thinks this is an opportunity to work on forgiveness and healing." He knew his voice sounded cynical.

Grace shook her head in confusion. "He wants Jacob to forgive the Nazi who did horrible things to him?"

"Not exactly. It's not so much a question of forgiving the Nazi, but forgiving himself."

"What? He was a victim, not the sinner. Jews were herded into railroad cars, starved, beaten, gassed. They didn't hurt anyone."

"Yes, but Jacob and these others lived when so many died. To survive, Jacob told me he watched a friend get clubbed to death and didn't try to stop it."

"Wouldn't he have been killed if he interfered?"

"Probably. But that doesn't take away his guilt. He said he was too weak and should have been stronger, done what was morally right. And it isn't only that one thing. When he was in the infirmary and shared a bed with a dying man, Jacob ate the man's dinner. He hates himself for taking away that last pleasure."

Grace played with the little knobs on the chenille bedspread. "How sad. Poor Jacob. I mean, who wouldn't steal food rather than starve? Besides, the dying man might not even have been able to eat it."

David watched Grace as he shed the remainder of his clothes, pulled on his pajama bottoms, and sat down again on the sheets. "Come to bed, hon."

Grace sighed and rose from her chair. "Jacob must have such a burden of pain." As she raised her knee to climb into bed, she leaned over, index finger flapping at David. "And don't you leave me out again."

Rebecca opened the Strauss' front door and invited David into the living room where Jacob was shaking hands with a youngish man, maybe thirty-five—younger than David, anyway—with dark hair and wearing an expensive businessman's suit. Jacob introduced him as Len Barenholtz. Four other men milled about whom Jacob introduced as Stu Kornhauser, Daniel Meckler, Joel Fried, and Rabbi Abram Meschen. They were a range of ages from mid-thirtiess to fifties, all shorter than David, who was five-feet-ten-inches, and, all dark-haired. The rabbi looked like a scholar with his gold-rimmed glasses, rumpled pants, and full beard.

While they chatted, David tried to fit the names to the people. Len of the expensive suit looked like a lawyer—a slick one who knew his way around corporate boardrooms and could argue cogently about anything. Someone you handled with kid gloves if you wanted him to stay on your side. Joel was his foil. He looked fifty, though he was probably younger. Slim, with long fingers and neatly-trimmed nails, like a pianist. He only glanced at the person speaking to him; mostly, his eyes were on the floor. Someone you helped, if you could. David was surprised he had agreed to attend.

Daniel reminded David of the fairy tale about the Billy Goat Gruff. He had gray facial hair, bags under his eyes that made him look ready to cry, and a tic in his neck, sort of like a goat when it shook its head. He told the rabbi he didn't want the meeting to go on long because he had to get up very early to get the bread baked in time for the store opening. "You'll want your challah fresh tomorrow, no?"

That left Stu. Slender, close-cut curly beard. Seemed self-assured, though he used imperfect grammar, at least according to Grace's strict standards. He said "for you and I," which David did as well and then got corrected. Likely in his forties, probably had a shop, maybe along Lee Road or Taylor. A lot of Jewish stores there.

Within a few minutes, they all took seats on the couch and folding chairs, approximately in a circle. Jacob sat on David's right, next to Joel and Stu. The rabbi was on David's left, and then Daniel and Len. Jacob opened the meeting. "Permit me introduce my neighbor, David Svehla. He was in OSS during the war and liberated the Dora camp."

Rabbi Meschen spoke up. "That's where Jacob was."

All eyes turned toward David, then back to Jacob, who looked calm, in control. "Now, David is teacher and lawyer, and as I said to you, he has found a former officer of the S.S. who is professor at Case. One who was at Dora. One who was very bad. One who is often in my dreams."

As Jacob's voice trailed off, David nodded to the group. "Pleased to meet you all." Then he motioned for Jacob to continue.

"We know already a little of the stories of the war for each one. For Len, his family lives in this community since a long time. He has lost relatives and one person he has found, who lives with him now. For Stu, he was prisoner of war. For others, arrived more recently . . ." he nodded toward Joel and the gruff man, Daniel, ". . . the stories are like mine, of months or years in the camps, the members of the family who disappeared."

While David listened, he scanned the group. Joel and Daniel stared at the floor. Joel sat rigid and still, his hands clasped in his lap. Daniel's chin jerked to the right every ten or fifteen seconds. Len and Stu had their eyes on Jacob, alert as watchdogs.

Jacob went on, "The name of the Nazi is Gerhardt Adler. He is chemical engineer, fuels expert." Jacob took a deep breath. "He lives on Fairmount Boulevard a few miles from here."

Stu sat up. "My God. We could be passing him on the street, standing in line behind him. My nephew might have him as an instructor."

"Yes," Jacob said. He looked at each man, his eyes inviting a response yet not insisting.

Rabbi Meschen clasped his hands and cradled his knee. "This is such an important issue; I didn't want it shunted to a back burner, let alone ignored. If we believe in justice—and we do—we need to act on that belief." He looked about and received nods of agreement. "However, the presence of this man, Adler, also brings up many old feelings of fear, of anger, of helplessness, and they, too, must not be shunted aside."

Daniel, with a single tic to the left, responded. "Excuse me. The war is over. We agree that what those swine did cannot be forgotten or forgiven. We're boycotting German businesses and could stay away from Adler, too. I'm fine keeping a good distance."

"In general, I agree," the rabbi said. "Adler will find a gentile to alter his suits and will hardly notice the change. Yet, Jacob's world has received a shock. He knew this beast well, and now, he cannot feel safe."

Joel interrupted in a soft voice. "How can any of us feel safe?"

All eyes moved from Joel to Jacob, who raised both hands, warding off objections. "I think that God gives me this opportunity to heal." Jacob closed his eyes for a moment. "I want to know if Adler has shame for what he did, if he remembers me, and if I can forgive him. If I have the faith to go to the end."

Joel shivered. "You . . . you don't have to do this, Jacob. No one will blame you."

From across the circle, Daniel added, "I want nothing to do with any Nazi ever again."

Jacob nodded. "I understand. That is right for you."

The rabbi spoke, "What you want to do is brave, Jacob, and we all support you. Right?" He looked around the group who nodded, slowly, as if pain came with each decision. "How do you want to begin?"

"I'm not sure. I hope others have ideas."

David looked around the circle. Most of the men stared at the floor. Joel wiped his eyes. This was embarrassing. Where should he lead the discussion?

Daniel grimaced and shifted his weight to the front of his chair. "I'm not comfortable with this. I lived through the hell once. I don't want to return."

The rabbi balanced his elbow on the arm of his chair close to Daniel. "I think Jacob is speaking mostly of today, of the pain he feels now and wishes to be rid of. Perhaps you, too, have these feelings?"

Daniel opened his mouth, bristling as though about to deny a false charge, then shut it. "I eat too much. If there is food left on the serving dish at dinner, I cannot stand it. We do not waste any food in my house."

Joel spoke up, so softly David could barely distinguish the words. "I am afraid. Afraid of the dark, of confined spaces . . . of loving people."

David kept his body still and his mouth shut. The rabbi was doing a fine job.

With a shift forward in his position, the rabbi announced his plan to speak. "The start of forgiveness comes when the two parties meet each other. Jacob has expressed his desire to meet this Adler. How can we be with him?"

Daniel rose. "I'm not going to meet him. I must leave now."

The rabbi held up his hand. "There is no need for us to be there physically. In fact, that might not be a good idea. It might bring on an angry, defensive response."

"I'll be there," David said. "I'm happy to push Adler, accuse him, back up Jacob as needed."

The group responded with silence. Len and Stu looked thoughtful, Joel nervous, and Daniel on the verge of sliding off his chair and out the door.

Rabbi Meschen spent a few moments on each face and then spoke. "The rest of us will need to pray and decide if we will join you both. Let

Lorelei Brush

us meet again next week, on Wednesday, here at Jacob's." He turned to his host. "That will be all right?"

Jacob agreed.

"Bring your ideas of how this confrontation can be orchestrated to be safe and healing. Ask others, if that seems right. We are doing hard work here, all of us. I thank you."

Daniel grumbled that he didn't think he could come. The others left, lost in thought.

When Jacob closed the door on the men, he clasped David's arm. "I know this was not what you wanted, but please, come. We need time to get used to the idea of Adler and get over the panic at seeing his like again."

David nodded. "I'll be here."

When he got home, Grace was already in bed, reading. She stuck her finger in to mark the page. "What happened? How did it go?"

"My God, they carry around a lot of pain. All of them."

"I can imagine."

"The group didn't make any decisions, just talked. We're meeting again Wednesday."

"And what did you say?"

"I didn't say much at all. I let Jacob do the talking."

A breeze through the open window rustled Grace's hair, blowing a few strands into her face. She put up a hand to hold one back. "This is a new picture of you. You're always out there, talking, moving. Tonight, you listened."

"Yeah, well, all this *is* new for me."

"I think I like it."

David got home after nine on Monday to find Grace seated at the kitchen table, hands folded on its top, staring at the wall. He set his briefcase on the floor and shrugged out of his overcoat. "What's the matter?"

"Sit down." She patted the chair next to her.

David obliged, throwing his coat across the table.

"Hildie and Davy came home from school looking like street urchins, covered in mud, faces scraped. Davy was holding on to Hildie's shoulder and near tears. Hildie said Tim and another boy went after Davy, down on the vacant lot. They called him a tattletale, a rat, a skunk, and I don't know what else." Grace laid a hand on David's arm. "Davy's doing his best to handle this. Don't get fired up, just listen." The pressure on his arm held it down.

He held up his other hand. "Okay, okay."

"He got a kick in the leg, that's all."

"Where were his friends?"

"Apparently, they'd already disappeared down the block. Davy was trying to capture a toad."

"So, how'd Hildie get involved?" He pushed his chair back, making that fingernails-down-the-blackboard screech against the floor, and tried to recover that patience to listen.

"Well, she and Karen got to the vacant lot and saw Tim knock Davy down. She charged Tim, like a bull. You know how she puts curled fingers at her temples and lunges forward? Davy said she hit Tim behind the knees, and he went sprawling in the mud. According to Hildie, she was going to smash into the other boy, too, but he backed away."

David felt a rush of pride. "Hildie knocked the kid down? God, what a pistol."

"Oh, please, don't encourage her. I've been thinking about this a lot. I'm glad she helped Davy out of a fix, but you know I don't approve of solving problems this way. I don't like what's happening around here."

"Yeah, girls shouldn't be the tough ones."

"David, you're missing the point. It's the fighting. I want you with me in trying to stop it."

David reached out for his coat and sighed. "I guess I'm going to visit the Donleys' again."

"No, that's not what I mean. You went there once; that's enough. We need help. This isn't just a thing between Tim and Davy. I know Tim's threatened Karen, and this evening I called several other mothers. Tomorrow, six of us are going to talk to the principal. A number of fathers will visit the Donleys. How about you join them?"

David picked some lint off his pant leg and slowly looked up. "Feels like you're taking away some fundamental male right: protecting the young."

Grace reached a hand out to enfold one of his. "Not at all. I'm trying to give you the strength of thousands."

Late the next afternoon, Grace reported that the mothers' meeting was an anticlimax. The principal knew about Tim Donley from his teacher and the reports of several children, and she had already organized the teachers to supervise the children's coming and going with a special eye on Tim. She hoped the fathers' actions would be more decisive.

David was surprised to find Jacob in the group who met outside the Donleys'. They shook hands. "Has Tim done anything to Karen?"

Jacob seemed to be standing at attention on the sidewalk. "Not physically, but he has menaced her. I do not accept this."

When they had all introduced themselves, the men walked to the door. David knocked.

Donley opened it and said, "Shit. What now?"

David cleared his throat. "Tim hurt my son again. He's beat up or threatened all of our children, and we want this to end. Is that clear?" He moved forward into Donley's personal space, lifting his foot to step into his living room.

Donley filled the doorframe. "What a lot of pansies these kids are. A man ought to be able to fight." He stuck his hands on his hips. "I suppose you're all going to take me on now? Think you can beat me up and make a difference for your kids? Well, just try it. I can lay you all out."

From his position on David's right, Jacob spoke, his voice confident. "My daughter is seven. It is interesting that your ten-years-old boy is picking on a child so much smaller and more vulnerable."

It wasn't a threat, just a statement. A very clear statement.

Donley's jaw dropped.

A second man stepped forward. "Tim tripped my son on the baseball diamond so he wouldn't reach third base."

Another of the men raised his arm and shook a finger at Donley. "Tim kneed my son in the back, and we had to take him to the hospital because of the blood in his urine."

A fourth man said, "We want your assurance these behaviors won't be repeated. No more attacks on our children. Or we go to the police."

Donley blustered. "All right, all right. Now, get off my property. I want to see the backs of you lot." Then he stepped into the house and slammed the door.

As David told Grace when he got home, "Donley may do nothing; he might beat his kid again, which will only make the boy lash out, but Tim *might* choose kids his own size the next time. I don't know."

Grace threw up her arms. "Oh, David, what good has all this done?"

His excitement faded. "Jeez, nothin' physical went on. Just a threat to go to the police. Isn't that what you wanted?"

She turned and walked to the sink, grabbing its edge with both hands. "I want the violence to stop. Maybe Tim won't keep on bullying our kids, but we've no assurance of that, and you seem to be pushing Tim at older kids. Maybe this is the last time you'll confront Mr. Donley—or maybe this will escalate. I don't think Davy and Hildie are any safer, and now you're in the ring, too."

He walked to her, turned her around, and took her in his arms. "Oh, Grace. We'll work this out. As you wanted, now I'm part of a posse." He kissed her head.

"Don't you dare tell me not to worry my pretty little head about it." Her voice was muffled by his coat.

"Some good did come out of this."

"What?"

"I know Jacob's a good man to have along. How's that?"

Lorelei Brush

She pulled out of his embrace, pushing hair out of her face. "That's a *small* comfort. And I suppose it's good you talked instead of fought. But I still don't like it."

David took off his coat, thinking he'd done what he could. "We okay now?"

Grace nodded, dropping her hands to her sides. "I guess. For now."

CHAPTER 8
MAY-JUNE 1955

Just before his first period physics class on Wednesday, David wrote the homework assignment on the blackboard. He did this each day in each class so students couldn't legitimately claim they had no idea what they were supposed to do. John Adams High School had sure changed from the early 1930s when he'd been a student. Kids back then—mostly from second- or third-generation Eastern European immigrant families—were eager to learn, conscientious about completing homework, and serious about using their education to improve the status of their families. Now, there were way too many kids biding time, occupying space with no intention of doing any work.

He turned as he heard heavy sniffs. A senior girl, a Hungarian with neatly teased hair, was wiping her eyes and trying hard to stifle her sobs. He walked the few steps to her and put a hand on her arm. "What is it, Judy?"

"Oh, Mr. Svehla, they stole my lunch money again."

"Who did?"

"They'll kill me if I tell."

David debated pushing her a little, getting an affirmation of the punks he'd watched from his window: a small brotherhood of dropouts who hung around the gate at the school entrance and bullied kids to give up their lunches or money. When he'd reported them to the principal, Broz had a janitor go ask them to disperse. The boys had returned the next morning.

David fished in his pocket and handed her a couple of bucks in change. "Sorry we haven't been able to stop that. I'll alert the police again. The boys stay just off school property, so Mr. Broz doesn't feel he has the authority to stop them."

"I know. I usually come in a group, like the principal said, and they just heckle us. I was late today."

"Well, you sit down and take some deep breaths. You'll be okay."

She nodded.

As fourth period came to an end, the crowd in the hallway coming to and from lunch was getting rowdy. David stepped out to calm things down and felt someone push a note into his hand. He glanced behind, in the direction the person must have been walking, and saw one of his best students—a boy headed for Ohio State in the fall, a baseball player with a batting average over .500. They caught each other's eyes when the boy looked around for a moment. David guessed the reason for the subterfuge, which was confirmed by the note. "Rumble at the end of classes."

Not again. These were happening every week or so now that the weather was warming up. David sighed. He could tell Broz, but that had brought little action in the past. Broz would say he'd stand at the front door (he usually sent his assistant principal) and make sure no non-students came in. Only, the rabble that started the fights would make their way in the locked back doors as students opened them to go home or to the playing fields. Well, he'd warn the office, and today he'd be there to break it up. As he turned into the teachers' lunchroom, he felt a smile curl one edge of his lips. He might even enjoy the encounter.

David ended his last class promptly, stepped into the hall, and listened. The rumbles usually began away from the office, on a corridor with English or home economics classes where female teachers predominated. He heard a short scream and ran toward the English wing. A gang of six boys had positioned themselves in an arc around the door of a classroom. David heard the switchblades click into place, and a tall kid gave an order to take care of the punk who'd refused to pay up that morning.

When three tenth-grade boys dared to exit the room together, David waded through the hormone-charged lot of no-goods, yelling for them to break it up. He faced off with the large punk of a leader and ordered him to hand over the knife. When the kid laughed, David slammed the boy's knife arm to paralyze it and kneed him in the balls. As the kid crumpled in pain, David grabbed him by his leather jacket and threw him against the wall. Then he turned in a crouch. "Any other of youse boys want to take me on?" He pivoted slowly, his back protected by the classroom door, and his eyes following the five attackers still standing. No one rushed him.

In less than a minute, a couple of policemen appeared around the corner from the office with Broz trailing behind. The punks who were mobile took off and were out the exit door before the police reached David. The kid on the floor fake-cried, and the policemen looked David up and down. For a moment, he thought he was going to be accused of assault and stood straight to face them.

Seemingly on cue, the English teacher, Mrs. O'Keefe, opened her classroom door and pushed in front of David, hands on her hips. "Don't you even think about criticizing Mr. Svehla. He saved the day. What we need to do here is thank him."

David thanked her and explained to the police what had happened. Broz hemmed and hawed about how this just shouldn't go on in educational institutions, and the policemen nodded. They called an ambulance to take the instigator to the hospital, and everyone went home.

As he drove toward Cleveland Heights, David chewed on this problem of bullying and how it had gone on in Germany, not only with Hitler as bully-in-charge, but at all layers of the bureaucracy, even in the displaced person camps. Oh, not among the Red Cross personnel and the medical staff. But it had sure affected Jacob. When he was well enough to travel, he'd been moved to a DP camp near Strasbourg, as that had been his childhood home. David had visited him there when he was stuck in an aging army barracks and terribly lonely. Rebecca had been shifted to a different area, and the camp personnel had verified that no one in Jacob's family had survived. David found him sitting on an overturned washtub, rocking back and forth with his arms held tight across his chest. He squatted next to him, a hand on his shoulder. "Where's your coat, Jacob? Didn't they give you a coat?" It was May, then, but still not warm.

"It was taken."

"By whom?"

"A man. A kapo."

"He had no right. I'm not gonna let this go by. Is he here in the camp?"
Jacob nodded, still rocking.

David pulled off his army jacket and wrapped it around Jacob's bony shoulders. "Come with me. We're going to get you a coat."

"They said we could have only one, and I had received mine."

David took Jacob's elbow. "Then we'll find yours."

It didn't take long. The thief was standing at the door of another barracks, ordering someone to get him extra bread.

David tapped his shoulder, and when the man turned around, it was obvious he was much better off than most in the camp. He had muscles in his arms that stretched the coat's sleeves and a stomach large enough to make buttoning the garment difficult. In German, David said, "I'll take that coat back now." He grabbed one lapel.

The man whipped around, arms raised for an assault, but David used his shoulder to heave the man against the building's door and his fists to send him to the ground. Then he backed off, gestured for the coat, and repeated his polite request.

The man wiped blood from his mouth onto the coat and slowly took it off.

David handed it to Jacob. "Sorry about the blood. We'll see if it can be cleaned."

Jacob touched the softness of the wool and smiled. "Thank you. He was a bad kapo, took what he wanted."

David stared down at the kapo still on the ground. "If I hear that you have stolen from my friend, I'll find you and you *will* regret it. Understand?"

The kapo, looking at the ground, nodded.

With his hand again under Jacob's elbow, David guided his friend—now warmly clad in a long coat—to the mess hall. "We need to talk about your upcoming marriage and trip to the States. I have an idea."

Lorelei Brush

At the second meeting with the men David thought of as the "temple team," Rebecca handed coffee around and then disappeared into the kitchen. David again took stock of the group: Rabbi Meschen circulating to welcome each man; Stu and Len chatting with a good deal of hand-waving; Joel picking up one family picture after another from the top of the piano. David caught Jacob's arm on his way by. "Is Daniel not coming?"

Jacob shook his head. "He said he was busy. I think he does not wish to remember."

"Ah. You okay?"

"Yes. I am remembering much."

When they were seated, all faces turned toward Jacob. "I must speak about Adler, so you understand. I know you trust me when I say he is cruel man, but for those of you not in labor camp, you may not know what I mean. I give you idea. Adler was senior S.S. officer in camp. He had rules for the guards. One said no beating unless prisoners try to escape. What did this mean, in practice? While a guard viciously beat Bertrand, my friend, for being late to roll call, Adler turned his back and chatted with another guard. If he did not see, the beating did not happen. Bertrand tried over and over to stand up. He could not do it. Adler pointed to him, made his hand into a gun, and mimicked shooting Bertrand. The guard did so. They left his body in the dust as warning to the rest of us."

The rabbi groaned and folded his hands in prayer.

"The worst memory is what Adler did to my father. When Papa grew ill from sadness at the deaths of my mother and sister, I persuaded him to go to hospital. Each day or two, all men in hospital lined up to be examined and rated. Those in worst condition were shot. My father could hardly stand when Adler ordered the most ill to be killed. The guard made Papa stumble to the side of the crematorium, shot him, and left him where he fell. But he was not dead. He froze in the cold when I was at work. I heard later of his quiet moans."

The room was silent for several minutes. David thought of his own dad, still healthy in his seventies but getting frail. He'd kill anyone who hurt the old man.

Rabbi Meschen said, "Jacob, you paint very vivid pictures. I believe we are all committed to working with you to confront this man and help those images fade."

Len of the lawyerly suit cleared his throat. "I'd like to hear what sorts of actions we've all come up with."

Jacob turned to David. "You speak."

David settled his forearms on his thighs, leaning forward to make the conversation more intimate, more an exchange among friends. "I think it's clear the law won't help us because Adler's done nothin' illegal in the U.S.—well, that we know of—so we have to expose his crimes in Germany."

Stu Kornhauser, the owner—David had learned—of a series of dry cleaners, said, "We've got this boycott going of German goods. Why not extend it somehow? Do we have to get this close to him?"

"The boycott's a good start," David said, "but it's unlikely to affect Adler. He may not even have noticed it. We need to ratchet things up a bit. Jacob and I would like to confront him publicly. Invite a bunch of reporters. Catch him when colleagues are around, humiliate the bastard."

Jacob put his hand on David's arm. "We will do nothing illegal." He seemed to be assuring both the group and himself. "We will make him uncomfortable, push him to speak of what he did, to say he was wrong."

Joel looked from David to Jacob, stirring uncomfortably in his seat. "Why do you want to do this publicly?"

David chose to answer. "If we did this in private, or Jacob tried to talk to him alone, Adler could refuse to speak, walk away, blast him with anger, or throw him out before he says what he needs to say."

"Probably a man of big ego," Len said. "Well, he'd have to be, wouldn't he, with the rank he held in the S.S. I'd think he'd be attracted by a group wanting him to lecture. An invitation to public recognition seems like a good carrot."

David opened his mouth to expand upon that idea, and then decided to keep quiet and let the others toss around possibilities. He crossed his arms and sat back.

Joel spoke up in his quiet voice, "But the whole thing could backfire. Right there in public. Adler could yell at Jacob, humiliate him, and then storm out. He could leave at the first mention of his wartime activities. In a hundred ways, he could get around you."

It was Jacob who responded. "But then at least I will know that he is not sorry for what he did. I will know that I have only to forgive myself."

Very quietly, Stu asked, "I still don't get what you have to forgive."

"I survived."

Joel nodded. "That's the toughest part. We did what we had to and survived."

David watched the men eye one another and leave unasked the question of what exactly Joel and Jacob had done. The rabbi shifted in his chair. Glancing at Jacob, David said, "I'd like to start the confrontation with Adler, with Jacob beside me. We'll make it to-the-point, and I promise you, we'll make him sweat."

Len sighed and pinched the sharp pleat of his pant leg. "Are you sure we can't aim at his money?"

The rabbi shook his head. "This isn't a financial issue, it's emotional. Even if he paid a lot of money, it wouldn't remove the hurt and pain he's caused. It's too easy for us to throw money at a problem."

Stu pulled on his curly beard. "You gotta make him talk about the war."

David saw a grimace cross Joel's face. "If you told him the topic of this meeting was the war, he wouldn't show up."

Len nodded. "You've got to feed his ego. Tell him you're going to give him an award for his scientific discoveries, that kind of thing."

Joel came back with, "I don't even want to think about rewarding him." The disgusted look on his face made David think it likely he wouldn't show up for any such ceremony.

Len cleared his throat, then pressed his hands on his knees. "I've got an idea. Most of you have met my cousin, Samuel Goldstein, the Chief of Research at the Lewis Flight Propulsion Lab here in town. Sam and I were talking the other day about the lab's wanting to coordinate more with Case. Adler's a natural, seeing as how he's their fuels expert. I'll bet Sam would be willing to push negotiations with the Case administration and suggest Adler be part of the shared resources."

Joel groaned. "You really gonna reward Adler? What kind of a response is that to what he did?"

Len waved his hand as though erasing the comment from a blackboard. "It doesn't mean Sam really will use him. It's just a ruse to get the man to show up. But Adler may even prove useful to the lab. I don't know. It'd be a nice turn of events to have him work for one of us for a change. Anyway, it's a start, an idea."

David threw his hat into the ring. "I like it. As Len suggested, it'll feed his ego, so he'll show up. And then he's ours."

Rubbing his hand across the back of his neck, the rabbi commented, "Who's coming to this event? If a lot of us show up, Adler will know something's going on other than recognition of his scientific prowess. Have you thought of that?"

It took David only a moment to respond. "Case staff and professors will come, and staff from Goldstein's lab, and newspaper reporters—lots of them. We want this public, so let's make it as big as we can. My brother works for the city, and he can be sure we get coverage from the *Plain Dealer* and the *Press*."

Stu, relaxing his body, held up a finger, "I'll let the editors of *The Jewish Review & Observer* and the *Jewish Independent* know. They'll send reporters." He smiled. "They love stuff like this."

Once unleashed, the men suggested TV and radio personalities to invite and other men from the temple. They sounded committed. David took it all in and imagined hurling accusations at Adler. God, he'd enjoy it.

The atmosphere in the room seemed to lighten once there was a plan and a to-do list. David decided to be Devil's Advocate. "Gentlemen, we do need to look at possible difficulties. What if the Lewis Lab doesn't want any part of Adler? What if the negotiations with Case and the labs reach an impasse?"

Len waved those problems away. "Then we'll figure out another public forum. Sam'll find out who else is courting Case for a partnership."

Stu said, "Yeah, let's not give up on this idea just because it may not work. Nothing's a sure thing."

David smiled. "I'm up for a risk or two. It's been kind of boring these last few years." He paused for the laughter to subside. "Other difficulties?"

This time it was timid Joel who put an idea forward. "What if Adler turns the tables on us, like calling the police, getting us thrown out of the meeting, bringing in Case's lawyer for defamation of character or disturbing the peace, or suing us? I don't know, but couldn't there be that kind of retribution?"

Len said, "You're right, Joel. There might be. It's another risk. But if we play this right, Jacob tells his story and asks Adler whether he's sorry. We've done nothing illegal or immoral or threatening."

"The whole thing still makes me nervous." Joel hugged his chest.

Len nodded. "Let's plan carefully. I'll talk to Sam; you all make the press contacts you've mentioned. We'll meet next week, here, and work out the details. Okay?"

Everyone agreed.

The rabbi held up a hand. "One other thought. Len and David, you're lawyers. Sam, whom you may involve, is a professional with a high-profile job. We don't want anyone to lose his job over this or—perhaps worse—tarnish his reputation. Much as you might want to move fast, let's take time to consider all the potential impacts. Use caution, please."

David strolled home, listening to the quiet sounds of the night. The June bugs had started up. A light breeze brought the hint of summer to come. And he felt small bursts of excitement that he was about to do something big. Oh, he'd be careful, but perhaps not cautious. He'd tell Grace the outline; she'd get on board, he was sure.

At the third meeting of the temple team, everyone sat around Jacob's dining room table. Each of the men had a notebook or scratch pad along with strong coffee. Len grabbed the group's attention. He'd had a long consultation with Sam about Lewis Lab's collaboration with Case, summarized on a sheet of paper he held in his hand. It was covered with small, neat script. "It took some doing to convince Sam. He's wanted a partnership with Case for some time. That idea hit home. But he's got a couple of stipulations." Len looked up at Rabbi Meschen. "He shares your sense of caution."

"First, the science and the project have to be real. There has to be an intention on both sides to make the partnership work. He can't take the chance that this will destroy opportunities for future collaborations or break a fundamental trust between the lab and the university." He looked around, probably checking that everyone agreed.

Joel pushed his hand through his hair, making him look like Einstein demonstrating static electricity. "I've been working hard to accept that we're giving Adler a reward. I try to focus on the cost for him, but it doesn't seem very high."

David said, "I'd say, at the least, he'll be embarrassed or maybe humiliated. At the most, he might lose his job or any hope of joint work with other more modern labs."

Joel rocked his head back and forth as though considering these options.

Len waited a moment before continuing. "The second stipulation is that he doesn't want to know any details about what we're doing. I told him we wanted to talk to Adler in a public place like a celebration of winning a contract; that's all."

David nodded. "Deniability."

"Right. He'll be as surprised as Adler and able to tell the press and Case's president he had no idea what was coming. After all, he's committing himself to work with these two men over time—perhaps a long time. Are we agreed on these requirements?" He looked around at the nodding heads.

Jacob asked, "So, what happens next?"

"Sam has a meeting scheduled with Adler later this week. He's got a series of studies in mind, all under a contract he has with the military. They'll work out Case's role over the next few weeks, bring in the appropriate administrative and finance staff."

David tried to contain his impatience. "How long before they'll be able to announce the plan, should it all work out?"

"Sam's thinking July if all goes well."

David took a deep breath. He had to wait. He'd make himself wait.

Jacob thanked Len. "It does not seem real . . . this idea that I stand before Adler to speak words I have not dared to say."

Rabbi Meschen stirred in his chair. "I want us to go into this venture with our eyes open. We know our intentions are honest, even good. But we also know there will be consequences—some that we'll like, some not."

David wondered what the rabbi had in mind. "Let's think about this. Adler may say he regrets what he did—sort of an anticlimax, good for Jacob. Then we leave. Or, he may bluster and deny it all. We push a little. He continues to deny a role. Jacob knows there's no atonement coming, so we leave. Or, Adler may refuse to answer the accusations. He is humiliated, and we leave. I'd guess the problems you're thinking about, rabbi, concern what happens after we leave."

"Yes."

Quietly, Joel put a question in. "What's the likelihood he'll sue for slander?"

Len and David exchanged glances. Len answered. "I don't think he'd choose that route. It would open him up to detailed questions of his wartime assignments. I also don't see repercussions from Case or Lewis Lab. Sam's a good manager. He'll take care of any complaints from the lab and calm any ruffled feathers in the collaboration with Case."

The rabbi broke in. "I see other threats, too. One is the press. They could take this idea of Nazis in our midst and run with it. And who knows where? What I do know is that few of us want to go back over that territory. We don't want to be in the limelight and expected to drag our families with us as we are interrogated about past events we'd like to forget."

Joel swallowed hard. "I've never told my wife what I went through—well, not much. She doesn't need to know, or my children."

David waited for the others to chime in, and when it was silent for a time, asked what the second threat was.

The rabbi sat back in his chair. "A bigger problem. We must not be naïve here. Adler got to this country because our scientists, our military, and our politicians wanted him here. And still do. They are the real sleeping tigers that we're kicking awake."

David flashed back to Williams' letter warning him off, the warning he chose to ignore.

Len took up where the rabbi left off. "Sam works for the military-industrial complex. That's why he needs to stay outside of what you're doing."

David had to cut in. "What *we're* doing."

"David, I'm in the background and mean to stay there. I support you. I'll even come to the ceremony, or whatever it's going to be called, but only with the understanding that my name won't be associated with any action that can be construed as anti-government."

"Hey, you know what we're doing isn't illegal or anti-government. It's anti-Adler."

"In your eyes, perhaps. But it is a protest, which the government doesn't like. They brought Adler over and kept him here, even after they had no specific use for him."

David mulled this over. Was he, were any of these men, too scared of their reputations to take this step toward justice for Jacob? He couldn't stop now, but the others?

Stu accepted hot coffee from Rebecca, who had stayed in the kitchen until now, no doubt listening to the arguments. He spoke. "We all need to be careful. We've been told. We've heard the stories, the accusations against Jews. It's odd. We ate up this idea of the American Dream with a chicken in every pot, a house in the suburbs, two or three children, and a dog. That's fine. I like my piece of that. But it kind of leaves out the abstract stuff like justice. Sometimes, it seems, it's not okay to ask for that."

David said, "I fully support the judgment that this is a time when it's not only okay to ask but necessary."

Len pointed at David. "You do know that you might lose your teaching job over this?"

"You're serious? You think it's possible the backlash will go that far?"

"I've heard it happening more than once."

David bristled. Were they trying to scare him out of this action against Adler? Setting him up to be the scapegoat if this failed? Or were they just nervous, throwing out unlikely possibilities? "Perhaps I'm naïve, but I believe that the words in our Pledge of Allegiance about justice for all are true and that Americans believe in the idea. More than that, I'm willing to test the theory."

Len looked around the circle. "Okay. Looks like we're all with you." Turning to Joel, he said, "And, yes, it is a risk, a big one."

Nearly two weeks later, Jacob knocked at the Svehlas' back door. Grace let him in. "David is home?"

"Yes, yes. Come in."

David strode in from the living room. "You have news?"

"Yes. We have a date: Wednesday, July 20."

Grace's hand covered her heart. "I feel a knot in my stomach. Just what are you going to do?"

David put a hand on her arm. "We're organizing a meeting at Case where I'll ask him about the war."

"You sure that's all you're doing?"

David exchanged looks with Jacob, who nodded. "It is the plan."

With a slow intake of breath, Grace put a hand on Jacob's arm. "It is very brave of you to face him again."

"I feel, in my heart, I must speak. It is time." He smiled at David. "I want to thank you that you give me the chance."

"You're welcome, Jacob. But, you know, I'm doing this for me as well." They shook hands.

When Grace pushed the door shut, she leaned against it as if she needed its support. "I see you need to go through with this, and it isn't just anger making you do it. I'm all for helping Jacob. But confrontations make me nervous."

"Why?"

"You have this desire to wade into a fight. You relish confrontations, mental and physical. I suppose that's helpful for the practice of law—well, the mental type. But my parents taught us to work things out among ourselves, not confront. I'm frightened of what this killer might do."

"In front of the university president and the press? In his best suit? In a college classroom? I don't see him brandishing a gun or getting physical. Will he be angry? Sure. But so will I."

"I know."

The ducks, the ducks. David wanted all the ducks in a row. The next morning, he called Chet from his office, told him the barest outline of the Adler plan, and asked him to contact press liaisons. Chet thought Ted Hessoun would like the idea, urged David to call him again, and said he'd get a hold of a couple of guys he knew at the *Press*. A week later, Chet had made his calls and David had triggered a small avalanche at the *Plain Dealer*. Hessoun wanted details. Why should he attend? What was David really up to?

"How am I going to convince my editor I should even go if I don't know why?"

"Tell him this joint venture is going to make scientific breakthroughs for the space race, and you want to be in at the beginning."

"Yeah, I could say that. Is this related to that call you had me make to Wright-Patterson?"

David hadn't revealed the name of the Case faculty involved and didn't wish to. "Tell you what. First thing after the ceremony, I'll give you all the inside information. You'll have an exclusive."

"Promises, promises. I need something now. This have anything to do with the guy you asked me about?"

"Ted, we need this under wraps for now. I'm giving you an early heads up. You'll be getting a press release from Case. Show that to your editor."

"Chet know any more about this?"

"No. And Chet keeps his mouth shut. No need to pester him."

"Huh. Well, we'll see."

As David hung up, he saw movement in the back yard. Davy and Buddy. They'd been upstairs with the trains when he shut himself in the sunroom. Grace must have rousted them from their hangout and sent them outside to play. Nice, sunny, June day like this. He got up, moseyed over to the window, and stuck his hands in his pockets, jangling change.

Look at that! They were wrestling, and Davy was on top. David whispered, "You go for it, kid. Show him the moves I taught you." Then Buddy caught one of Davy's legs with his own and flipped Davy to his back. They rolled in the grass, sat up laughing, and threw handfuls of the green stuff at each other.

Not what you call a rout, but Davy tried. Grace, at least, would be pleased that the boys came out friends. After all, every interaction didn't have to have a winner and a loser. Yeah, but who wanted to be the loser?

CHAPTER 9

JUNE–JULY 1955

David and Jacob met several times to try out accusations, discuss follow-up barbs, debate which emotions to show and which to hide, and pick the story Jacob wished the press to broadcast. David gloried in his attack, rehearsing it over and over. He'd massacre Adler. Jacob ate himself up with worry to the extent David thought he might not be able to go through with it. But he went to temple each day, talked to members of the team, and gave David his word that he would be ready for the event.

The day of the press conference dawned hot and muggy with the temperature predicted to rise into the nineties. David and Jacob rode downtown together, David energized by what was coming and Jacob subdued. They parked on Carnegie and climbed the stairs to the campus. A large banner hung over the entrance to the Smith Building, proclaiming it the place to enter. A crowd of perhaps forty people had filtered into the Fuels Lab for the ten o'clock performance. David and Jacob stood toward the back of the group, which clustered around a long laboratory bench at one end of the large room. The place stank of oils and chemicals and the wax a janitor had used on the floor. David ran his finger along the bench behind him. Its surface was gritty and the table pockmarked. A burst of laughter made David turn around. He saw Adler swell with pomposity and Jacob, at David's side, stiffen.

Case's president, a heavyset man with a receding hairline, opened the proceedings. "Gentlemen, the Case Institute of Technology is extraordinarily proud to announce its renewed collaboration with the Lewis Flight Propulsion Laboratory. With the intensification of the Cold War, it is critical for the United States to extend its knowledge of rocketry and space flight. Finding appropriate fuels is central to our ability to build superior rockets and conquer space. The combination of the talent associated with Case's Fuels Lab and that of the Lewis Lab is sure to make a significant difference in our battle against Communism." Mild applause erupted. "To tell us more about the upcoming work, I'd like to introduce Dr. Samuel Goldstein, head of research at the Lewis Lab." More applause.

David pulled out his handkerchief and mopped his brow, then his neck. He saw the sweat on Jacob's face, tapped his arm, and thrust out the white cotton square. Jacob startled, as if coming out of a trance, looked down, and shook his head. Was he going to break? David scrutinized the man: shoulders back, eyes focused, absorbed in who knew what fantasy, but not backing away. He'd do.

Dr. Goldstein, thoroughly professional with his well-trimmed salt-and-pepper hair and thin-striped navy suit, shook the president's hand and turned to the assembled group. "Thank you. I am very pleased to represent the Lewis Lab today and celebrate our upcoming collaboration with Case's Fuels Lab. Though much of the work we'll be doing is classified, I can tell you that we've pushed for this collaboration because of the groundbreaking research of Dr. Gerhardt Adler on liquid hydrogen as a potential rocket fuel. For those of you members of the press, please be sure to pick up a copy of the official press release, right here on the end of the lab bench." He picked up a stack of paper and riffled it before replacing it on the bench. "And now, let me introduce Dr. Adler, distinguished professor of chemical engineering and head of the Fuels Lab, to tell you more about this research."

This time, louder applause. David assessed the crowd, counting maybe ten men taking rapid notes. Most of those wore slightly out-of-date suits. The ones clapping looked more like professors or graduate students. Some of them were in shirtsleeves. David debated taking off his jacket and decided against it. He wanted the power of proper dress, even when the day was hot and the damn suit baggy. He glanced again at Jacob. If eyes could bore holes, Adler'd be a pincushion. "Breathe, man, breathe."

Jacob slowly turned his head to David, inhaled deeply, and turned back to Adler.

David suppressed a grin. God, they were gonna destroy this guy. He floated into a daydream, imagining his hands on Adler's neck, squeezing the life from him. What would his OSS trainers suggest as the best attack on this fit physical specimen? It didn't matter. He couldn't touch Adler. Violence on his part would turn public opinion to Adler's side. No, today required pulling hard on the reins to halt all his fighting impulses.

Then Adler spoke. "Thank you, gentlemen. I have worked on rocket fuels for many years and am pleased that the Lewis Lab recognizes the importance of my research. Hydrogen is the fuel of the future for rockets. We have already solved many of the problems related to thrust, exhaust velocity, and specific impulse using this fuel, and the collaboration with the Lewis Lab will allow us to move forward more quickly in our research. It is very difficult to work with liquid hydrogen. It is dangerous to handle, difficult to store, and hard to obtain. As you can see, looking around this room . . ." he paused, waving his hand to indicate the length and breadth of the lab, ". . . this lab is filled with outdated equipment and is far too limited in size to do the testing that is needed. The Lewis Lab has recently purchased a hydrogen liquefier, which will help me immensely with supply issues."

David winced at the intended insult to Case's facilities and glanced at the university president, who frowned. Adler sure wasn't winning friends at his place of employment. Looking at the audience again, David saw a couple of guys who'd checked out, a few a little confused, but most hanging on. Adler probably thought he was demonstrating his own brilliance, but he sure came across as an arrogant asshole. Besides, it was real stuffy in here. David wanted to get his own show on the road.

The president put on a smile. "Gentlemen, if you'll come upstairs with us now, you can sit down, and we'll open the session to questions."

Hah, David thought, *show time*. Sweat ran down his sides from under his arms, and his palms were damp. He took a deep breath and whispered to Jacob. "Five minutes 'til we're on."

Jacob nodded once.

From the Fuels Lab in the basement, the crowd snaked up the stairs to a recitation room on the first floor. David had pressed for this venue for the confrontation because the listeners would fan out in its chairs, nearly surrounding Adler, and it would be easy to block his access to the door, which opened at the ends of the rows of seats. Adler marched the ten steps to the lectern. The guests from the Lab took seats, and then the lecture hall doors opened again, admitting fifty to sixty men recruited by the temple team, all dressed in dark suits, who spread out across the back of the room and in front of the door. The rabbi ducked his head and raised his hand in a small wave.

Goldstein made no comment on the new arrivals and walked to the microphone to open the session for questions. Adler stood behind the lectern, his deep-socket eyes wandering about the room and his scar showing white as it peeked out from the neckline of his shirt. For at least a minute, the reporters murmured to each other and glanced at first one and then another cluster of men in black. Finally, one of them raised a hand and stood. "Ted Hessoun, the *Plain Dealer*. What are the next steps in this joint venture?"

The answer came from Goldstein: "We'll be meeting frequently together over the next few months to plan our joint research. We have an excellent team at the lab, which will be supplemented by Dr. Adler and his team from Case."

Adler nodded. "The facilities at the Lewis Flight Propulsion Lab are more extensive than Case can afford, so the faculty and graduate students will have greatly increased opportunities to pursue their research agendas."

David, seated in the second row, raised his arm, and Adler pointed at him. David stood. "Isn't it true you began this research at Peenemünde in northern Germany when you were an S.S. officer?"

Adler paused, his eyes mere slits. "We are not here to discuss that. Have you a legitimate question about fuels or this collaboration? If not, we will pass to another question."

David leaned forward, balancing on the back of the seat in front of him. "Actually, many of us are here to discuss your activities, all aspects of your research." David felt the rush of adrenaline, like the best of skating competitions when he flew off the starting line and surged ahead of his competitors. "You were at Peenemünde." He made it an accusation.

Adler drew up to his full height with the rigidity of an officer's call to attention. "I was. We did excellent work there."

David, too, stood at attention. "Excellent science, perhaps, even when you moved with the rocket installation to Nordhausen. But at what cost?"

"The war is over. I work now in the U.S. so the Free World will beat the Soviets into space." He was the commandant once again. He ruled, and others were meant to shut up and listen.

"Unfortunately, the war is not over for many of the people in this room who mourn the losses of their mothers, fathers, siblings—whole families." For David, and he suspected for Adler, they were the only people in the room. Everyone else was furniture.

Case's president strode to the podium. "Gentlemen, gentlemen, this is a press conference announcing a beneficial collaboration of institutions. Let's return to the issue at hand—the scientific breakthroughs we see in our future and the positive steps that the Case Institute of Technology is taking into the future of rocket science."

David waited for the man to finish, then spoke again. "You didn't stop at science. You watched over the Dora labor camp, and you were brutal." If he couldn't use his fists to punch Adler, he'd sure use his words.

For a moment Adler's façade cracked—irritated, dismissive. "Ach, du liebe Zeit!" Then he grabbed both sides of the lectern and jabbed at David with his chin. "I did the job I was assigned. It was wartime."

David moved up a row, gripping Adler with his eyes, daring him to show weakness and look away. "No, you went beyond your assigned duties. You personally beat to death your workers for minor infractions or no infractions at all. You—"

Adler jerked his body around to face Case's president. "I need not stand here and listen to these hostile accusations!"

The president cleared his throat. "Sir," he said to David, "I don't know who you are or why you're doing this, but you must desist at once." He looked around, probably hoping to see police of some sort, but his eyes stopped at the phalanx of men in front of the door.

"My name is David Svehla, and in the final days of the war, I arrested Herr Adler on behalf of the Allies for crimes against humanity." He moved yet closer to the podium, only a few feet away, and fixed his gaze on Adler's eyes. "I know what obscenities you committed against defenseless concentration camp laborers. I saw the results in the corpses that littered the compound."

Jacob limped up beside David, removed his suit jacket, and rolled up his left sleeve. No one moved. All eyes followed the white fabric. One fold, two folds, three folds. An undercurrent of murmuring flowed through the crowd. David heard exclamations like "My God," "Look at that," "Poor man," and "Not these Jews again."

Jacob's gaze never faltered. "I also know you well, Sturmbannführer Adler." Standing at attention, he raised his left arm above his head, the tattooed number on display for all to see. Then he recited the number, as though reporting in a morning roll call.

Adler and the president froze in place. David watched the president's eyes dart around the room, no doubt wondering who would get him out of this mess. The graying man tried valiantly, "Gentlemen, Mr. Svehla, I assure you that Case will look into your allegations. But now, it's time to disperse. We have a small reception planned in the foyer. Please join me there." He threw his arm out to indicate the exit doors.

The line of black suits in front of the door drew closer together.

David caught a hand motion of the president, calling a student to his side. In a whisper, he sent the student out. The "soldiers" at the door parted for him, and David knew he and Jacob had a limited amount of time to wrap this up.

Jacob began quietly. "You have certainly noticed that I have difficulties to walk. It was not always so. One very cold day in November 1944, you called us outside to stand in cotton shirts and trousers."

The only sounds in the room were those of the reporters whose pens scratched across their pads.

Adler's eyes shifted from Jacob to David and back. Jacob ran his story in a monotone. "When the snow started to fall, a new man in the camp called to you, said he was freezing cold. I was in front row. I turned to identify this new man, to tell him later we must keep silent. You strike me with your cane—you, in your warm winter uniform and gloves. My ligaments tore, here." Jacob indicated the outside of his knee. "When I fell to the ground, it was not enough. You smiled and pressed your heavy boot on that place."

Several listeners moaned in sympathetic pain. Even David, who had heard the story before, winced. The straightforward recitation heightened the tension in the room.

The president turned to Adler, a look of pained astonishment on his face.

David spoke, index finger pointed at Adler. "It's time you acknowledged your role and paid for your actions." He shot the finger forward with each noun and verb, imitating the fist punches he yearned to make.

Adler's face creased with anger. He yelled, "I did nothing wrong," executed a precise quarter-turn, shoved aside two men blocking the door, and stormed out. Several reporters elbowed their way to the door, buzzing with questions.

David turned to Jacob and squeezed his shoulder. "You okay? You were magnificent." Jacob looked about to collapse as the temple team gathered around him. Several reporters leapt to their feet and crowded around, firing questions. David strode to the lectern and announced that he and Jacob would answer any questions the press might have.

Rabbi Meschen took Jacob's arm and walked him to the podium. Then the team dispersed, and without haste, melted away.

The reporters bunched up in front of the microphone, launching a barrage of questions: What was Jacob's full name? What camps was he in? How did he get to the U.S.? Why wasn't Adler prosecuted at Nuremberg? What was David's role in the service? Where did he work now? How did he know Jacob? And so on. Jacob spoke in a clear voice, answering each inquiry until the question of why Adler wasn't prosecuted. Jacob shrugged, and David stepped in to make sure the press got the point of this revelation. "All of us in the U.S. have an ethical dilemma left over from the war.

We need the scientific knowledge of Germans like Adler. They're helping the U.S. military and its related industries. But do they get a blanket pass for the atrocities they committed? Should we welcome them openly and freely into our communities when, like Adler, they're not even ashamed of what they did in the war? Do we truly believe in justice and paying for one's crimes?"

The hubbub that followed pleased David no end. He and Jacob held center stage for perhaps fifteen minutes, until the president, surrounded by several police officers, announced that the meeting was over. Jacob's weak leg trembled from the stress, and David took his arm to help him down the corridor and across the yard toward the car. As they paused on the steps down to the street, a couple of reporters hurried by. One said, "Adler's bolted. I checked his office and the Fuels Lab. Secretary said he'd gone."

The other asked, "You know where he lives?"

David smiled and patted Jacob's arm. Mostly, he was proud that Jacob had mastered his fear and put on an Academy Award-winning performance. But also, deep down, he was proud he hadn't succumbed to his fighting urges but donned the robe of a lawyer and argued his case effectively. Yes, Adler had become prey.

David hardly tasted lunch. He was riding on air, so much so that he described the encounter twice, elaborating on the details.

Grace listened without comment, pushing food around her plate.

Davy grinned. "You really got him, Daddy."

"Yes, we did, Jacob and me." And then the phone rang, the third time since they'd dug into their sandwiches. Another reporter for David.

When he set down the receiver that last time, Hildie asked to be excused to go to the Strausses', and David said he'd go with her.

"Why, Daddy?"

"To check on Jacob, see how he's doin'."

Hildie ran on ahead. The thought that she'd probably heard enough and didn't want to be caught having to listen to more of the morning's affair made David smile.

A weary Jacob met him at the door. The man's pale face looked drained, his arms hanging loose.

"You okay?"

Jacob leaned against the kitchen door. "Full of relief. Tired. Okay."

David nodded. "Yeah. Me, too. Want to drive over to Adler's and see what's goin' on?"

Straightening up slowly, Jacob said, "I do," as though he was surprised at his own reaction.

Adler's block of Fairmount Boulevard had cars parked along both sides of the divided road, at least two policemen directing traffic and people, and a host of reporters and cameramen clustered around the two driveway entrances. When David pulled the car to the curb, he turned to Jacob. "There'll be more questions. You ready?"

"It will be for the best." He got out and, shoulders back, limped to the nearest cluster.

The reporters pounced, turning away from the house and directing the cameras and microphones on Jacob. Faced with their onslaught of questions, David called the group to order. "Listen up, you people. Jacob's going to tell more of his story. You can ask questions afterwards."

Jacob closed his eyes and took a deep breath, then looked up at the crowd. "Dora was a labor camp. In '43 and '44, the Germans needed a place the Allies cannot bomb, to build the V-1 and V-2 rockets. They forced us to make tunnels in a mountain, to work with little light and no fresh air, twelve, even sixteen hours a day. The scientists ruled us, with Adler most powerful. It was Adler who pushed the guards to give us no food, to beat us, and to kill us." He paused again, and in the silence the cameras whirred. "Adler." He flicked his hand toward the house.

David moved to the microphones, hoping to give Jacob a few moments to breathe, and repeated his request for a debate in the press on this business of employing German scientists who had been active Nazis.

A reporter called out, "Are you a member of the Communist Party?"

David drew up to his full height. "I am not now, nor have I ever been, a member. I served my country in the OSS during the war. Never was, never will be, a Red." This question enraged him. He'd followed the Mc-Carthy hearings, read about the investigations of the House Un-American Activities Committee. Everyone had. He believed the country should be cleared of commie sympathizers, though McCarthy and H.U.A.C. had gone overboard. Who was this guy doing the asking? The press was probably full of "fellow travelers."

"Isn't that why you're attacking Dr. Adler?" came a voice from the crowd. David searched for the face. It was hidden. His temper was fraying: who was that asshole?

"Sounds like you're a Communist. You don't want science advanced in this here U.S. of A."

Jacob eased up to the microphones. "Here today we speak of Adler. My friend David and myself, we hide no illegal activity. But Adler yes, there is much in his past. He has not paid for his crimes."

As David worked to control his anger, he ran through the possible responses to prove his loyalty. In the silence between questions, he heard muttering in the back of the crowd. A number of men turned around, looking up the driveway to the house. A few peeled away and turned camera equipment in that direction. And then David saw the cause of the defection: Adler's teenage daughter was walking toward them. Dressed in a conservative white blouse and navy skirt, she looked poised and determined. The reporters shot questions her way. A policeman hurried to the hedge that separated public and private property and kept the reporters on the public sidewalk.

Greta's voice shook yet came across clearly. "Why are you persecuting my father? He is a good man, working for the U.S. My mother is crying inside the house, afraid to come out. I thought this was a free country where people could live in peace."

The girl had broken the spell of the moment, and David's anger dissipated. He looked at Jacob. "Seems like we've had our time in the spotlight. Shall we leave it for her?"

Jacob seemed mesmerized by the poised young girl and smiled. "All right."

Once in the car, he commented, "I would like that my daughter grow up like this girl. I mean, grow up and be able to say what she thinks."

David pictured Karen, then Hildie. "Yeah, I see what you mean. I hate the lip I get from Hildie, but she has spunk." He'd never thought of her comebacks, her sauciness, as good before. God, she was like him.

CHAPTER 10

JULY 1955

Early Friday morning, a day and a half after the confrontation, David sipped coffee across the kitchen table from Grace. The children were still asleep, and she was in her nightgown. He really didn't need coffee—he was so pumped up by the Adler thing. He rustled the pages of the *Plain Dealer*, looking for news of his exploits.

"Grace, listen to this." He folded the paper back, creased the fold, and then took the target page in both hands. "'This reporter spoke with five concentration camp survivors yesterday, all of whom have broken years of silence, emboldened by the actions of Jacob Strauss. Earlier this week, Strauss accused a Case professor, Dr. Gerhardt Adler, of unspeakable crimes . . .' Yeah, yeah, yeah. Here's the good part. 'The university has launched an investigation to ensure Adler is in the country legally and not wanted for crimes in Germany.'" He looked at Grace over the top of the paper. "Look at what's happenin'. We got all kinds of coverage. It just keeps getting better."

"You've certainly stirred up a hornet's nest." She fiddled with the handle of her coffee cup, which drew his attention to the tabletop and then to her face.

"Yes, I have. Yesterday's *Press* said reporters were hounding military and government sources for an explanation of how he got into the U.S. Truman's okay with bringing scientists into this country as long as they weren't Nazis." He smacked his lips. "Is there more coffee?"

She stared at him and tilted her head toward the pot. "Why don't you check?"

He sat, lifting his cup. Grace did not rise, and he let the cup clatter into its saucer. "All right. Spit it out. What's wrong?"

She met his eyes, stare for stare. "I'm glad Adler's been exposed, I am. And I hope the cause of justice is served and he's punished for what he did."

"Good." He sat back and crossed one leg over the other.

"It's the undercurrents I'm scared of." She pushed loose hairs behind her ears.

"What undercurrents?"

"This Communism thing. I scanned the *Plain Dealer* while you showered. Even that article you were reading asks whether you're a Communist. I suspect reporters are checking membership lists, talking to your colleagues and our friends, and contacting the FBI, spreading your name far and wide."

"So? They're not going to find anything."

Grace took a deep breath. "Did you see the editorial?"

David flipped to the right page and spotted the headline: "Is Svehla a Communist?" He skimmed the lines, getting angrier with each accusation. "How dare they say that it's a well-known fact that OSS personnel consorted with Communists in the war!"

"Did you?"

"I can't talk about that. You know the rules."

"Yes, I do."

"And look at this." He slapped the paper. "A veteran who often has a beer with Svehla at the VFW on Miles Avenue reports that he has described interactions with Russians during the war."

"Did you?"

"Well, I told them a story. But it wasn't about negotiations or sharing information; it was about a massacre."

"It doesn't sound good."

David pushed his chair back, scraping the floor. "I'll stop this."

"What are you going to do?"

"I got friends."

Lorelei Brush

David marched into his home office and called Hessoun at the *Plain Dealer*. It was still early, but the reporter had told him he liked the dark hours.

"Ted Hessoun here."

"Time to follow through on my promise to give you an exclusive."

"Okay. What you got?"

"It's this business of my bein' a Communist. Never was, never will be. You know Chet. You went to Adams with him. We were raised red-blooded Americans. Ma wouldn't have put up with Communist ideas in the house. Besides, we've always voted Republican, hated FDR and his New Deal. We don't like giveaways. We put ourselves through college; others should, too."

"Yeah, so?"

"You read that editorial on me this morning? Where's it all coming from? That's what I want to know. Feels like I got H.U.A.C. or McCarthy dogging me. How about you find out?"

"I don't know. The public's bored with H.U.A.C., and McCarthy's a thing of the past after the army trial last year."

"Well, someone's after me."

"Tell you what. I'll make a few calls. No promises. We'll see."

David's second call was to Chet, who was still at home. "Can you put a stop to these nonsense rumors?"

Chet laughed. "You got yourself knee-deep in muck, didn't you?"

"C'mon. Use your connections and get me out of this."

"I'll try. Jeez, maybe I can be the one to get the bullies off *you* this time."

"Yeah, well, thanks in advance."

The phone rang while the receiver was still warm from the call to Chet. Figuring it was a reporter—and primed to set the record straight—David answered.

A voice growled. "You commie. Ought to be taken out and shot. We don't want your kind around." The phone slammed down, making David jerk the receiver away from his ear.

What the hell? This business was getting out of hand. He'd been so sure people would believe in his loyalty once they knew his war record; he hadn't prepared for an onslaught of accusations and hatred.

Almost immediately, the phone rang again. David stared at it, angry and a little off-kilter. It stopped ringing at the third sound. David relaxed until he heard Grace's footsteps coming toward his office.

"It's for you. The man wouldn't give his name, just spit out, 'Gimme that David.' You want to take it? I . . . I suppose I can tell him you aren't home."

A spurt of anger ran through him. He'd tell this guy where to get off. "I'll take it."

She turned and hesitated, her hand on the door handle. "I don't like this."

"Me either." He picked up the phone. This caller was more graphic. David caught himself before answering in kind, suddenly afraid he'd only generate more bad publicity if these callers talked to reporters. Instead, he gently pushed down the button and cradled the phone. Then he ran his hands down his face and went to talk to Grace. She was in the kitchen seeing to the children's breakfast.

"I think you should just let the phone ring, hon. You, too, kids."

Hildie looked up as she chewed on her jelly toast. "Why, Daddy?"

"I've had a couple of nasty calls. I don't want you to listen to these crazy people."

Grace narrowed her eyes. "All right." It was almost a question. "You have appointments today?"

"A few. I should be back by late afternoon."

"I'm going to Karen's," Hildie announced.

Grace picked up Hildie's empty plate. "Tell Rebecca I may be over later."

When David cruised down East Scarborough a few hours later, he saw a closed van parked across from his house. As he turned into the driveway, two men got out and strolled toward him. He shut off the engine, leaving the car in front of the garage to avoid being trapped in a space too small for maneuvering. Taking his time to slide papers into his briefcase, he watched the men in the rearview mirror. Friendly or not? Hard to tell. No slouching, no smirking, nothing disrespectful in their bearing. No obvious weapons. He opened the car door primed for battle.

"You David Svehla?" This came from the taller of the two, in a blue suit worn for the third or fourth day by the looks of the creases. Dirty blond hair, dark eyes.

"Yes. Who are you?" Blue suit seemed to be the spokesperson. The other guy, in a darker gray suit, hung behind blue suit's left shoulder.

"We're from the *Plain Dealer.*"

"You got IDs on you?" He'd keep this as pleasant as possible, but he was sure going to find out who he was dealing with.

Each of the men handed over a press ID. Blue suit was Thomas Higgins; gray suit was Gary McDonald.

David allowed his shoulders to relax. "What can I do for you?" He handed back the IDs.

"Ted Hessoun said he'd talked to you. We want to get as much background for your story as we can. About what you did in the war, why you decided to expose Adler. Could we go inside?"

"It's nice out today. Why don't we sit at the picnic table in the backyard." He indicated the wooden table and benches under the seckel pear tree. He wanted to keep this follow-up out of Grace's kitchen.

They had to brush off stray leaves and bird droppings, to which task David donated his handkerchief. Gary opened his notepad and pulled a pen from his shirt pocket.

Tom led off. "Tell us about your war."

David stripped down his experience, carefully editing out what he was forbidden to describe and those items he didn't wish to see in print, like any association with Mickey Mouse. He could imagine the taunts. "I enlisted in the army on December 8, 1941, was assigned to the Chemical Warfare Service, worked initially developing army war materials, volunteered for intelligence in '43, trained for OSS in Washington, shipped out in '44, did my assigned jobs, and returned home in the summer of '45."

Gary wrote it all down in a sort of shorthand that David had no chance of reading upside down.

Tom kept up the questioning. "What was your assignment that involved Jacob's labor camp?"

"Tom, you seem like a straight guy, so let me be straight with you. I can't talk about that. See, the OSS asked us all to take an oath at the end of the war not to discuss what we did. It's still top secret, given this Cold War we're in. I pushed the limits saying I was at Dora. That's as far as I can go."

"How about that story you told on meeting the Russians?"

David threw up his hands. He'd never outrun that tale. Should have kept his mouth shut at the VFW. "We can talk about our training, which was where that story came from. We used a lot of 'what if' scenarios, where we had to decide what we'd do. The Russian massacre was one of those."

"So, it didn't really happen?"

"Only in a classroom."

"Anything else you can tell us about that time?"

"Sure. I'm a loyal American. I served my country with honor and was proud to do it. I used the GI bill to get my law degree, and I believe the American legal system delivers justice for all—or it does, if used properly."

"Right, right. Who were the men you brought with you to that press conference?"

"Friends of mine, of Jacob's. Men who wanted to support him, who knew what he'd gone through."

"Jewish?"

"I didn't ask." This interview had definitely taken a left turn, and David didn't like it. "What was important, what we were doing there, was pointing out that a criminal, a brutal man, had a position of responsibility in our community. That's what we need to focus on here. That's what you need to write more about."

"Yes, well, we'll be talking to Jacob, too, maybe some others. Thanks for being so candid."

Gary closed his notebook and stuck his pen in the plastic holder lining his shirt pocket.

David watched them walk back down the drive, reviewing what they'd asked, what he'd said. Hessoun better be watching them, better make sure they stuck to the facts, to Jacob's story.

Determined to stem the flow of the VFW leaks, David strode into the hall that evening and picked up a beer. He heard catcalls from a couple of directions. Some guy he knew only to wave at yelled, "Found any more Nazis?" The men with him guffawed.

David threw away the question with a wave of his own. "Naw, one's enough." Then he sauntered over to the table that held Mac, Bill, Sarge, and some others whose names he'd forgotten. As he said hello, Sarge asked, in all seriousness, if the scuttlebutt was right that the feds were after him. David shook his head, adopting a nonchalant look. "I'm a patriot, and they know it."

"Oh." Sarge's body relaxed.

David checked out the others. Bill grinned. The guy next to him stared at the cardboard coaster he was twirling. Mac gave him a high sign. No one else looked at him. He gritted his teeth.

Bill pointed at Sarge and then David. "Dave here ain't no Red. Don't-cha know that by now?" He patted the empty chair next to him. "I been telling everybody that I know the man who's found that Nazi." His head bobbed in affirmation.

"You also tell the press I consorted with Communists in the war?"

Bill furrowed his brow. "Huh?"

"I read this morning that someone at the VFW said I interacted with Reds in WWII."

With his face now wreathed in smiles, Bill nodded. "Sure. I told them about your story and killing them horses."

David leaned forward, hands gripping the edge of the table. "Bill, I wasn't cutting a deal or working with Communists. That story was about massacring commies."

"I know that. I'm not stupid."

Sarge laid his hand on Bill's shoulder. "I guess the *Plain Dealer* reporter interpreted the story a little differently."

"Oh, gosh, I'm sorry, Dave. Can I buy you another beer?"

David opened his mouth to give Bill a proper dressing-down and thought better of it. "Sure, Bill. Thanks." He emptied his mug down his throat and passed it across the table.

The others were quiet. Mac raised his eyebrows. Someone said the Indians really had a chance at the pennant this year thanks to Bob Feller's pitching. David sat with them, joked along until he realized their discomfort with him was not going away. "Mac, you got a minute?"

Mac saluted the others with his mug. "Later, guys." He followed David to an empty table in the corner.

After they were seated, Mac took a long pull on his beer. "What's up, Cap'n? More than this commie thing?"

David hunched over his beer. "The paper hit me hard, like they want people to believe I trumped up the charges about Adler. My wife's upset." He looked up at Mac, anger oozing out of him. "I'm thinkin' that, somehow, that damned Nazi won. The press doesn't want to go after him. Seems like he's just getting more money and more status."

Mac raised his eyebrows. "My offer to lose him on Lake Erie is still open."

"I don't think we ought to go that far. But thanks for the offer."

Setting down his mug, Mac crossed his arms on the table, leaning over them toward David. "Look at the facts here. Adler got out of Germany. We think that's good 'cause people are better off in this country than in Germany: more food, good jobs, homes to live in. But Adler had to leave his country, most of his relatives, his friends, and the future he'd planned."

"Yeah, but he's got a great job."

"Number two: The man's been exposed and that'll follow him for a long time, maybe all his life. Sure, he's got a job and a nice house, but think about the finger pointing of neighbors, parents of his kids' friends, people at church." Mac sniffed and dragged his wrist across his nose.

"I don't think he cares. He's got such a big ego, he probably doesn't notice the snubs."

"I'll bet his wife does."

"Well, yeah." A small voice murmured to David never to underestimate wives.

"Face it, he's going to be isolated for the rest of his life."

David shook his head. It just wasn't right. "His kids are getting a better education than mine, growing up with privileges I can't afford."

Mac smiled. "Didn't you tell me you agreed with Jacob that we aren't at war with the children?"

"Shit. You shoulda been a debater." He punched Mac's shoulder. "You gonna dispose of that Communist label, too?"

Mac took another swig and licked foam from his lips. "You and I know it ain't true. However . . ." He looked down for a moment, then straight at David. ". . . there's another little matter I got to tell you about. I—ah—had a call from an FBI guy—about you."

"What?" David knew all the OSS men were under casual surveillance to make sure they didn't reveal any secrets from the war. He scanned the room. Hell, that new guy at the bar could be FBI or CIA. Still, no one in listening distance, not with the canned music playing. They could talk.

In a quiet voice, Mac went on, "He asked about you and warned me to keep my mouth shut. I figure he meant not to mention the call to you, and also not to talk to the press or say anything about what we did in the war."

David blew out his pent-up air. The walls were closing in. "I'm not a damned Communist. It's common knowledge we liberated camps and arrested the S.S. in charge. I haven't spilled any secrets. There's no reason for the FBI to go after me."

Mac stuck up a warning hand. "I got it, Cap'n. Just wanted to let you know you're in their sights."

David pushed his hair out of his face. "Jeez. If it's one thing we all learned, it's how to tell a story with scrubbed facts. When I think of the tales I've made up for my son . . ."

"I suppose the good news is you only promised to shut up for fifty years. You can tell him the truth when he's an old man." Mac grinned.

David raised his mug in agreement. "Here's to living that long."

CHAPTER 12
JULY 1955

David slept badly on Friday night, unable to get comfortable and dreaming of a tiger trapped in a small cage. It paced the perimeter, stopping to pull at the bars with its teeth and roar. In the morning, he cut himself shaving, and by the time he got downstairs for breakfast, he could only growl a stony, "Good morning."

Grace shook water from her hands and pointed to the coffee pot. "You'd better have some coffee. I made it strong. Then read the editorial about you. You're not going to like it." She leaned forward, almost bowing over the sink. "I want to hit somebody."

Startled, David sat down hard. With a wet thumb, he separated the paper's pages and found the article. The headline leapt from the page, *Svehla Admits Lying.* "What the hell?"

Grace sat down catty-corner to him and folded her hands on the table.

He held the paper at arms' length. His damned eyes weren't as sharp as they used to be. *David Svehla, the man who accused Case Professor Gerhardt Adler of crimes against humanity, admitted yesterday to lying on multiple occasions about his role in the war. When asked to describe his true experiences, he refused. When asked to verify even the simple story he'd related to fellow veterans, he admitted it never happened.* "I can't believe this!" He scanned to the next paragraph. *It is interesting to ask why he portrayed himself as anti-Russian. One reasonable assumption is that he is covering his actual Communist ideas.* "I'm being railroaded. This is trash, all of it." He looked for affirmation from Grace to see her wiping away tears. "Ah, hon, you know this stuff isn't true."

She blew her nose and crushed the Kleenex in her hand. "It's half-truths. But, David, it gets worse."

He read on, his exhales audible and angry. *Interviews with neighbors expose Svehla as a housebreaker. Two of them, Douglas Vaughan and Henry Calloway, reported his using a set of thief's tools to get into their homes.* David sputtered and swore under his breath.

Svehla also refused to identify the men who accompanied him to the meeting where he leveled the heinous accusations at the distinguished professor. He denied knowing whether they were Jewish, which was obvious to the reporters in the room. He is apparently a part of a Jewish cabal aiming to discredit a fine academic. Dr. Adler is involved in critical work for the United States in our Cold War with the U.S.S.R. Is it possible that Svehla's intent was to disrupt our development of the weaponry needed to win that war?

He crushed the front section and tossed it across the table. "They can't get away with this. I won't let them. It's outrageous. I'm calling Hessoun. What the hell is he up to?"

David stomped into his office and dialed Ted's number. He let the phone ring twenty-two times before slamming down the receiver. With only the man's work number, he headed back to the kitchen for the White Pages.

Grace was fixing cereal for the children and raised her eyebrows as he entered.

"Just getting the phone book. He wasn't in his office."

Hildie announced she was having a banana with her Cheerios. As he flipped pages to the H's, she added, "Are you mad, Daddy?"

"Yes."

David read the number, recited it aloud, and hurried out.

He heard his daughter. "What's wrong, Mommy?"

"It's what we talked about yesterday. Some people are calling him a Communist."

David grumbled. His kids shouldn't have to deal with this shit.

"Why?" Hildie sounded a little too unsure for David's comfort.

He shut the office door, certain Grace would reassure her.

A child's voice picked up the Hessoun's home phone and promised to get his dad.

"Ted, I thought you were on my side. What's going on with the article in today's paper?"

"I didn't write any article. I'm still trying to get answers." He sounded defensive, like he really didn't know about the article.

"Didn't you read it?"

"Give me a minute."

David drummed his fingers on the desk.

"God. Look at that, there's no byline. Odd."

"You swear you weren't a part of this?"

"Yes. In fact, I'm going to track this guy down. He's stealing follow-ups that are mine."

"So, you didn't send two guys out yesterday to interview me, a Thomas Higgins and a Gary McDonald?"

"No. Never heard of either of them. I don't think they're on the PD staff."

"Damn. They showed their IDs. I've been a fool. Should have called you to verify before I said one word. I won't make that mistake again. The only reporter I'm talking to is you."

"Okay by me. I'll see if I can get a lead on the imposters. Now I think I've got a story."

By 0930, David had listened to a flow of invective from three more callers, told two reporters he had "no comment," and had taken the phone off the hook. He'd also proved to himself there was an extra click on his phone each time he picked up the receiver. It was bugged.

He caught glimpses of Grace through the glass in the sunroom doors. She was pacing back and forth across the living room.

When she thrust open his office door, her words spilled out. "There are people gathering outside. Ten, maybe fifteen men. I'm going to call the police."

David slewed around in his chair. Two men were pulling signs out of a black sedan. He read, "Throw the commies out."

"I'm going out there. I'll deal with this."

"There are too many of them." Her voice wavered.

His whole body contracted with rage, but he stood tall and steady as a rock. No one could threaten his family and get away with it.

When he opened the front door, several men rushed forward yelling insults.

"You, commie, get out! And take your Jew-boy with you."

Jacob? They were after Jacob, too? No, no. He was the *victim* here. David contracted his hands into fists, picking the first man he'd assault if it came to that.

One older man in a WWII uniform whose jacket could no longer button across his stomach called out, "You're a disgrace to the army."

Among the men with steno pads, one brandished his pen. "Who else is in your cell? Who recruited you?"

David stood on the small front porch, fighting back the urge to explode in rage and tell these idiots where to go. His OSS training hadn't prepared him for this scenario. He mustered up his best teacher's voice, the one he used to halt the rush of thirty teenagers' hormones. "Quiet!" As the noise level abated a little, he added, "I'll speak when I can be heard. I will not yell."

Instead of listening intently to him, the group of men, like starlings, turned in a wave to look down the street. Jacob limped into sight and across the lawn to join David. In a whisper, he reported that Grace had called him.

David's impetus was to hug him, but he glared back at the intruders.

"You support this Communist? You a Red, too? You part of his cell?"

David couldn't tell who said it, but he felt Jacob bristle.

In a slightly raised, tight voice, Jacob answered. "When you gather in front of David's house, when I hear you accuse an innocent man, I hear not the voices of Americans but those of storm troopers. They came to Jewish homes, to people who were lawyers and electricians and shopkeepers, and yelled at our doors. They did not seek the truth. They came to destroy.

Surely you do not forget Kristallnacht, that night Hitler's brownshirts destroyed Jewish businesses and synagogues?"

A couple of men backed into the street. Another looked embarrassed.

Jacob took a step toward the crowd, right to the edge of the porch. "I thought I left this behind in Germany. My wife and child hide now in our house, very scared. I do not accept this. You must give respect or leave."

One suited man let his placard drop to the ground. Another poked at a friend and jerked his head to suggest they take off. Low murmurs replaced the strident catcalls. Many seemed to bide their time, but after a moment's silence, started again. "We aren't here for you, Jacob. It's David who's the traitor."

"Yeah, it's David who's turned on the U.S. of A."

"He should be run out of town on a rail."

"We don't want his kind around here."

David laid a protective hand on Jacob's arm. "Thank you. You don't need to stay. It's my problem."

"I cannot leave, not now." He stood rigidly facing the wrath of the protesters, now numbering at least twenty.

David yelled over their vitriol. "Let me repeat to you gentlemen. I am not, nor have I ever been, a member of the Communist Party. Nor do I support communist beliefs. I am a loyal American."

Several people crowded toward the porch, their questions, comments, and accusations piling one on top of the other.

As David pointed to one of them, a serious-looking and well-dressed man, he heard Hildie's angry shout. "Get off my property!"

From around the edge of the house came a youngish man backing toward the street, his hands in front of him as though warding off blows. David's furious seven-year-old, with a baseball bat over her shoulder, marched toward the hapless demonstrator. "Get off."

A photographer snapped a shot of child, bat, and adult shielding his face.

The crowd sniggered, which caused Hildie to startle. She stopped, taking in the mass of men, and ran to the porch, clambering up over the rail to tuck herself in behind her father.

David put his hand down to smooth her hair.

Most of the mob took only a momentary pause before shifting their focus back to David, shouting once again.

In the middle of the third or fourth of David's attempts to reiterate his innocence, a boy's voice called out from down the street, "Mr. Svehla." At first, David was so involved, he barely registered his name, but several men turned at the sound, allowing the panicky voice to be heard. It was Davy's friend Buddy holding him up and guiding him toward the house. The boys looked like a soldier bringing his wounded comrade home. Davy cradled his right arm with his left. His nose dripped blood down his shirt, and his left eye was a slit. The photographer snapped it all.

Hildie ran to the porch rail. "Davy, Davy, what happened?"

David headed down the steps, uneasy about the look of his son's arm.

Davy groaned.

Buddy said, "It was six or eight boys, yelling 'commie, commie.'" He made a two-note chant, the higher note on the first syllable.

David swore under his breath. It wasn't Davy's war. "Thanks, Buddy. For bringing him home."

Buddy hung back, seemingly unwilling to leave, eying the crowd of men.

David knelt on one knee, his hand touching Davy's arm. The men circled around, and David ignored them. Davy's arm wasn't spurting blood; the bone hadn't come through the skin, but the way his hand hung affirmed a bone was broken. The puffy parts of his face were bound to turn black and blue, but the nose didn't look broken.

David scooped up his son, taking care not to jostle the broken arm, and carried him to the house. Hildie followed close behind.

Davy stared at all the men. "Who are they, Daddy? Are they going to hurt us?"

David squeezed his son, just a bit. "Don't you worry about them. They're going now. We'll go find your mom."

One reporter of the age to be the father of a young child asked, "What happened? Who did this?"

Davy turned his head into David's shoulder. "I want to go inside."

A reporter pushed in front of David. "Your son in a lot of fights? He pick on other children?"

Hildie hung onto David's pant leg.

With Jacob clearing a path, David faced his accusers. "My son was beat up because of the lies you've written about me." He looked into each face as he passed them, memorizing their features. "Stop harassing my family."

Jacob whispered, "Go. I shall take care of this."

They both looked up at the sound of a police siren.

Several men rushed to their cars, and David rounded the corner to the back of the house. A few moments later, he settled Davy on a kitchen chair with Grace hovering next to him.

Buddy sidled just inside the door. "You aren't a Red, are you, Mr. Svehla?"

David looked up from examining his son's face. "No, Buddy, I'm not. Davy isn't one, either." He tried to sound neutral, nonthreatening, but he seethed and thought it was probably showing.

"I thought you weren't." Buddy eased open the screened door. "I . . . I better go." He let the screen door bang shut behind him.

Grace murmured to Davy for just a moment, then narrowed her eyes at David. "Get the car. Now."

"You call the police?"

"Yes."

"The mob's dispersing. Not sure I like getting the police involved."

"Get the car. We'll leave Hildie with Rebecca."

David angled Davy into the back seat, propped his arm on a pillow, and backed the Studebaker out of the garage. He vacillated between plans for revenge against his attackers and walking away from the vulgar storm.

Davy looked gray.

Grace slid in beside her son, told Hildie to take the passenger seat, and knocked on the back of the driver's seat. "Go, now."

David headed to Jacob's and then downtown to University Hospitals.

Davy's breathing was ragged and punctuated by sniffs and small cries. "Why'd they pick on me, Mommy?"

"Because they're bullies. You're not a commie. See if you can take a deep breath."

"I . . ." He hiccupped. ". . . can't."

"You keep trying. Think of being a Hardy boy. You like those books, right? Sometimes Frank or Joe has to go to the hospital, and they're brave. Remember?"

David interrupted. "You know the boys who did this?"

"Yeah, I think. It was—"

"David, this is not the time or the place. Just drive."

Later, when Davy's arm was being X-rayed, Grace said to him, "I will not live this way. I won't have my children in the middle of your fight."

David whispered back. "I didn't ask for this, and I'll fight my own battles."

"But you've dragged us all in with you."

"I can't ask these men—"

She waved a dismissive hand. "Don't you tell me there's nothing you can do. You've done too much already. You and your fighting. You've crossed a line, David. I won't have the children subjected to scenes like this morning. We will not be prisoners in our own house, wondering if men are coming to burn it down."

"That's taking things a bit far, isn't it?"

"Don't you dare minimize what happened. We were threatened. Davy was accosted."

"I know, I know. It's not what I want for the family either."

She sat up, rigid. "Just so you know, I'm taking the children to the farm for the rest of the summer. You can sort this out without us."

"Please, I—"

"Don't you dare argue with me. This is our children's safety we're talking about."

David rubbed his face, appalled at what was happening.

"In September, when it's time for school, we'll see where we are. That's the best I can do."

When they returned from the hospital, David opened the screened door and tore off a scrap of paper in Jacob's handwriting taped to the inside door. *Please call me.* He stuck it in his pocket and looked up to see Grace getting Davy a snack. Good. He'd handle this new problem right away, by God. "I'm going over to get Hildie."

Grace was chatting with Davy about how he could get his friends to sign his cast and nodded at him.

Jacob met him at the door. "Davy?"

"He's fine. And—um—thank you for this morning."

"Of course. And you found the message?"

"Yes. What's it about?"

"After the men went away, I stayed to talk to your neighbors. A car I did not know came into your driveway, and a man got out. He knocked on your front door and your back door. I went to see him. He said he was from the government and you should call him at this number." Jacob handed David a business card printed with the name of Donald Jones and giving a local phone number.

"Any idea who he is?"

"It is difficult to say. Not a reporter, I think. Not like the men in the morning. Too nicely dressed."

David nodded. "Thanks." He turned the card over. Blank. He called to Hildie.

"She is good with Karen."

"Yeah, well, thanks for keeping her. I need to clean up this mess and at least get the family out of the middle of it."

David trudged home a few steps behind his daughter, conscious of sticky sweat under his arms. Got to be the FBI. He was not going to put up with nonsense from them.

Grace's and Davy's voices came from the second floor. He called to Grace that they were home and watched Hildie climb the stairs. Then he steeled himself and crossed the living room. Once behind closed doors, he sat down at his desk and dialed.

"Don Jones here." Jeez, the name was so common, so innocuous, probably fake.

"This is David Svehla, returning your call." He'd play Mr. Mild-Mannered Gentleman while holding razor-edged focus.

"Ah, Mr. Svehla. I'm with the FBI, and I'd like to talk with you about some serious matters." The voice had the tone of a priest about to chastise an impenitent parishioner.

"How about now?"

"This isn't something that can be discussed over the phone. Could you come to my office?"

David's lips twitched. He was gonna take this guy. The man was an amateur. "Sorry. I'm just back from the hospital because my son was beat up. I do not feel it's appropriate for me to leave the house. Why don't you come here?" Always better to command the ground on which you meet the enemy.

"All right. I'll be there in half an hour."

David hung up the phone and thought about his office set-up. First, he removed the fan that usually sat in a window. Better if the guy got hot and uncomfortable. Should shorten the interview. Second, he took one of the two chairs facing his desk down to the basement. He'd sit behind the imposing carved structure and make Jones take the subservient position. Third, there'd be no offer of refreshment. By God, he'd be in charge. Polite but firm. No way was he going to get railroaded into making any more stupid statements.

Then he went upstairs to let Grace know that a man was coming to see him. She was in their bedroom facing a suitcase wide open on the bed. "You sure you need to leave?"

She stopped and looked up. "Yes. My brother can drive us out to Chardon tomorrow."

He rubbed her arm. "I don't want you to go."

"It's no longer your choice."

"Yeah, I can see that. But I still don't like it."

"I don't feel safe here, wondering where the next attack is coming from, who I'm going to find in my kitchen, whether I'll get screamed at if I answer the phone. You're going to do what you need to do. I'm doing what I need to do."

He bent to kiss her, but she turned her head away. He flashed back to that trapped tiger of his dreams and growled to himself.

When David answered the doorbell a half-hour later, he scanned the visitor's I.D. and extended his hand. Jones was a fresh-faced, college kid type. Certainly hadn't seen service during WWII, and probably not Korea. White, short-sleeved shirt, starched collar, and navy striped tie. Newly polished black shoes. Piece of cake. But was he the real McCoy? "Before I talk to you, I'm gonna make a call, make sure you didn't fake that badge."

"Please, call my supervisor. He's—"

"Oh, no. I'll decide who to call."

David escorted Jones into the sunroom and shut the doors. He sat behind his desk, dialed zero for the operator, and asked for the number of the local FBI office. It took several minutes to get to a supervisor, but the man did acknowledge Jones and give a decent description of him.

David hung up and sat back against his chair. "You *seem* to be who you claim."

Jones, the young agent eager to prove himself, launched a barrage of words. "We've received some disturbing information about your activities, Mr. Svehla, and I've been asked to investigate."

"What information?"

Jones sat on the wooden chair, a yellow legal pad on his lap, his hand ready to take notes. "I'm sure you know what you've been up to."

Throwing down a pathetic gauntlet, trying to take charge. David picked up his knife-sharp letter opener. "Where did the reports come from?"

"I'm not at liberty to say."

Rocking the letter opener back and forth, David caught the late afternoon sun and flashed it at Jones. A kid's trick. "So, someone could have made up the accusations."

Jones twisted his face away from the light. "Mr. Svehla, the reports that you are a Communist sympathizer and a rabble-rouser came from reliable sources. I am here to ask you questions, not answer your questions."

Contrary to his words, that tilted head looked submissive. "Mr. Jones—if that is your name—I'm a lawyer." He laid the letter-opener down and clasped his hands over it. "When someone is accused in this country, he has a right to know what he is accused of, who the accuser is, and what the evidence is against him."

The FBI agent squirmed in his chair and then leaned forward. "You have not been accused of a crime, as yet. This is a time of fact-finding. Now, I'd appreciate it if you would answer my questions."

In his turn, David leaned forward, his eyes narrowing. "Mr. Jones, I spent WWII in the OSS. I swore my loyalty to the United States of America, and I have done nothing to break that oath. I am not nor ever have been a member of the Communist Party. The man I confronted at Case is a known Nazi and S.S. officer who should have been tried and convicted for the atrocities he perpetrated."

Jones met his eyes, then focused on his yellow pad, writing furiously. "I understand you were in the Russian sector after the war ended."

David blinked. He'd said he'd arrested Adler at Nordhausen, which was in what would become the Russian sector. "Yes, before the area was turned over to the Russians."

"Would you please describe your duties?"

"Since my war activities remain classified, I can give you only a general picture. Most OSS officers, myself included, saw firsthand the Nazi atrocities and, at times, were a part of liberating concentration camps. That, I believe, is as far as I can go."

"Did you not meet and consort with Communists?"

Sure, he'd met with Communist informants at the direction of his superiors. Back then, they were trying to locate people and papers that would

Lorelei Brush

help the U.S. It didn't matter if the sources were Communists. But how did this lower-level agent find out? What had he been told? Must have been someone senior in the OSS, someone who knew he wasn't a Communist, but Jones's accusation was plausible. Not good.

David kept all emotion from his face, offering Jones a blank stare. "This is the last question I will answer, and my response is: Absolutely not. If you have further questions about my OSS activities, I suggest you call Dr. Bruce Williams in Washington, D.C. or ask Bill Donovan." David rose.

Jones finished writing a paragraph. "Please sit down, Mr. Svehla. I have a number of additional questions."

David strode to the double doors and threw them open to the living room. "Out. Now." He remained standing only a few feet from Jones' chair, letting his anger show in the threatening look on his face. He pointed to the outside door.

Jones looked confused.

As David contemplated picking up the agent and carting him to the door, Hildie erupted into the living room. "Daddy, Mommy says we're going to the farm tomorrow." She looked at his face and then at the man sitting in the sunroom. "Who's that?"

"He was just leaving."

And so, Jones picked up his paper and pen and walked out the door. "I don't know where the farm is, Mr. Svehla, but you can be sure I'll find out."

David held open his home's front door, saying nothing but watching until Jones had unlocked his car and driven away. Then he looked down and ruffled Hildie's hair.

CHAPTER 12

JULY 1955

David had another sleepless night as he debated how to get out of the mess he was in. His thoughts wandered from how to prove the falseness of the Communist label to how much he wanted to keep Grace with him. He looked over at the contours of her figure, lit by the streetlamp outside, and saw her back stubbornly toward him on the bed. When she awoke, he reached for her and asked her to stay. He felt weak, vulnerable.

She sat up slowly and curled a leg under her so she half-faced him. "I can't, David. The children come first."

"I've been awake all night about this. I didn't know my actions would cause this firestorm. I never imagined I'd be made the bad guy and that you and the kids would be drawn in."

Grace studied her fingernails. "But that's what's happened. I don't even want to think about what's next."

David slid his hand across the bed to touch her thigh. "Neither do I. At Jacob's, we talked about consequences like these. I guess I wanted to humble Adler so badly, I refused to face the possibilities."

"Yes. And I'm worried about this obsession, about what started it. Is it revenge? Or something more?" She stared at the dim light through the front windows as though mesmerized by the waffling curtains and a soft dawn.

"You gotta respond, hon, when you believe somethin' is wrong. My mistake was not anticipating a response like this."

Grace swiveled to face him full on. "You sure it's not more than 'something wrong?' Oh, that doesn't matter now. I hate all this—these threats, my house invaded, the obscene phone calls. Hildie said the man she chased away was going through our trash."

She rose, pulled on her robe, and tied its belt. Grasping the carved pineapple at the corner of the headboard, she asked, "Why didn't you tell me this 'meeting' was a major press conference? I feel like the rug's been pulled out from under me, that our marriage isn't the one I'd agreed to, that I can't trust that you have the family's best interests at heart."

He pushed himself up against the bedstead, thankful for its support. She wasn't going to like his answer, but it would be the truth. "I didn't want the story to leak out. I'm sorry if it seems like not trusting you. It wasn't that. It's a . . . well . . . a habit OSS taught me, to hold my cards close to my chest."

"I'm not a faucet, David, or a poker opponent. I can keep my mouth shut." She rubbed her forehead. "I'd think you'd know that by now. When, in our fifteen years of marriage, have I spoken out of turn?"

He stared at the place where the ceiling meets the wall, running through his memories and trying to tamp his rising anger. "I . . . can't think of any time." Was that the only reason he'd kept quiet? He turned to her. "Look, I'm not so good at team stuff. I like bein' in charge, being out front, strutting my stuff. It's why I like us having a division of labor, so I have my responsibilities and count on you for yours."

She stared down at him, and he thought she was weighing his words on a balance. "I'm not trying to take away your freedom to 'strut your stuff.' I don't want to know the details of your law cases or where you are every minute. I just want you to redraw this line you have between us. I'd like to hear from *you* that you're training Davy to fight, not from friends. I want to know beforehand that you're going to be in the news and we may have our lives ripped apart. These things matter. They impact my life and the kids' lives."

Backing a few steps away, she leaned against the closet doorframe and crossed her arms over her chest. "You had a team there at Case—Jacob and his friends. But I wasn't permitted to join, even in spirit."

Lorelei Brush

"I didn't tell all those men the details of what I'd planned, just Jacob. But I get your point. I'll try. It won't be easy. It's like breaking the habit of years."

Grace nodded but with hesitation. "There's something else, too."

David groaned. "Oh, God. What?"

"You get a lot of joy from fighting."

"Joy?"

"It's like you came alive when you backed Adler against the wall, threatened Donley, and when you twisted that FBI man into a knot and threw him out."

David narrowed his eyes. "Sometimes a little intimidation is perfect for proving a point. Fighting fire with fire. It worked with Adler. It's the language he understands, and it built public outrage. For a time . . ."

"Perhaps. And now someone is turning that tactic against you."

"Well, maybe—"

"David, I'm worried about you."

"About me? I'm not going to let these assholes railroad me. I'm gonna track down the sources and prove them wrong." His words spilled out. He knew he was wound up, like a snake preparing to strike.

Grace sighed. "Yes, you're going to fight. And when you get wound up like this, your anger comes out at me and the kids."

He blustered, sitting up straight, his face turning red. "I have a lot to be angry about. This reaction in the press—"

Her hand swept across the space between them, erasing the sentence. "All right, all right, stop. Listen to me. All year, I listen to you disparage teaching."

"Wait a minute. You know what I do at Adams. My job hardly touches on science these days. It's all about animal control."

Holding his gaze, she kept on. "Then transfer schools."

He rubbed the back of his neck. "There's no better alternative. The good teachers are all fighting to get into the few decent schools left in Cleveland. I thought the law degree would give me an out, but the only clients I have are from the old neighborhood. They have plenty of legal problems and no money to pay a lawyer."

"So, quit teaching. Join a law firm. Work for the city."

"Don't be silly." He waved his arm in a dismissive gesture. "Why would I trade one bureaucracy for another? I never get along with bosses."

Grace smiled, not in a good-humored way. "So, you're stuck with battles to fight on all sides?"

Hit it in one, except he hadn't focused on the pattern she described. Looking away, he wondered if he could break it. That would please Grace, but would it please him? "I see what you're saying. But it's who I've always been."

Grace shook her head. "It's not who you have to be. I watch you escalating arguments, lobbing bombs here, there, wherever." She tossed imaginary balls in several directions, then jammed her hands on the bed and leaned toward him. "You don't have to answer every accusation of these idiots. You don't have to keep teaching at Adams. Do something different, expand your law practice, make peace with your mom."

"Ah, c'mon. It'll take two to change what goes on with Ma, and she's not about to change her tune." Imitating his mother's high voice, he added, "Why aren't you more like your sainted brothers?"

Grace shook her head. "It's been years since you lived with her. Declare victory or a truce, and move on."

"My mom won't quit. Every time I talk to her, she's got a complaint about me."

She took a deep breath and threw up her hands. "So stop responding. Chet doesn't get rattled when she harps on the mess he's made of the house with all of his stuff stacked up under the tables and in the hallways. He laughs it off and keeps building more stacks. How about ignoring her comments, changing the subject?"

He didn't want a fight with Grace, not this morning. Not when she was leaving. "Okay, okay. I'll work on it."

"When, David, when?" She threw both arms into the air.

"When I have some time."

Lorelei Brush

At breakfast, Davy's face was a kaleidoscope of colors from broken capillaries and an eye swollen shut. He teared up as he crunched too hard on the toast Grace had made. David sipped his coffee, alternating between anger at being dressed down and sadness at the reality of his family's desertion.

"Daddy?"

"Yes, Hildie."

"I don't want to go. I want to stay here. I can help you fight."

Grace stopped buttering more toast and turned to glare at David over the top of her glasses.

It felt like a test. He produced the "right" answer. "Thank you, sweetheart. I'm glad you're on my side. I think this'll all blow over soon, but I'd feel a lot better—and so would your mom—if we knew you were safely out of the line of fire."

"There were a lot of bad men here yesterday."

"I don't think they'll come back."

"What if they do?"

"I'll be smart about it. I promise."

She nodded as she chewed her Cheerios. "You call if you need us, okay?"

David grinned. "Okay."

When Grace and the kids left, David returned to the kitchen, poured himself more coffee, and returned to the question Grace had raised. Was there more to this Adler deal than righting a wrong? Was it revenge? He shook his head. He didn't know.

With some trepidation, he opened the paper. Today's diatribe again appeared on the op. ed. page: *Evidence Builds Against Svehla*. The writer castigated Hildie's aggression, painting a picture of an angry child facing a frightened man and ignoring his gesture of surrender. He—David assumed a man had composed this drivel—even suggested that Davy had started a fight. The words came close to applauding an unknown "victim" who had turned the assault around and clobbered Davy. Grace was right that his fighting every accusation wasn't paying off. And he felt stymied by that oath he'd taken—and by knowing he had a prodigious set of enemies. David ambled to the front window and stood, shifting the change in his trouser pocket as he sipped. Who were his enemies and who his friends?

He set his coffee cup down and picked up the phone.

Thankfully, Chet answered. "You've sure stirred up a hornet's nest."

"Yeah, yeah. I want to talk to you about Hessoun."

"Huh? What about him?"

"How well do you know him?"

"I'd say very well. It's been thirty years, you know."

"So, he's a friend from school? And you trust him?"

"Yes, I do. Why the questions?"

"I'm wondering if he's the source of this bad press. He denies it, but, well, he must be getting pats on the back down at the *Plain Dealer* for this 'big story' he's uncovered."

Chet was silent for long seconds. "I see your point. I'll talk to him."

"Thanks. I need friends that I'm sure of."

When David put the receiver in its cradle, the phone rang. He stared at it, considering letting it ring. Instead, he picked it up, ready to press the buttons and cut off the call if it was more vindictive rhetoric.

"You know my voice? No names, please."

David came to military attention. "Yes, sir." It was Colonel Williams.

"Go to a phone box and call this number."

David memorized the digits, reciting them repeatedly until he could see them on a blank wall. He hurried upstairs to collect the random change he deposited each night on the top of his dresser, working out the location of the nearest pay phone available on a Sunday. Probably the gas station down Lee Road.

Ten minutes later, he was there, feeding quarters and dimes into the black metal box.

Williams answered on the first ring. "David, you've stirred up a God-awful mess and it needs to stop. I had a call today from J. Edgar Hoover. It wasn't pleasant."

Adrenaline flooded David's body. By God, he was known across Washington—except the tone of Williams' voice made it clear that he was known as a troublemaker rather than a hero. "Yes, sir, of course."

"Well, he's got the FBI's weapons aimed at you. And he's not alone. There's a powerhouse from the Pentagon, a senator or two, and the presidents of a couple of major businesses supplying the military. You get the picture?"

David leaned against the glass wall of the phone booth, pushing his hair back out of his face. "I'm sorry to hear that, sir. I was aiming for justice for all these—"

"I know, I know. And we've got chaos here in D.C. People seem to think the kind of publicity you generated could ruin Operation Paperclip and force the U.S. to send the German scientists home where they'd find welcoming offers from the Russians." Williams' voice lingered on the last word.

David opened his mouth to argue the purity of his actions and then shut it again. Williams didn't want any rebuttal. He was stating the situation and surely had actions in mind. "That was not my intent. I'm sure you know that."

"I believe you, David. However, I spent most of yesterday afternoon and evening on the phone pacifying the tigers. Your statements about your actions in the war and the implications about how scientists like Adler got into the U.S. are on the edge of acceptable under your OSS oath. I suggest you cease talking about any of this. I hardly need to say that, if I am to calm down the storm around here, you must stay out of the press and out of Adler's way. Do I make myself clear?"

David reeled from his second dressing down of the day. He almost stood to attention but was just too tired, way too tired. "Yes, sir. Message received, loud and clear." He was to take whatever accusations came at him, hide, and hope Williams could calm things down. The whole idea rankled. Look where his good intentions had got him: in deep shit.

Over the next week, the vise squeezed tighter. The only business client David had, Mac's marine engine company, phoned to say they were shifting their legal work to another lawyer. When called on this, Mac apologized, said he'd fought the decision but was overruled. Those editorials had been too scathing.

By Wednesday, David was down to a handful of clients who were either personally loyal—like Gladys Thompson, still appreciative of his intervention when her drunken husband broke down the door and beat her—or afraid no one else would handle their affairs for such a small fee.

Thursday afternoon, he had a call from the high school principal.

"David, I've got some unpleasant news. There was a letter on my desk this morning making the argument that you're an inappropriate person to teach children and requesting that I fire you."

"Who wrote it?"

"It's official."

"But I have tenure. I can't be fired for no reason."

"Well, it says you're disloyal. There's a reference to the likelihood of your being a 'subversive.'"

"I'll fight this."

"That's your prerogative."

David ground his teeth and wondered if Broz was gloating.

When his Ma reached him on Friday, David tried to follow Grace's advice and keep calm through what he was sure would be an unpleasant exchange. The resolve lasted less than a minute.

"The neighbors are talking. I went down to Spivak's store last night, and three men stopped talking when I walked in. Sophie Spivak saw me and fled to the back room. She always comes out to chat. It's you. Look what you've done!"

"Ma, I didn't—"

"The worst part you don't even know. They came to see Chet. He wouldn't tell me much, but they threatened to have him fired. This is his *life*, this job. Do you realize what he may lose because of you?"

"Ma, Ma, wait. Who came to see Chet?"

"That's not all. They've questioned George. You know George is struggling to make enough to feed and clothe his family. Do you want to ruin him, too?"

David yelled. "Ma—I didn't ask for this. Stop blaming me for all the evil in the world. I could use a little support from you. I tried to get some justice, and all I hear from you is—"

She hung up on him.

He slammed down the black receiver and swore. After pacing from kitchen to office, checking out the windows that no "enemies" lurked in the bushes, he returned to the kitchen and dialed Chet at work. But when he tested the words he'd say, figuring they might well be overheard, he placed the receiver in its cradle. Better to call later from a pay phone and hope "they" hadn't bugged Chet's phone as well as his own.

What a colossal mess. No stable job, a fragment of legal work, disgust from his mother, a broad swath of relatives who might be accused by association, and an empty house, which he would have to sell if he didn't earn any money.

Saturday morning, before heading to the farm, David took his coffee into the back yard. It could use a mow, but he didn't have the energy. He moseyed behind the garage and stared at Grace's Victory Garden. Lots of beans ready to pick. He should do that and take them to Grace to can. Somehow, that felt like too much for him—finding a basket to put them in, bending over to pick, moving the basket from plant to plant, hoisting it onto a hip, fitting it into the car.

As he stood, frozen by indecision, Jacob appeared around the corner of the garage. "I knocked, and you did not come, so I try out here."

"I'm going to see the family in a bit." David meandered down the rows of vegetables toward his friend.

"How are you?"

David tossed his cold coffee onto the grass. "I sure hope I never have another week like this one. Skewered by the press, fired from teaching, dropped by most of my clients, and deserted by my family."

"Want to sit down a moment? Your picnic table?"

It occurred to David that it probably hurt Jacob to stand on that leg for any period of time. "Sure."

They strolled to the table under the pear tree and brushed fallen leaves and twigs from the benches.

"Do you pick these pears? Eat them?"

David set his cup down. He didn't want to discuss pears, think about how he should volunteer to do the picking, ask Grace to make pies or jam, and give them as gifts to Jacob and Rebecca. He eased onto the bench. "I should."

"I have thought much about you this week. I remember, in the camp, how so many bad things happened. Some men gave up and died. Some of us resisted to stay sane, to feel human. We had to be clever. The guards must think that we obey the rules while we sabotage the rockets. One day, I wired a component incorrectly so a fire would start when the rocket was launched. It would explode in the sky. I dreamed about that explosion for days."

"And did it? Blow up?"

"I do not know. It did not matter. You see, I beat them in my heart."

"Oh."

"David, you are free to fight as you choose, in your heart."

"It's hard to see how."

"But you are lawyer. There must be cases to read."

A weight rose like steam from David's shoulders. Williams hadn't said to stop thinking, stop reading. Others had been falsely accused. Some must have fought back. He looked up and drew strength from Jacob's sad eyes.

CHAPTER 13
JULY 1955

David made the first two turns on his way out of town by rote, lost in the quandary of what to do. As he turned from South Taylor onto Cedar Road, he checked the rearview mirror and spied the edge of a blue 1953 Dodge turning behind him. Wasn't that the car that was parked a couple of doors down the street from his house this morning?

Sure. Sure it was. Damn. What kind of spy was he not to have planned for this? Stupid, stupid. Any FBI agent worth his salt would be able to find the addresses of all of the Svehlas' relatives in short order, but David wasn't going to be the patsy who revealed the location of his family without a fight. They were throwing down a gauntlet.

Without a hint in his speed that he'd seen them, he approached the light at Warrensville Center Road, made a right as the light was changing to yellow, and trapped the Dodge with a red. When he was out of sight of that light, he turned right into a block of stores and snuck behind them. He left the engine on and, on foot, crept to the edge of the buildings. It wasn't long before that Dodge showed up, moving slowly across the last intersection. He memorized the license plate: AX 433, like they were trying to ax him—one in a long line of deviants. After the car had passed, he returned to his Studebaker, located his Ohio map, hurried back to his viewing post to watch for the Dodge retracing its steps, and glanced at the map until he had figured out a circuitous route to Chardon. Usually he'd take Mayfield, maybe Route 6, but today the countryside was safer.

Fifteen minutes later, having seen no blue Dodge pass by going to the left, he headed out in that direction. Every thirty seconds or so, he checked the rearview mirror. Three times he pulled over and watched for several minutes, noting the license numbers of the passing cars. It took him twice the usual amount of time to get to Chardon, but he arrived without a tail.

After saying hello to Grace's cousins, Frances and Ben, and listening to the kids chatter about how Hildie had ridden bareback on Minnie, the farm's horse, with Davy leading, he asked Ben if he could park the car in the barn.

Ben was a tall, spare man. Not a pound of excess flesh on him, not much hair left on top, and not one to use two words where one would do. He stared at David for a long moment and then nodded.

David pulled up to the barn doorway and heard the tractor fire up. Ben steered it between the horse stalls and the milking pen, and David tucked the Studebaker in behind. Together, they closed the heavy barn doors.

"Trouble?"

"'Fraid so. I was followed, at first, coming out here."

"Ah."

David had never felt close to this taciturn man and had no idea if that "ah" meant he understood and approved of hiding the car or hated the idea and condemned David for the need of such subterfuge. And he wasn't going to ask. Ben had taken in his family.

Davy and Hildie met their father just outside the barn, Davy in a waiting mood, Hildie bouncing with excitement.

"Want to see me ride, Daddy?" Hildie danced a few steps alongside.

"Sure." After all, he had little to entertain him these days.

Hildie turned brightly to Ben. "Will you put the bridle on her?"

He jerked his head toward the barn. "You do it."

Hildie ran for Minnie's stall with David and Ben strolling behind.

Ben supervised Hildie's preparations and boosted her up on Minnie's back. She gathered the reins in her hands and walked Minnie out of the darkness into the sunny driveway.

David swelled with pride. He couldn't ride a horse, and he wasn't sure he'd want to try it bareback. "Good job, Hildie!"

She guided Minnie out to the road, turned her around, and returned. "I'm good with horses, Daddy."

"That you are."

Davy was kicking at the half-buried stones in the driveway. As Ben and Hildie took Minnie back into the barn, David looked his son over. "Your bruises seem to be healing. How're you feeling? Arm okay?"

"Yeah. This cast itches."

"Huh. Let's go in the house." Their feet crunched on the driveway. As they passed the gnarled fruit tree, David had an urge to swing a leg over the lowest branch and shinny up a ways. "That looks like a good climbing tree."

Davy shook his head. "It has ants. I squished about a hundred." He pointed to the trunk.

A few more steps. Davy kicked one of the stones in his way. "I wish I were brave."

David winced. "You were brave when the doctor set your arm."

"Not really."

"Davy, what happened at the vacant lot with those boys?"

"They surrounded us, yelling 'commie.'"

David could see tears forming in his son's eyes. "Sounds like you were ambushed."

Davy kicked another stone. "You would have fought and beat 'em all."

"I don't think so, son. Not an army like that."

More of the story spilled out. "Buddy and me were playing catch. Tim tried to hit my face. I stuck up my arm, and he hit it hard. I fell. That's when I heard the bone snap." Davy stared at the ground.

David conjured up an image of beating Tim's dad to a pulp. "Doesn't sound like a fair fight to me."

Davy sniffed, lashes wet. "Are you a commie, Daddy?"

David put his hands on Davy's shoulders and squatted down to face him. "This is really important for you to understand. There're a lot of people calling me a Communist. They're wrong. I'm a patriot. It's the USA I fought for in the war, and it's our country I believe in."

Davy sighed. "Good. I didn't want you to be a commie."

David rubbed his forehead. "There's another thing you need to understand. Everybody loses sometimes."

Davy swiped the back of his hand across his leaking nose. "You don't, Daddy."

"Yes, I do. All lawyers do."

"But you never got beat up."

David coughed a laugh. "Who told you that? I got beat up plenty of times."

A gleam appeared in Davy's wet eyes. "Really?"

"Sure. See, it's important to pick your fights. Only fight if you got a good chance of winning."

Davy scuffed his foot across the dirt. "I'm no good at fighting."

"Well," David started, "you could practice. Or, you could try a different approach."

"What do you mean?"

"You gotta find your opponent's weaknesses."

"Tim doesn't have any." Davy slowly shook his head.

"Everyone does. You know that Nazi Jacob and I confronted?"

"Yeah."

"He was a terrible bully. Very proud, always had to be in charge and admired. You'd think he had no weaknesses. But Jacob and I found one: he hated being humiliated.

"Tim has weaknesses, too. I know a couple, and you may know more. Like, he always comes with sidekicks. I think he's afraid of facing anyone alone."

"Yeah, he's never alone." Davy shook his head over and over.

"He might be, one day."

"Maybe."

David stopped and squatted down. "Davy, this is really important, so listen up. Bullies like Tim pick on kids they know will respond. You can stop responding."

Davy tilted his head. "You mean run away?"

David ran his tongue around the inside of his mouth. "Suppose Tim calls you a coward or a sissy or something bad. You could answer back, 'I use my brains, not my fists.' Then take Buddy's arm and march away. Or, you could play in our house or Buddy's yard and let Tim hunt up kids his own age to pick on."

"I don't know. It feels like I'm a coward."

"No, you're not. You're smarter than he is."

Davy looked up again at his father. "Are you gonna stay here?"

Out of the mouths of children. "No, but I'm pickin' my battles, and I'm gonna fight only the ones I can win. But you—you can't beat up a gang on your own. For a time, while I sort out this commie business, you'll need to stay here."

"What about school? What about Buddy?"

"We'll see. We'll see."

His conversation with Grace had to wait until mid-afternoon, under a hot sun and in the midst of the vegetable garden. She'd suggested they pick the corn, beans, and tomatoes for dinner. He, of course, knew nothing about how to choose ripe ears of corn or beans that were crunchy and not mealy. Grace was a pro. She gave him the bushel basket to carry, took him to a patch of seven-foot high corn stalks, and broke off a dozen ears.

"Why'd you come *here*? There's a whole field of this stuff behind the barn."

She shaded her eyes with a hand and looked up at him. "It's field corn, for the animals. And talking about crops is not why we came out here." She threw several ears of corn into his basket.

David had to maneuver to catch the incoming missiles. He lowered the basket to his knees as tomatoes and a couple of green peppers dropped in over the corn, then a trio of cucumbers and a bunch of flowers. Flowers? He kept his mouth shut.

Grace put her hands on her hips and canted backward, compensating for all the bending over she'd done in the picking. "Go on over to the bench under the grape arbor."

He trudged across the yard, feeling sticky with sweat, and longed to get past Grace's anger. When he dropped down onto the bench, he pulled out his handkerchief to wipe his forehead and the back of his neck. "Seems like the kids are adjusting fine to the farm."

"In some ways."

"Yeah?"

"Ben isn't. He's asked more than once how long we'll be visiting." The last word sounded annoyed, like it was in quotes.

"You *could* come back home."

She squinted at him. "You know that's not an option, not now."

"No."

"But this isn't a long-term solution either, David. We're all sharing a bedroom with two twin beds. The kids tried to sleep together, but Hildie kicks and keeps waking Davy, so she's on a pallet of blankets on the floor. Ben and Frances are feeling crowded, and I feel guilty at their paying to feed us."

"Good thing they grow their own food."

"That's not the point. We're eating what Frances would have put up for the winter."

David took a deep breath. "I'm going to fight my dismissal from Adams. I'm owed a hearing before the school board."

She threw up her hands. "More press, David? More reporters? More confrontation? Broken windows this time? Someone setting the house on fire?"

"I don't think so. I'm not talking about Adler anymore. I've been warned."

"Warned? By whom?"

"My OSS boss."

"Oh, God. It's all over the country. What have you done?" The worry lines between her brows deepened.

"He's trying to stop the stories, the retribution."

"And you're going to bring it all up again?"

"Not if I can help it. I'll argue about due process, about moral and ethical issues, about what teacher tenure means."

"But the reason you've been fired is Adler. How do you avoid talking about him?"

He probably couldn't. "It'll be a private hearing. Just me, a quorum of the board, a few witnesses. No observers. No press."

They sat silently, her hands kneading each other, him watching, gauging her mood. He felt a crevice widening between them.

"Hon, if this dismissal holds, I won't be able to get another teaching job. I may get disbarred. I've gotta fight." He reached for her hand, but she kept them intertwined. His stomach clenched as he returned his hand to his lap.

Her voice sounded small and tight. "How long will this go on?"

"I hope not long. Maybe a couple of months? Please, hang on with me."

"Your cases always have motions, objections, postponements." She rubbed her hands down her face. "Okay, I'll enroll the children in school here. I know the principal; he's a distant cousin. They'll use my maiden name."

David closed his eyes on that announcement and shook his head. "I . . . um . . . understand, I guess." He had a vision of his kids on the other side of a widening crevasse, belonging to another family. A shiver ran through him.

He guided Grace's chin so she faced him. "I wouldn't cause this kind of pain if I could figure out any other way."

She shook her head to slough off his hand. "I know, intellectually. It doesn't change how I feel."

David drove home into the setting sun in turmoil, intent on getting his next steps right. Time to consolidate his allies, figure out how to use them. It would be a small unit: Mac and Jacob, for sure; Chet, perhaps; Hessoun, if he proved trustworthy; and maybe Williams, from afar. He'd study his dismissal letter and review any cases of teacher dismissal since the war. Then he'd find out all he could about the seven school board members. Chet probably knew them. He'd work out good arguments that they might buy. This would be the biggest case of his life. And he'd be representing himself.

As David approached the house, he went on full alert. The Dodge sat in place—empty. David drove past and parked several houses down from his own. Keeping to the bushes and trees on the shadowed lawns, he crept to the next-door neighbor's front yard and used the oak as a shield. He made out a stream of light moving around his office. Goddamn FBI. They'd crossed a line here.

What did he have in his file cabinet or his desk that might be incriminating? Nothing from the war. Nothing that tied him to Russians: he had no such ties. Did they plant something? Did they find the correspondence with Williams? Could that be used against him? Unlikely, but he didn't want them to see it, misconstrue yet another piece of evidence. Okay, they were inside, but he wasn't going to let them get away with the breaking and entering. Should he rush them and physically throw them out, wait to see them leave, or something else?

David stepped lightly to the street and scanned it in both directions. All quiet; no walkers, no watchers on front porches. He slipped up the street to his Studebaker and pulled the flashlight out of the glove compartment and tested the light. Worked fine. Then he returned to the house and crept around the front to the sunroom. He heard a male voice whispering. Okay, two of them. Then he turned his flashlight on full and shone it through the window. The intruders, dressed in black, fled toward the living room and split up, one heading toward the front door, the other toward the back. David ran toward the back of the house, not wanting streetlights to illuminate his actions. A slight shadow of a man shot from the backdoor and through the next-door yard, leaped the fence, and disappeared in the darkness. David wasn't far behind him when a chain-link fence loomed up. He couldn't make it over, grabbed and shook the fencing, and swore.

He retraced his steps and jogged to the street. The second intruder was in the Dodge, pulling away.

Damn, they used better tradecraft than he'd given them credit for. And, well, they were in a lot better shape than he was. Seething with indignation at the invasion of his home, he acknowledged that it was probably good that he didn't catch them and do them real harm.

The kitchen door was unlocked. He flipped on the light switch, and his eyes landed on the address book on the breakfast table. He and Grace always kept it under the phone, out of the way of spilled food. Okay, so now these guys definitely had a list of his friends, relatives, and clients.

He hurried into the sunroom. The Venetian blinds on the front windows were closed. Not very smart if they meant to hide the fact of their entry. He only closed them when the afternoon sun was hot on his back, and they'd been open when he left for the farm. Still, they hid him as he separated a couple of slats to check the street. No parked cars.

He yanked out the top drawer of the file cabinet. The folders sat more neatly than usual, but only a little, a subtle difference. He dove in, anxiety rising again, to find the correspondence with Williams. Should have taken it to the bank days ago. Gotta be vigilant, and he'd been lax—stupidly lax. Insufferable that he'd lost his rights to privacy, to the sanctity of his home, that his wife and children had been threatened, his options for making a living torn away. He pulled file after file out of the top drawer, evaluating contents, asking himself if anything was missing, anything incriminating, and hanging onto his temper by a thread. The Williams letters were gone. Had he said anything incriminating? Anything that contravened his OSS oath? He closed his eyes and conjured up the contents. He'd mentioned the T-Forces and the Field Photographic Unit. Might be new information for the FBI, but he couldn't see how they could use it against him. Maybe he was okay, maybe. But the FBI also knew he'd contacted Williams and been warned off. They might use that.

He picked up the bankbook from his desk. Their savings account had less than $1,000. Not bad for a teacher, but the family wouldn't survive forever on that. He paced from room to room, checking on the street and securing all windows and doors. Maybe he'd try poker again. He'd be one formidable opponent. Except that Grace hated that, and no one would play with him.

CHAPTER 14

JULY-AUGUST 1955

Sunday afternoon, David cruised around the neighborhood to locate all the pay phones, keeping his eye on the Chevy in his rearview mirror. Two different men in the front seat. Same crew-cuts, same summer suits. He hoped to keep the G-Men inside this new car and wondering what on Earth he was up to. He answered their curiosity by pulling into the Texaco station, asking for a fill-up, and going inside the office to pay. Sure enough, it had a phone on the wall where he'd be partially hidden from prying eyes, and it was only a few blocks from home. Feeling pride in his subterfuge, he returned the Studebaker to his garage, went into the kitchen, and from its shadowed interior, watched as the Chevy secured a parking place across the street. He eased out the back door, kept the house between himself and the Chevy, and crossed his rear neighbor's lot to the next street. Then he hotfooted it to the Texaco station and called Hessoun, intending to get as much information from him as possible and give nothing away.

"Ted, you've been quiet. You find out anything?"

"Yeah, been busy, meaning to call you. You're in a heap of trouble."

"I've noticed."

"I saw the memorandum about you that came to our editor. Plain bond paper, no watermark, so unlikely to have come from someone at the *Plain Dealer*. No signature; not clear who it's from, but official language. It suggests, just short of ordering, the editor to print the paragraphs that followed the intro, and that's what he did."

"He know who it's from?"

"I asked. He stared me down."

"So?"

"I asked why the story had been taken from me, why I didn't get to do a follow-up."

"And?"

"He said this was much bigger than our little paper."

"What did you make of that?"

"Well, he's tied into politics, may even run for state rep. one of these years. Certainly willing to grant favors for future support. Could be it came from Washington; could be local. FBI's not a bad guess, but I couldn't print that, couldn't swear to it."

So, powerful men believed in the memo and wouldn't be helpful in identifying its source. Hessoun wouldn't either. "Why no articles these last few days?" David looked out the window toward the gas pumps. No Chevy, no one looking toward the office.

"Well, I asked if I could do an article. Gave him a couple of ideas. He said—and this might be good for you—that we were letting it go for now."

"Don't know if that's good or bad."

"Bad for me. But, hey, I'll give you a call when I hear something. I'm still hoping for that exclusive."

"One of these days . . ."

"Yeah, yeah. By the way, I had a talk with Chet."

"Oh?"

"Don't play dumb. Sources are important in this job. So is protecting those sources."

"So?"

"So, you schmuck, you're potentially a valuable source, and I'm not about to lose you."

"Thanks."

Lorelei Brush

David thumbed through the stack of mail and let all of it drop to the table but the white business envelope from the Board of Education. Sure enough, he had thirty days to request a hearing, if he wished to contest his dismissal. He used his trusty two-finger typing method to fire off his request and drove the letter to the post office.

It was Monday, August 1. Unlikely they'd set the date for the hearing a day before they had to, given the slowness of the wheels of bureaucracy. Their lawyer would want every possible hour to prepare a watertight case, just as David did. That made the starting date Wednesday, August 31, at the latest.

So, he'd start in the law library at his alma mater to brush up on relevant cases. Cleveland-Marshall catered to the workingman, and the library had long hours. If he was lucky, Alberta, the new librarian (and a contemporary of his in the class of '50), would be there when he arrived bright and early in the morning, full of information. He'd be humble—he felt humbled—no matter if it cost him some pride. He needed every live body he could muster to help out.

David smiled at her care-worn face and offered his hand. "I'll bet you didn't expect to see me here. Truth is, I'm in trouble, Alberta, and I need your help."

She shook his hand, though the action was not accompanied by a smile. "I imagine so, given what the papers have been saying."

"I'm not a Red. You remember that debate we all had our second year, about the New Deal?"

This time, a smile creased her face. "When you called our constitutional law professor a commie for supporting the Civilian Conservation Corps? Heavens. I hadn't seen that much animation in him the whole term! I was afraid he'd have a heart attack when you went on and on about how his ideas were on the slippery slope of socialism to Communism."

David paused before answering, betting that she'd dwell on that pleasurable vision. "I haven't changed my mind. But, because of all this press, I've been fired from my teaching job. I've asked for a hearing, and it's only three, four weeks away."

"Oh, dear. Well, what can I do for you?"

He ticked off a list on his fingers. "A copy of Ohio's loyalty oath, the law on teacher tenure, all the stuff you've got on teacher dismissal in Ohio, and cases clarifying the Fourteenth Amendment's due process."

She jotted down his requirements in her own shorthand and then tapped the pen against the list. "And then you need to study everything we've got on subversives in government positions, starting maybe with the Alien Registration Act of 1940, you know, the Smith Act. Then look at the Internal Security Act of 1950, the McCarran Act. Someone may bring that up."

"Yeah. The school board *might* stick to the tenure criteria but most likely they'll throw the book at me."

"It'll be too tempting to pass up. So, be sure to review the Compulsory Testimony Act of 1954. It makes it very clear you can't use the Fifth Amendment; they'll consider it an admission of guilt."

"Okay. Anything else?" The weight on his shoulders seemed to increase tenfold as he contemplated the potential losses he faced—his jobs, family, friends, status, pride. Her voice called him back to the library counter.

"You could go back further, but start there. And you'd better check a couple of executive orders, especially 10241."

David took a deep breath and sighed it out. "What's that about?"

"It might be that the hearing requires a 'preponderance of evidence.' But Ike's said there only needs to be 'reasonable doubt' of loyalty to dismiss a government employee."

"And the state's agreed?"

"You'll have to see. The idea is planted." She jotted some names down on her pad. "Then you'll have to track how those have been applied to people accused of being Communists."

"The Rosenbergs, Alger Hiss."

"They're the biggest names, but not alone."

"Right. And I haven't got a lot of time." He could feel his blood pressure rising, his muscles tensing. This would be the fight of his life, and he didn't like the company he seemed to be assigned.

By Thursday night, David was exhausted. His eyes burned from so many hours reading small print that he kept rubbing them. Not that it did any good. He slumped at the kitchen table, trying to find the energy to scare up some dinner. Food shopping hadn't made his to-do list, so he'd be relegated to the fruit cellar in the basement where Grace kept all the food she'd canned or made into jelly. They'd had a bumper crop of green beans. Somehow the canning took away their taste.

The phone rang at his elbow. He answered on instinct.

"Hey, David. It's Mac."

Relief flooded through him—no invective. "Good to hear your voice." Now, how to tell him he was likely being overheard.

"I been down to the VFW. Guys are talking."

"I bet. Lots of talking going on around me, too. Even from friends when they think I can't hear." He let his voice linger on "friends" to show the listeners were quite the opposite.

"Roger that. Can you swing by? I got a call today that might interest you."

"Sure. But how about we rendezvous at the VFW tomorrow night? Say 1730 hours?"

"You sure that's a good idea?"

"No, but I want to know how bad it is. We'll be early, catch guys as they come in."

"Okay. I'll be there."

David heard Mac's reluctance. Showing up there was taking a chance. But he might find an ally or two, people he could call on at the hearing. Okay, so he was an optimist.

As he walked the garden rows, searching out dinner, he wondered what Mac wanted to tell him. Those damnable FBI listeners. Intolerable that he couldn't talk openly on his own phone. This was America, for God's sake, the land of the free and the home of the brave. Ha.

After consuming his vegetarian supper and feeling decidedly unsatisfied, David picked up the packet of envelopes into which Grace divided the money from his paycheck. He'd been pulling from them every Saturday morning, and this weekend would be no different. Except, only one envelope had any money: Entertainment. What irony. With a sigh, he dialed Ben's number. He and Grace were careful in these phone conversations, avoiding anything that might be misconstrued by the extra listeners, but both of them knew it was important to keep up the façade of using this phone, being in regular contact.

After the usual check-in about the kids, David came to the point. "Hon, our envelopes need refilling, and I'll have to dip into our savings account."

"Oh, goodness. Already. This is scary. The children will need school clothes soon. And supplies. I need to give Ben and Frances more money for food."

"Yeah. I'll bring cash with me Saturday."

"How much do we have in savings?"

"About a thousand."

"That won't last very long with you out of work."

Determined not to show weakness, David stood tall and told lies. "I'm betting this hearing will clear me. I'm working all day every day on it." Well, the work part was true.

"And if it doesn't?"

David imagined a rod of steel up his spine. "I'll sell the car. It's worth a good deal. We'll get a clunker, and Mac'll help me keep it going." God, he didn't want to do that. He didn't want to lose the '53 Commander—or depend even more on his generous friend.

"It's good you still have friends. You know, when the children start school, I'll bet I can find a job here, maybe in the drug store or as church secretary, maybe a cook."

"Oh, Grace. I hate that idea. Let's wait and see what happens."

After a too-long pause, she said, "Are you still expecting a miracle?"

Lorelei Brush

After a grueling day among law tomes, David drove to the VFW. Not many cars in the parking lot yet, and Mac's Ford was easy to spot. Mac himself was seated in the shadowy corner, facing the door with two beers in front of him. David sat with his back to the room. Not a good position for a spy who should watch for possible threats, but probably all right for doing a little business before testing his reputation with other vets.

"I'll keep my eyes open," Mac assured him.

"So, what've you got?"

"I had a phone call last night. From Colonel Williams." Mac took a long swig of beer and set his mug carefully on the table.

"And?"

"He wants to talk to you. Privately."

"Anything else?"

"The sooner the better."

"Message received, loud and clear." David closed his eyes and shook his head.

"Anything I can do?"

"No, thanks. Time to take the temperature of this room, see where I stand. You want another beer?"

"Sure."

David strode to the bar and ordered.

The bartender hung up the towel he'd been using to dry some mugs, put his knuckles on the bar, and leaned toward David. "We don't serve commies."

The room went quiet, like dominoes falling, as the guys nearest the bar shut up and the silence spread.

"I'm not a Red, Bernie. I been coming here for years. You know me."

A few chairs scraped the floor, and David could hear the rustle of fabric and then the footsteps as men approached. Mac appeared at this side and leaned an elbow on the bar, facing the incoming traffic.

"That's not what I hear. Your kind ain't welcome in this establishment."

David turned around. "C'mon, guys. We're all vets. We fought for our country because we believe in our democracy."

A big man, arms across his chest and legs spread, squinted at him. "You told us about talking to Russians. How do we know what else you said to them?"

"I told you I *killed* Russians."

Sarge loomed up next to the big guy. "Not what the papers say."

The big one took a step closer. "Yeah, we're hearing about lots of youse fellow travelers pretending to be loyal Americans and sending information to Moscow." He rolled up his sleeves and showed off forearms honed by daily stoking of the steel furnaces.

Maybe ten men drifted into a semi-circle around David.

The bartender spoke up. "No fighting in here, men. This commie was just leaving."

Mac plucked his sleeve and jerked his head toward the back door.

David considered a fistfight for just a second. He was angry enough to do some damage. But it was a bad idea on too many levels. What had he told Davy? Time to be smart. He saluted and walked in front of Mac to the door. So, he'd tested the waters with the vets, and the situation was as bad as he'd feared. No use dreaming he'd have support from that direction. Not even Sarge, who'd leaned toward his side. And he knew where Williams stood. If he wanted support, he was going to have to do some serious groveling. The thought made him grind his teeth.

The whole way home, David checked the rear-view mirror every minute or so and watched his tail. The guy wasn't even disguising his role, just staying a car or two behind. He even used his blinkers to signal each turn. It was like living in a pressure cooker with the heat turning up. He swore and then promised himself not to explode.

Filled with determination to show emotions he didn't feel, David pulled into his garage, closed it up, and wandered into his kitchen. He turned lights on and then off as he progressed to the bedroom and lowered the shades. Leaving the bedroom lights burning, he snuck downstairs in the dark, out the back door, and over to the nearly deserted Texaco station. In the office, he pointed to the pay phone. "Just need to make a call."

The attendant nodded and went back to the paper he was reading.

Holding all his anger at bay, David filled the box with quarters and made the call. "It's David Svehla, sir. And I know I owe you an apology for all this negative publicity. I'm sorry you have to handle the mess I've created in Washington. I do apologize. And I do thank you for helping me out."

"Ah, David. Apology accepted. I've been watching the Cleveland papers and know you've been true to your word not to speak publicly again about Adler. I believe I've calmed the waters here, but if matters erupt again on your end, Washington will retaliate."

"Yes, sir. I know that. And I am very, very sorry about all this." As groveling went, this wasn't as bad as David had feared, but it wasn't comfortable either, as he lied. He wasn't sorry for confronting Adler.

"I want to talk to you about your decision to fight your dismissal from teaching."

"I believe I can argue my case without bringing in Adler or—"

"Yes, yes, that's good. But please understand the utmost need for privacy. You must ensure your hearing with the school board is private—no press. And you must leave the FBI out of this. Do not underestimate their capacity for retribution."

"Yes, sir, I won't. Do you know anything I *can* use in this hearing?"

Williams changed his tone from admonishment to encouragement. "Perhaps. Read about the Army-McCarthy hearings." He paused. "See if you can find the Edward R. Murrow broadcasts on McCarthy, maybe late October '53 and early March '54. He's taken a very thoughtful, courageous approach. And see what you can find about Owen Lattimore, an academic accused of being a subversive. He managed to fight the charges successfully."

It felt like the world had shifted. Williams was on his side, tipping the balance. David hung up the phone and took a deep breath.

David's tension collected in his shoulders the next morning as he drove the long miles to Chardon. How was he going to find all that stuff Williams mentioned? Sounded like some of it would only be available in Washington—that subcommittee testimony—and he couldn't afford a trip, either in dollars or time. The clock was ticking way too fast. Who did he know in TV who might get him old Murrow broadcasts? Had they been discussed in the Cleveland papers? He stretched out each arm and shook his wrists. He had to get himself unkinked.

He'd call Hessoun again. That was his best chance. A journalist would at least have easy access to the *Plain Dealer* archives. Maybe he could get the Murrow scripts or copies of the shows. Well, David would ask, see just how far the man was willing to go for him.

Forcing a smile, he cleared with Ben that he could use their phone. He picked up the receiver and listened deeply for any sign of being overheard. Nothing. So he dialed Ted's home.

"I think I've got somethin' for you."

"Okay, shoot."

"I want you to search the *Plain Dealer*'s files for 'Owen Lattimore' and any commentary on Edward R. Murrow's broadcasts about McCarthy in October 1953 and March 1954."

"What for?"

"The FBI seems to be using illegal means to get people convicted for being subversive."

"Whoa. Could be good. Could be too hot to handle."

"But you're tempted?"

"Yeah. Let me get pen and paper, write down those names and dates."

David heard him open and close a drawer.

"Okay, Lattimore and Murrow. Repeat those dates."

David complied. "Can you get scripts from the shows?"

"Sorry, I'm not that connected. You think of trying Dorothy Fuldheim? On WEWS? She loves a good story about an underdog, loves sniffing out government corruption. Not the same network as Murrow, but don't they all know each other?"

"Good idea. One more thing. You know anyone with the Washington, D.C. papers?"

"Don't think so. Just call the papers. Somebody'll be interested. And let me know what happens."

Boy, he'd have to be careful if he made the calls himself. Make up a good story. He could do that. Get creative. Like any good spy. "Any chance I could use your phone to make the calls?"

"I don't think so. Can't put my family at risk. Sorry about that."

During the next week, David racked up at least a hundred bucks in long-distance charges on a series of pay phones, following lead after lead, source after source, and sitting on hold far too long for his comfort and his wallet. He told them he was a graduate student studying the ramifications of the Smith Act. Pretty damn close to the truth—always a good strategy.

Hessoun found little in the paper's archives. His suggestion of Dorothy Fuldheim, however, struck pay dirt. She managed to finagle Murrow scripts from someone and was having them sent to her. He had a nice lunch with her, telling her that his story had to be confidential, and giving her just enough detail to get her riled up and ready to dig. As instructed by Williams, he didn't mention Adler, focused on the idea he was doing research, but she probably knew just how personally relevant this research was. And he might have to pay up later. Funny his bedfellows these days. A year ago—heck, four months ago—he would have laughed if anyone told him he—a conservative Republican—would be seeking help from Dorothy Fuldheim—a staunch Democrat. Times had sure changed.

Still, he was making a case, beginning to see how to fit it all together. Time to find out about the men he'd face in court, the lawyer who would present the case against him, and the school board members who would sit in judgment of him.

He called Chet.

"You comin' out from under your rock? Got your job back yet?"

"Jeez, Chet, you know the hearing's set for August 29. I need your help."

"You keep me outta the courts, David. I had enough of the FBI when this all started with you. I ain't speaking at your hearing." His tone was certain but followed by a laugh to lighten the sting.

Family support personified. "Can you tell me about the school board members? I need to know who I'm up against. Also, you know the lawyer they're going to use? Fritz Saunders?"

"Hmm. The board's split—four Democrats, three Republicans. Average age, late forties. I think five of them are vets. No teachers. All of 'em have kids. I'll have to check on the lawyer. He's new to the Director of Law's office. It'll take a call or two to get his story."

"Could you do a short bio for each one? I'll have four or five on the panel, I figure. And the lawyer. I'd like to know their big issues, what gets them going, day jobs, anything that might help me make my case."

"And you need it tomorrow?"

"How about lunch on Thursday?"

"You pay."

A week before the hearing was scheduled to begin, David got a note in the mail. "Call me." The postmark was Washington, D.C., so he called Williams' number from a pay phone.

"I have with me a copy of a memorandum from Hoover to his staff about something he called the 'Responsibilities Program,' which he used to ensure people he believed were Communists would be found guilty of subversive acts. It's dated March of this year and orders his staff to stop the use of blind memoranda and vague charges from anonymous informers. I believe the Cleveland office has ignored this memo, and I'm sending you a copy. Use the information wisely and only if you must. What's a safe address?"

David thought a moment. "Try c/o Marshall Gentile, 3437 Clarendon Road, Cleveland Heights. I know him; he's right around the corner, but not involved with me in any way."

"Okay."

Like manna from heaven.

CHAPTER 15
AUGUST 1955

David emptied his briefcase onto the plaintiff's table in the hearing room of the county courthouse and organized the file folders in the order of upcoming witnesses. His sense of this careful organization offered a small boost of confidence, critical to him in this arena where his fate would be decided by others. He glanced across the small aisle at the defense team, three men from the Director of Law's office, chatting amicably. One lawyer wasn't enough for the board, apparently. Yet another sign they were throwing the book at him. Ten or twelve feet in front of his table was a dais, one step above the floor, holding a long table and a line-up of chairs for the board. No occupants yet, but it was early. To the right of the table sat the chair for witnesses.

He fastened the middle button on his suit jacket and hoped it covered the extra material bunched around his waist and cinched by his belt. It hadn't been possible to eat heartily these past weeks, not with his limited funds and non-existent cooking skills. God, he missed Grace. Thank goodness Rebecca had slipped over with a casserole from time to time. Len, the lawyer from Jacob's temple, had even shown up for a visit, bearing a basket of food and some inside information on a couple of school board members. That was a pleasant surprise. Mac had taken him out for burgers twice, so, sure, he wasn't starving—nothing like the poor guys in the Dora labor camp. Good friends stood by him, and that meant a lot.

With his costume adjusted, he approached the defense's table, hand outstretched. "Fritz, glad to meet you again. I see there are five chairs set up for the board." The two young lawyers behind Fritz Saunders stopped talking mid-sentence and turned to stare at the alleged subversive. David felt like a freak show at the circus.

Saunders had sandy hair, neatly trimmed, and an athletic body. Not tall, not thick in the shoulders—more like a runner's physique. Seemed wound up today, more so than when they had met to discuss the list of witnesses. When he shook David's hand, it felt like a competition in squeezing. This opposition didn't care to lose at even minor sports. "Yes, we might see five, maybe four. Evans wasn't sure if he'd make it."

Chet had reported to David that Evans was a building contractor who had a couple of big contracts with the city and a lot of friends in the political in-crowd. Even though Evans was a veteran—and David could play to his sympathy for a fellow vet—he had little hope for Evans' support. Not an independent-minded man.

One of the junior defense lawyers said, "I heard the superintendent called him and begged him to come."

Saunders turned, his face creased and a forearm waving in the air as though trying to shut the underling down. "Well, we'll see, won't we?"

David nodded and pivoted, taking in the high ceiling, long windows, polished wood, and carved railings. Without a jury and an audience to liven it up, that deep brown mahogany weighed down the atmosphere and David's mood. He liked to play the crowd, hear the murmurs of support and even the odd Amen to something he said. Well, he'd asked for this private hearing, followed Williams' rules, and this was a part of the price he had to pay. He was alone, physically and psychologically. The rest of today's small world would be, at best, suspicious and at worst, hostile.

By 0930, five school board members had settled into their straight chairs, their faces grim. Ray Evans was on the left. It made sense that he'd place himself as far from David as possible.

Next to Evans sat Dar Patek, and then Sam Grabski, Dennis Rogers, and Marvin Glanz. Chet had generously provided pictures of each, along with their bios. David felt his stomach churn the doughnuts he'd eaten for breakfast. It was one thing to hear about these men, another to see them in their dignified suits and starched shirts.

David, as plaintiff, led with his opening statement. "Gentlemen of the school board, we are here because the superintendent of schools has dismissed me using the grounds defined in the law as 'other good and just cause.' The 'cause' is described in preliminary documents very generally as 'acting in contravention of the Ohio Loyalty Oath,' which I freely signed in 1949. It states, and I quote, 'I, David Svehla, do solemnly swear that I am not a Communist and not a member of any organization advocating any seditious practice or overthrow of the United States government by force or violence.'

"These accusations are serious. They question my patriotism and may bar me from future employment opportunities. To contest them, I will present witnesses who can swear to my loyalty to this country and to my excellence as a teacher." David scanned the faces, stopping at each one to make eye contact. All looked serious; he clearly had their attention.

"The evidence on which the defense bases its case is contained in a blind memorandum replete with innuendo and sparse in facts. The memo is supported, we are told, by evidence in a sealed envelope. I am not privy to the contents of the envelope, as they are deemed 'confidential,' and I don't believe you'll learn the specifics, either. We're all being asked to believe in mere accusations. This is hardly what constitutes 'due process' under the Fourteenth Amendment to the U.S. Constitution."

Evans tilted his head at the word "innuendo" and looked to Saunders for guidance. Marvin Glanz nodded perceptibly at the mention of due process, though it could have been a tic. Glanz was the one bright light in this dark room. Jacob had told David the man was a lawyer whose family owned a popular bakery where hundreds bought challah on Fridays. Glanz was the family's exception in his choice of career. He didn't take the easy or expected path in his life or his work; Chet had added that Glanz knew the law and was very likely to stand behind due process—and agree with David's arguments.

"I asked for this hearing to clear my name and have my job restored. There is only a single precedent for these hearings in the state of Ohio, *Applebaum v. Wulff et al.*, July 25, 1950, heard first by this board and then taken to the Court of Common Pleas of Ohio, Cuyahoga County. You may remember the proceedings?"

He saw Grabski nod. After all, he'd been on the board since the war. A staunch Republican, he owned a series of car dealerships. Everyone in Cleveland knew his jingle from the radio and TV. A tuneful chorus sang, "Give my regards to Grabski," just as enthusiastically as they'd sing their regards to Broadway. He was as extroverted as his commercial and outspoken in campaign speeches about the importance of every child pledging allegiance to the flag every morning. Being "soft" on potential subversives did not seem at all in character.

"The attorney general of the state of Ohio said school boards must admit 'only trustworthy evidence.' I would argue, and I think the attorney general would agree, that a sealed envelope does not constitute 'trustworthy' evidence. On this ground alone, the board can decide to reinstate me. But my due process rights under the Fourteenth Amendment also give me the right to know who my accuser is, what I am accused of, and what the evidence is against me. You see, I don't know; I have to guess, and so will you." He stopped to give the board time to digest this important point, realized his tie was nearly choking him, and loosened it a tad.

"I can think of only one act that might question my loyalty: I made an accusation against Dr. Gerhardt Adler, an accusation of crimes against humanity. I did this out of moral outrage. He should have been tried in Germany for his crimes like the others taken to Nuremburg. In lieu of such a trial, I took it upon myself to expose him. For this, I am thought to be a security risk. I am not. I responded to one individual in what some may think was an extreme manner—though completely within the law—and it has led, I believe, to my dismissal. For all of you who are veterans and saw the atrocities perpetrated by Axis forces, I would argue it was impossible to do less."

From the defense table, Saunders called out, "Objection! I've been tolerant of the plaintiff's need to justify his actions, but he is going way beyond what is appropriate for an opening statement. He's giving testimony here, which belongs later in the hearing, when he is under oath."

David countered, with some heat in his voice, "This is a *hearing*, not a trial, and has more relaxed rules. I will testify later and am simply setting the stage now by presenting factual information on which to base later testimony."

The school board members conferred. Evans stood, adjusted the perfect Windsor knot on his tie, and placed both fists on the table. "The board is inclined to let the plaintiff finish what he wants to say, though we appreciate there is a difference between stating facts and giving testimony. Our esteemed lawyer, Mr. Glanz, has clarified it for us."

David felt a small rush of gladness. "Thank you, Mr. Evans. I have finished my opening statement and look forward to demonstrating to all of you that I am a good teacher and a loyal American, so that, in the end, you vote to reinstate me." He retired to his hard chair.

David had made eye contact with each member of the board, broadcasting sincerity. He'd spoken slowly, with a confidence he didn't feel. Evans, at one end of the seats, kept looking at Saunders, as though he could read his opinions of everything that was said—or read what *he* should have as an opinion. Glanz, at the other end, raised his eyebrows at David as if asking, "What's next?" Grabski and Rogers looked serious, Patek downright condemning.

Chet had described Dar Patek as an accountant who was worried about the rising cost of education, a man addicted to details, and a Republican. Though David himself was a life-long member of the GOP and hated FDR's socialist legislation, he'd found more sympathy among Democrats for free speech and holding to the requirements of due process. Patek, a Czech who had grown up in David's old neighborhood, wasn't likely to be sympathetic to a suspected subversive, whatever the evidence.

With a glance at his watch, David saw he'd taken longer than he expected. It was already after ten. Had he been too legalistic? His language had been clear; he'd stated his case. Time to move on, take notes on what Saunders had to say, and form his rebuttal. God knew he wanted to win this case—*needed* to win this case.

Saunders stood for his opening statement and, with a chuckle, strolled to the panel's table. "Well, gentlemen of the Cleveland School Board, you've just been subjected to quite a lecture. It sounded like the plaintiff thought you all were uninitiated into what these hearings were about, when in reality, he is the uninitiated one."

The board members chuckled along with him.

"As Mr. Svehla has told you, the Superintendent of Schools has dismissed him on the grounds of 'good and just cause,' which covers, and I quote, 'situations that may not have precedent, but would necessitate a teacher's dismissal.' Thank goodness this case has no precedent."

He held up a manila envelope thick enough to hold a few pieces of typing paper and shook it as he continued his remarks. "This sealed envelope contains the confidential information the FBI has sent me. It constitutes reasonable doubt that Svehla is loyal to the United States. I'm sorry that I can't share it with you, as it's highly confidential. I can say that the FBI, our nation's guardian of security, deems it very serious, and so do I. Surely a man with the file of a subversive should not be allowed to teach our children."

Evans said, "Hear, hear."

Patek stared at David, shaking his head.

"This country is engaged in a Cold War that could result in the destruction of us all. Each week, our children are practicing civil defense drills that force them to crouch under their desks. We hear daily from our president, our congressmen, radio and television commentators, and the press that there are hundreds of U.S. citizens who are passing information to the Soviets. We may well have found one of these, right here in Cleveland." Saunders actually sneered at David as he strolled back to the defense's table.

David's rage bubbled into his mouth, and it was only with the greatest fortitude he suppressed yelling *Liar!* Swallowing hard, he scanned the board. Would they take Saunders' word for it? Could his fate already be decided and this hearing a sham?

Lorelei Brush

The members leaned in toward each other and spoke in whispers.

Glanz announced a ten-minute recess.

After the recess, the board members filed into the room chatting. All David could hear were short comments like "I agree," and "Look's bad."

David called his first witness, the Superintendent of Schools, Gordon Bradford. The stately man in his fifties with a face that television viewers would love strolled through the double doors at the back of the room and greeted each of the board members by name. David ground his teeth. Nothing like a hostile witness to start with, but he had no choice. His dismissal came from the superintendent.

Bradford took the oath, promising to tell the truth.

"Mr. Bradford, would you take us through my case, starting from when you received a memo suggesting I be fired—labeled Exhibit 1?"

Bradford folded his hands and settled back into his chair, the picture of confidence. "I found the memorandum on my desk the morning of July 26 and forwarded it that afternoon to Mr. Paul Broz, the principal of John Adams High School, with a recommendation that you be dismissed. I think you have my recommendation as Exhibit 2. He followed through with the formal letter of dismissal to you on July 28."

"Was there a way to identify who sent the memorandum that appeared mysteriously on your desk?"

"My secretary attached a note to it, saying it was hand-delivered. She was told it was extremely important and I should attend to it immediately." He spoke with a hint of boredom, as though this information was trivial.

"And who delivered it?"

"She didn't get a name, just said he looked official."

"Do you get a lot of these blind memoranda?"

"No. But when I do, I pay attention."

"Could you give an example of another time you received a similar memo?"

Bradford sat forward in his chair and lectured. "Such memoranda are confidential, Mr. Svehla. I couldn't possibly reveal the details of any other issuance."

"Who do you think they're from?"

Bradford shifted to look at Saunders, who nodded. David assumed it was an okay, as opinions were admissible in a hearing of this sort.

"I thought it was likely from the FBI."

"And why would that be?"

"Just a hunch."

David had a bit between his teeth and was not letting go until his witness gave him some definitive information. "Did you check with their office?"

"Yes, I did."

"And what did they say?"

"They said they had a file on you with damning information." He drew out the last two words, as though making sure David heard every consonant.

David swept on as though Bradford had missed the point, determined to get at the insubstantial nature of the evidence. "Did you ask to see that file or what the information was?"

"I asked if I could see it and was told it was confidential."

"Is it your practice to follow suggestions in blind memoranda and those made over the phone?"

Bradford sputtered as he sat forward. "I consider that insulting. In my position, I'm expected to use good judgment in making decisions, and in this case, with corroboration from the head of Cleveland's FBI, a highly respected federal agency, I judged it correct to move forward with the dismissal."

"How often have you acted on such information in the past?"

"Objection!"

Startled, David slewed around.

An angry Saunders stalked his way to the board's table. "The superintendent isn't on trial here. Mr. Svehla's question is impertinent and irrelevant to his case."

David squared his shoulders as he faced the board. He was fully the lawyer at this moment, standing up for his client and brooking no interference. "It's very pertinent. If mine is the only instance he's ever acted upon, it's important to understand the reasons, to know why my case is special. If there are other, similar cases, it'd help to understand how his follow-up actions are similar or different."

Before the board could confer, Bradford raised his hand, waving it slightly. "Members of the board, I don't mind answering. You see, this case is unlike anything else I've encountered. I acted as I saw fit."

David considered asking Bradford if he worked for the FBI, but this was already a hostile hearing room, and David was afraid any more questions would just make things worse for him. He was a mere teacher; Bradford was the man in charge. Underlings should not be questioning their superiors.

Saunders had no questions, so David called Broz, his principal. Knowing this milquetoast for the coward he was, David considered—for a moment—bullying him. But that too was likely to backfire. Better to stick to the facts.

"Mr. Broz, would you describe your reaction to the letter you received from Mr. Bradford on July 27 concerning me?"

Broz shifted in his chair as though unable to get comfortable. "Well, I was surprised. I had no idea there were these issues with you."

"And what did you do then?"

"I called you. I felt you needed to be warned of your impending dismissal." He straightened his spine, looking more like the man in charge.

"And then?"

"Well, as I was instructed by Mr. Bradford, I prepared the official letter of dismissal. I should say that I talked with the board's lawyer about the proper language and cleared the letter with him." He nodded at Saunders.

David faced the board. "Mr. Broz's letter is now Exhibit 3, and my request for this hearing is Exhibit 4. Mr. Broz, would you summarize, please, the appraisals of my teaching ability over the years I've been at Adams?"

"Your ratings have always been high."

Saunders stood. "The defense accepts that Mr. Svehla has been an effective science teacher. There's no need to review the ratings and comments he's received."

How clever of Saunders. He was making sure the majority of the time in this session was devoted to potentially problematic issues and giving David little leeway to glorify the positive. So, David returned to his chair.

Saunders rose, smiled at the panel, and strolled over to the witness. "Mr. Broz, thank you so much for coming today. I just have one question. Have you ever had a problem with Mr. Svehla?"

Broz glanced quickly at David. "Well, yes. He's been missing more days of school than he should have."

"And what did you do about that?"

"I reprimanded him."

"So, he hasn't always been a model teacher?"

"No."

"Is there any other instance you'd like to tell us about?"

Broz shrank down in his seat, out of David's sight line. "It's not really a problem exactly." He sniffed, leaned sideways to get a handkerchief from his pants pocket, and wiped his nose. "But . . . um . . . one time he picked up a student, threw him against the wall, and punched him. It didn't look good. It's not the way teachers are supposed to behave."

Dennis Rogers went on high alert at this admission. Chet had reported that Rogers was a policeman, a Democrat, had a passel of children, and had spoken out about the recent spate of rumbles in the high schools.

"Objection!" David yelled, standing up. "Mr. Broz has not provided the context. He's made it sound like—"

Saunders held up a hand toward David in the stop gesture. "I'll restate the question. Mr. Broz, please describe this event. Clearly, the plaintiff feels you have misstated what happened."

Broz retreated further into his chair, if that was even possible. "A group of students had gathered in the corridor. David reported to me later that he'd been told a rumble was planned and had come to disperse the crowd. When I heard the ruckus, I called the police."

"This was certainly a problem for you, I can see that. We don't like attacks in our schools."

The members of the school board nodded their agreement.

If they only knew the seriousness of what was happening in their schools, they'd be appalled at the state of affairs. When was the last time any of them had been in Adams? And here they were, sweeping under the rug the threats to students, the bullying, and the weekly rumbles. David ground his teeth: he had to hold tight to his temper, be the lawyer and not the accused.

Broz shook his head several times. "No, sir, we don't like these rumbles. Parents come to talk to me, and they're angry. We get a bad reputation in the community."

David wasn't sure if Broz was saying he, David, was creating the bad reputation or the kids in the rumbles.

"And we don't want that." Saunders sat down.

David rose. He stared for a moment at Rogers, in the midst of the row of Board members.

"Mr. Broz, were there weapons involved in this rumble?"

The handkerchief came out again. "Well, yes, the ringleader and a couple of others were described to me as having knives."

"And was it the ringleader I am supposed to have 'picked up and thrown against a wall?' Your words, sir."

"Yes."

"What happened to his knife?"

"I guess you took it away."

"Was I armed?"

"I don't think so. I wasn't there."

"So, did the rumble proceed?"

"No, no, it stopped. The police arrived. And I had to deal with them, and then the ambulance men, and then the parents, and then the . . ."

"Yes sir, you had a lot to do." David paused, debating with himself about where to end this testimony, where it would benefit him most. He decided to clarify one more issue. "Sir, when you said Adams was getting a 'bad reputation in the community,' were you referring to me, to the school as a whole, or the rumbles?"

"Everything associated with rumbles."

"So, not me, in particular."

"No, no."

David looked at Rogers, who seemed to size him up a little differently, perhaps with respect. "I've finished my questions for this witness."

Evans turned to his fellow panel members. "Shall we break for lunch? Resume at 2:00 p.m.?"

Nods all around.

As the group reconvened, David detected the lethargy that came with the consumption of alcohol at lunch. The next witnesses on his list were fellow teachers: Newton Rider, who'd substituted for him in his physics classes; Mrs. O'Keefe, the English teacher who'd spoken for him after the rumble; and Janice Hanuchek, who had been his English teacher when he'd been a student at Adams and was on the verge of retirement. They were assembled on a bench in the hallway outside. David had said hello and thanked them for coming before he re-entered the hearing room. He liked them all, and he knew they might just put the board members to sleep. This was awkward. The lawyers of the defense team relaxed in their chairs as though they were on chaise lounges instead of scarred wooden chairs. He decided it would have to be the teachers next; it just made sense.

Evans called the room to order and gestured to David to continue his arguments.

"Gentlemen, I'd like to turn your attention to my teaching evaluations from the past several years, labeled Exhibit 5. As you read through these, you will see such comments as 'An energetic and inspiring teacher;' 'Contributes to the school not only by teaching but also through his coaching of the baseball team;' 'Good relationship with students;' 'Respected by students for his knowledge of the sciences and his classroom interactions–'"

"Mr. Svehla, the defense has already stipulated that you are a fine teacher." Saunders faced the board members and smiled. "There's no need to continue this recitation of skills, is there, gentlemen? We all have many other valuable ways to spend our time than on something about which there's agreement on all sides."

With shaking heads or waves of hands, the board agreed.

David turned to the bailiff. "Would you relay the message to the teachers that they need not stay?"

The bailiff strode out the door to do his duty.

So much for David's friends who had taken a precious day off to support him. He'd have to apologize to them. Seemed to be his primary communication these days, apologizing.

David bowed his head a bit to the board. "Thank you for that stipulation. It's important to understand that the school system will lose a good teacher if this dismissal holds." He paused, letting the thought sink in. "I'd like to clarify what happened in that incident described by Mr. Broz. My next witness is Officer Perry, the first policeman on the scene the day in question."

A fit man in his mid-thirties clad in full uniform, strode to the witness chair. After establishing the day, time, and place of the attempted rumble, David asked for a description of what the officer saw.

He sat at attention, presenting a picture of the consummate investigator. "Three of us answered Mr. Broz's call. We all work in the neighborhood and know the school. We'd been there before to break up fights. As I ran down the corridor, I saw the alleged perpetrator—whose name I won't mention as he's a juvenile—slashing at Mr. Svehla with a knife. When I got to them, the knife was on the floor and the boy in no condition to cause problems. It was a fine example of defensive fighting."

"Thank you for the compliment."

"Well, we police have a tough job in that neighborhood. Things'd be a lot worse if civilians hid and let the toughs have their way."

"Yes." David turned to Saunders. "Any questions for this witness?"

"Officer, I want to commend you for your service. We're all a lot more comfortable knowing the police force is available should any incident like this one occur. Now, I'd like to explore what happened after you arrived. What was the state of the young man alleged to have started this trouble?"

"He was shaken up, bleeding from one elbow. And his lip split."

"Was that from a blow administered by Mr. Svehla?"

"Yes, it was the deciding factor. After a solid jab hit his face, the teen slid down to the floor and chose to stay there."

"Was he sent to the hospital?"

"Yes. We called an ambulance. It's good to make sure there's no serious harm done."

"So, am I correct in saying that Mr. Svehla assaulted a student and sent him to the hospital?"

"I would say the student assaulted Mr. Svehla and ended up in the hospital."

Several of the board members smirked.

"Is this the kind of behavior we want from our teachers?"

With a perfectly serious face, the policeman replied, "In my book, it's exactly the sort of behavior we want. He risked his life to stop what could have been a fight with serious consequences for a number of students."

Saunders patted the ledge separating himself from the witness. "I'm afraid I would much prefer the police to take care of such matters."

Officer Perry sat with lips pursed until dismissed.

It was after 1500 hours, and David was worried. He wanted to end the day on a high note, a strong argument for his side of the case. But he had three more witnesses out in the hallway, each of whose testimony would build on the others, and he wasn't sure there would be time for all of them. Well, he'd have to risk it. After all, the board had already agreed its time was too valuable to waste on this upstart Svehla. He called Lee White, the editor of the *Plain Dealer,* who was also here as a hostile witness.

"Mr. White, there've been a series of articles in your paper about me, correct?"

"Yes, you created quite a stir with your interruption of that important ceremony at Case."

"Following coverage of that ceremony, there was a string of follow-up articles on me, right?"

"Yes, several."

"And where did the information for those articles come from?"

"I have my sources, and as I'm sure you know, they're protected."

"So, there isn't any evidence to which you can point with certainty? No evidence you could show this hearing for any of the so-called 'facts' of those stories?"

White grinned and looked across at the board members. "I'm sure you gentlemen know the press doesn't ever reveal its sources."

"Did you search for corroborative evidence from an independent source?"

"I made a couple of phone calls, yes."

"And could you describe the conversations?"

"No." He smiled and folded his hands. "They're confidential."

David could not let this man go without pressing further; he couldn't bear the arrogance. "Have you ever published a story that turned out not to be entirely accurate?"

White sucked in his breath. "Not knowingly."

"But it's happened?"

White exhaled audibly. "Yes. And if we do, we publish a correction."

"How do you discover the error?"

"Sometimes a staff member catches it. Sometimes a reader writes in, one who knows the subject well."

"I see. So, these articles had some clear facts that could be checked by readers."

"Well, yes."

"How interesting this is. I am accused of subversive behavior, and the alleged evidence is largely 'confidential.' How can anyone, editor or reader, be expected to make a fair and just judgment from blind memoranda and innuendo?" David raised his arms in a questioning gesture and trudged slowly back to his chair. He'd expected the stonewalling from White, but as he searched the faces of the board members, he couldn't tell if they got his point and agreed. It looked like a bunch of stoics behind the table.

Saunders rose, approached the witness stand, and shook hands with White. "Good to see you again, Lee. I'm only sorry it's under these circumstances."

"Yeah."

"So, in this country we have something often called the yellow press. Can you tell us what that is?"

"Ah, sure. It's those poor-quality papers that write false stories just to increase their readership, often painting very graphic images based on little information and lots of hyperbole."

"And is the *Cleveland Plain Dealer* one of those?"

"Heavens, no. We are a respected publication with awards to prove it. I wouldn't have anything to do with that type of paper."

"So, you would swear to this court that the material your staff put together for those articles came from reliable sources?"

"Absolutely."

Saunders, all business, retired to his corner.

David took that punch, stood up, and called Mac to the stand. As they'd discussed, Mac appeared in military uniform, complete with a chest of medals and commendations. They'd rehearsed this a number of times, as Mac had only a high school education and was nervous about speaking before these well-educated elected officials. He'd said they were worse, in his mind, than anything the Germans had thrown against him in the war.

"Mr. McKenzie, Mac, could you tell the board about our service in World War II?"

"Yes, sir. We were both members of the Office of Strategic Services. You served with the rank of captain; I was a technical sergeant. We spent most of the last year of the war working together."

"And, during that time, how would you describe my loyalty to the U.S. and my opinion of Communism and Communists?"

"Your loyalty was absolute, sir. I never had a doubt. I can't imagine your being a Communist. You've said many times how much you hate them Russians, how strongly you wanted the U.S. to turn around and declare war on the Communists, right then in 1945."

"And now?"

"I still don't have a doubt. When you share days and nights of fear and action in wartime, you get to know each other inside and out."

"Thank you."

Saunders cocked his head as he made his way to Mac. "You were a sergeant you said, and David was your senior officer?"

"Yes, sir."

"And you had a pretty close relationship?"

"Yes."

"Did you ever have to lie in the OSS?"

"I suppose. If we were interrogated, we'd have to lie. That didn't ever happen to me."

"Did you practice lying, you know, like in training?"

Mac screwed up his brow. "Well, there was a part of training that concerned what to do if you were caught."

"So, you're not unfamiliar with the concept."

"Everybody knows what a lie is. But what does that have to do with Cap'n Svehla? I haven't lied about him."

"It's a question of whether you're a creditable witness. But let's move away from that. Exactly what did you two do in the war?"

"That's classified, sir. We signed an oath when we mustered out that we wouldn't ever talk about what we did."

"So, we must accept your testimony, without a shred of physical evidence, that Mr. Svehla is loyal and not a Communist?"

"Yes. I am under oath, and I don't take oaths lightly."

Saunders turned away, shaking his head as though he found it impossible to believe this man.

This was not working out well, but David gritted his teeth and called Major Fleming, the senior officer in his reserves' unit. In just a few moments, they established David's rank and that the major had no reason to doubt his loyalty. "Did you read the stories about me in the *Plain Dealer?*"

Major Fleming, also in uniform, appeared at ease. "Yes."

"And your reaction?"

"Well, I was surprised. Maybe confused."

"And in the end?"

"I decided the articles were filled with accusations without clear evidence."

"And have you acted to have me dismissed from the reserves?"

"No, I only do that under orders."

David nodded. "Do you know Senator Karl Mundt, who represents the state of South Dakota?"

"I know who he is. He's a big part of the House Un-American Activities Committee."

"What do you know of him?"

"He chaired the Army-McCarthy hearings in the spring a year ago. Very impressive, they were."

"So, what happened at those hearings?"

"Well, they were supposed to see if the army was clearing its ranks of subversives. They came to a climax with an exchange between Welch, the Army's Counsel, and McCarthy."

"That would be Attorney Joseph Welch and Senator Joseph McCarthy, right?"

"Yes. Welch challenged McCarthy to deliver the lists of subversives he claimed to hold. McCarthy wouldn't do it."

"And then?"

Fleming grinned. "McCarthy brought up the fact that Welch had a member of his own law firm who was a suspected Communist."

"How did Welch react?"

"He turned around and accused McCarthy of something like cruelty. When McCarthy continued to talk about the young lawyer, Welch cut him off with this now-famous statement, 'Have you no sense of decency, sir?'" Fleming imitated Welch's irritated voice.

"And can you see that such questionable tactics are being used on me: innuendo about my character and no clear evidence of guilt?"

"It sure looks that way to me."

"Thank you."

Saunders passed David as he strode to the witness stand. "Do you know what Mr. Svehla did in the war?"

"I know it's classified. That's true of many of us."

"So, you have no proof of his loyalty."

"As far as I can tell, you have no proof of his disloyalty."

And on that pronouncement, the board decided to end the day.

As David filled his briefcase, he smiled to himself. He wanted to hug Fleming for ending the day with a standoff—not that he'd ever embarrass the guy that way.

And then the board caucused for a few moments. They called Saunders and David to their table and clarified that the board would reconvene the hearing on the following Tuesday morning since the next Monday was Labor Day.

David called Grace from their kitchen telephone, suppressing his anxiety at their FBI listeners, and reviewed the day's hearing. "I did the best I could, and I have some hope. I think I impressed Rogers, the policeman, and Glanz, the lawyer. It's going to be hard, but we've got to keep thinking this'll work out."

"I guess. Um, I have news, too. The Baptist church here on the square has an opening for church secretary. I can't type very well, but I think I can manage easy letters, and I'll like the interactions with parishioners. I won't make enough for us to move out on our own, but we'll be able to pay something more to Ben and Frances. She and I are making the children's school clothes, but I'm afraid there won't be anything extra for you."

"I'll manage. The car brought us another $1,250. It's money in the bank."

David replaced the receiver, feeling beat down by the difficult day and depressed by the conversation. A knock at the door caused him to turn around. Jacob and Len stood outside.

David hoped this was good news, as he had to turn his worry around and do some hard thinking about the rest of the hearing.

Jacob limped to a kitchen chair. "May we sit down? I should like to find how are you. The hearing was good?"

Bless Jacob. "It was probably as good as I had a right to expect. Not as good as I had hoped."

The men took chairs around the table, and David served coffee. He thought Len looked out of place as he sat, fidgeting.

"David, Marvin Glanz is a good friend, a lawyer I've worked with often, and a member of the same temple as Jacob and I. He called me right after the hearing adjourned."

Feeling a shiver of excitement—someone on his side?—David called himself to task. Len wouldn't be making such nervous movements if all were well. "What'd he say?"

"You made some good arguments, and he said he could see your training as a lawyer showing."

"That's good, isn't it?"

"Yes and no. It would be good in a court of law with a judge who knew the law, knew what due process meant, and could instruct a jury."

David's excitement dissipated and dread remained.

"Apparently, in their recess and lunch breaks, the other board members thought you were showing off and somehow putting them down. Certainly there was conversation that you embarrassed the superintendent. This caused some resentment. I think they want a humble, penitent man. Marvin said that they liked the jollying along they got from Saunders—not that it would work for you. Also, Marvin'll do what he can, but playing your part will be key." He pointed at David. "Be respectful but firm."

Jacob put his hand on David's arm. "Have faith, my friend. You can do anything. I know it."

"By the way," Len added, "Did you know Saunders was ex-FBI?"

CHAPTER 16
SEPTEMBER 1955

David sat at his desk, batting his pen against the sheaf of notes he had for day two of the hearing. He had to get through his anger that the arguments about due process were shoved away as unimportant. He tried casting the arguments in different words, exploring analogies that would resonate with the board or stories to illustrate why due process was critical to U.S. law. This whole approach just wasn't working.

What else did he have? It was no good to contest the paper's silly accusations against him—the misconstruing of his story at the VFW, for example—and no use bringing up the FBI break-in of his house. The board might well feel such an action was justified. When he'd reviewed everything he could from Williams' list, he hit snags there, too. It didn't make sense to bring up the Owen Lattimore case. The major evidence that the man was a Communist came in the form of blind memoranda. He had that in common with David, but Lattimore hadn't been cleared of the accusation. He'd won on a technicality. Frankly, there were way too many confidential sources and classified facts in this investigation. It was teetering on the question of who to believe.

September 6 dawned a colorful, early fall day. The cool air cheered David as he made his way to the garage. The sick, green Hudson that hunkered down inside, however, depressed him. His shiny Studebaker—collateral damage from this case. He shook his head as he gave the car a pat. Maybe, if the board members saw him in this heap, they'd feel some pity for him? Not likely.

All five members of the board who had attended the first day of the hearing returned for the second, along with Saunders' team. The defense looked freshly scrubbed and eager, while the board members seemed annoyed, like they'd much prefer to be somewhere else. David opened the session by calling Peter Kittridge, his across-the-street neighbor. At least he could let the board see he hadn't participated in any illegal entries. He stood, steeped in his confident attorney role.

"Peter, do you remember the Saturday last February when your wife had taken the children sledding and her house key slipped out of her pocket?"

Peter smiled and rubbed his hand over his balding head. "Hard to forget things like that."

"Tell us what happened."

"Linda, my wife, took the two boys—they're two and three years old—to that big hill in Cain Park. They had a great time tipping over in the snow and got soaked. It wasn't 'til Linda got home and checked her pockets that she discovered she'd lost the house key. The boys were shivering and probably complaining. I was off running errands. So, she found you."

"And what did I do?"

"You got your fancy keys—the ones from the war—and let them in."

"Have I ever broken in when not asked?"

He glanced over at the line-up of board members and shook his head. "No, never."

Saunders rose for his cross-examination. "Have you read the articles about David in the *Plain Dealer*?"

"Yes."

"So you know there's a question of his loyalty to this country?"

"Yes."

"Have you seen anything suspicious regarding David's behavior?"

"Not that I can think of."

"Have any foreign-looking people entered his house?"

Peter screwed up his face and raised his arms in a gesture that said he didn't know. "I suppose. His family's Czech."

"And these foreign-looking people go into the home, right?"

"Yes. You know, relatives do that." With this comment, he sounded annoyed.

"Are you aware that Czechoslovakia is behind the Iron Curtain?"

"Of course."

"And Communist?"

"Yes, but these people live in Cleveland. They're Americans."

"And do they have relatives behind the Iron Curtain?"

"I don't know. You'll have to ask David." He seemed to be dismissing the question.

"Aren't you worried about David's loyalty?"

Peter winced and shifted in his seat. "My family background is Estonian, and Estonia is also behind the Iron Curtain. I don't know all the details about David's family, but if your criteria for loyalty include no foreign-looking visitors and no relatives behind the Iron Curtain, I'm in trouble, too. Personally, I hate the Russians for what they did to my family and my country. I'm loyal to the U.S. and grateful to be here."

"Thank you. If I may summarize, then, you can't testify, without question, to his loyalty."

"I have no reason to question his loyalty. And I can say for sure he's never broken into my house without being asked."

"Back to the loyalty business. Your answer was that you don't know about David's loyalty. Right? Please, just answer yes or no."

Looking from right to left as though seeking guidance, Peter answered, "No. I guess not. Not for sure."

Saunders turned away, nodding as though assured he'd won that round.

The second neighbor told a similar story about David's alleged "break-in" of his house, an action he said was described inaccurately in the *Plain Dealer,* and Saunders again pushed the witness on David's loyalty. Same result.

Believing he'd made his point on this issue, David announced that he wished to take the stand and make a statement. Once under oath, he chose not to sit in the witness chair but to face the board, to pace a little, and radiate humility.

"At this critical time in the Cold War, we need to find the subversives in this country and root them out. With the visit of Don Jones of the FBI to my house, it was clear that I was of interest to them as a possible subversive. May I add here that I requested the presence of both the head of Cleveland's FBI and Mr. Jones at this hearing? They have chosen not to appear, but you have the testimony of the superintendent of schools and myself as to their interest in me.

"What I have done is show all of you that their accusations—and those in the papers—are truly innuendo and not fact. First, it's true that my heritage is Czech and I probably have relatives behind the Iron Curtain. But I don't know them. I don't even know any names. My family emigrated to the U.S. in the 1850s. And I'll bet most of you are members of families of immigrants. It's common in Cleveland. And that means most, if not all, of us are connected to people who live abroad—the Poles, Hungarians, Czechs, and Estonians—who got left behind. Does that make all of us Communists? A ludicrous assumption. Second, I didn't break into any neighbor's house; I helped people in need, as two of my neighbors have testified. These alleged 'break-ins' have innocent explanations. So, let's focus on the critical reason for which I'm here—the question of my loyalty to the U.S., a question that arises from my confrontation with Professor Adler, and the FBI's response, their choice to use blind memoranda and innuendo to suggest that I am a subversive.

"I'm hoping you all watch Edward R. Murrow, that excellent television commentator." He scanned the board's faces and saw nods. "I refer you to two of his broadcasts, one on October 23, 1953, and the second on March 9, 1954. The transcripts of those broadcasts form Exhibit 6, which you have all had a chance to see. Each of these transcripts criticizes the tactics of Senator McCarthy, tactics that are also being used on me. On the earlier show, Murrow described what had happened to a soldier named Milo Radulovich, who was discharged from the service following McCarthy's investigation of his loyalty. Murrow affirmed that the committee made their decision based on vague charges, testimony from anonymous informers, and guilt by association, as his father was a Communist. Do you remember that?"

Again, the board members nodded, though Evans' eyes went to Saunders before he joined in. Glanz was smiling.

David wondered for a moment what Saunders was thinking over there at the defense's table and how long he'd let this explanation go on. Then he let the thought go. This was his last chance to persuade all those stoics at the table. "Let me turn now to the second broadcast, the one from March '54. I'd like to quote from the script: 'Two of the staples of his—McCarthy's—diet are the investigation, protected by immunity, and the half-truth.' Murrow then describes two investigations using these tactics and concludes with, and I quote, 'We must remember always that accusation is not proof, and that conviction depends upon evidence and due process of law. We will not be driven by fear into an age of unreason.'"

David paused, evaluating the thoughtful expressions on board member faces. He was doing well. One more item to go. "Gentlemen, I'd like to turn your attention to Exhibit 7. It is a memorandum from J. Edgar Hoover to all of his offices, a memo sent in March of this year."

He paced to the center of the board's table. "Let me summarize it for you. Five months ago, Hoover asked all his agents to stop using blind memoranda or anonymous letters, that is, to halt the sort of innuendo that has been used on me. Apparently, the Cleveland office of the FBI didn't receive this memo or has chosen to ignore it. I am presenting it here to underscore the fact that there's no hard evidence against me that anyone has presented in this hearing. Everything you have heard is merely circumstantial evidence or innuendo, not fact. It's time to stop this murdering of character and return to our country's Constitution and its requirement of due process." David absorbed Glanz's slow nods, turned, and took the witness chair.

He stared for a moment at the clear blue of the sky outside and fought the sense that, try as he might, he was losing—that, at some level . . . well, he ought to lose. The U.S. had to go after potential subversives; it had no choice. But he was innocent and a proud man. He would fight to the end.

Rising slowly to his feet, Saunders ambled over to face David, Exhibit 7 in his hand. "I'm curious about this memo, Mr. Svehla."

"Yes?"

Saunders scanned it slowly from top to bottom. "Are you sure you didn't write this yourself? How could you possibly have obtained a real FBI memo?"

"I'm afraid the source must remain anonymous, but the memo is real. I'll swear to that."

Glanz cleared his throat. "A moment, please, Mr. Saunders. I've seen J. Edgar Hoover's signature several times, and I believe this signature is real. I realize I'm not a handwriting expert, but that is my opinion. And if I may, I'd like to point out that we do have an expert in this room. You worked for the FBI prior to joining the Director of Law's office, didn't you?"

Saunders squinted at Glanz, clearly unhappy with the question. "Yes, I did."

"So you must know Hoover's signature."

"I'm afraid I'm not an expert on handwriting either." His emphasis on "either" sounded like a put-down.

David was careful not to move a muscle to detract from the board's focus on Saunders.

"Duly noted," said Glanz, "but your educated guess?"

Saunders paused for several seconds, staring at the memo. "It could be. Or it could be a forgery."

He turned abruptly back to David. "Let's get back to that fundamental problem you talked about—the meaning of your confrontation with Professor Adler. You said you did it out of 'moral outrage.' I believe those were your words."

David nodded. "That's correct."

"Were we not at war at the time you claim to have met Dr. Adler?"

"Yes, it was April of 1945, not long before V.E. Day."

"People do things in war they would not consider doing during peacetime, Mr. Svehla. Surely you know that?"

David wanted to wipe that fake smile off Saunders' face. "And some people, in wartime, go far beyond their orders to commit acts that constitute crimes against humanity. For those, we held trials at Nuremberg and other locations. I would argue that Adler should have been tried then. I'm not privy to the details of how he escaped, but I could not let him go unpunished."

Saunders opened his mouth, but David held up a hand. "I'm not finished. It is important to remember what my friend, Jacob Strauss, went through at Adler's hands. I've heard the horrors of Jacob's life in Dora, and for those alone, Adler should be punished. That bully left my friend permanently maimed and in pain—seemingly for fun, or just because he could get away with it. 'Moral outrage' is exactly what such actions should provoke in all of us."

Saunders sighed and shook his head. "Another lecture. As though we were the ones here facing dismissal." He indicated himself and the row of board members, and then pointed at David. "It's you who have the problem, you who have no evidence you acted as a loyal American in confronting Adler, or that you will act in complete loyalty to the U.S. in the future. In fact, you broadcast the idea that our U.S. of A. acted in a nefarious manner in not trying Dr. Adler and in offering him a job in this country. That accusation shows disloyalty to the country you say you swore allegiance to. You seem to doubt the morality of your leaders and commanding officers. I'd call you a subversive right now, and I'm very troubled by what you may do next."

David leaned forward, speaking slowly and clearly into the silence. "None of us knows how we'll behave in the future. But intention matters, plans matter, our goals for our lives matter. My goal is to have a stable job, provide for my family, and live in the country that follows the rules of due process."

"Fine words, counselor. But we're very worried about your plans. And I, for one, am too nervous about your loyalty to take your word that you are an innocent. I'm siding with the FBI on this matter, without a doubt."

Saunders pivoted, picked up the manila envelope from his table, and held it above his head as he returned to face David. "Mr. Svehla, this is not flimsy evidence. Admit it."

"No, sir, I cannot. I believe the FBI have used innuendo to get me dismissed from my job because they have no evidence to prove my disloyalty."

Saunders shook the envelope. "So, you're saying that the evidence contained in this envelope is false?"

David took a few moments to calm himself and choose his words. "Since I don't know what's in that envelope, I can't say whether it's false or true."

"What you are doing, Mr. Svehla, is questioning the actions and veracity of a respected part of our federal government. How dare you?" He smacked the side of the envelope with his left hand. "The FBI is charged with our national security, and they are very worried about *you*."

With those words ringing in their ears, the board adjourned for lunch. David sat at a café table and stared at his food. The acid in his stomach gurgled. The implications of the hearing were daunting. That envelope Saunders kept flaunting had grown to mythic proportions. David was losing, no question. The flimsy envelope was crushing him. Okay, maybe the country needed Adler, but this was extreme humiliation for David.

He tried a spoonful of soup. It threatened to come back up. He had to face it; he had no chance. How naïve he'd been, going into the Adler confrontation! The FBI was going to shut him up out of fear that he'd search out other Operation Paperclip scientists, expose them as Nazi criminals, and create such a hue and cry that all of them would be returned to Germany—or accept jobs in Russia. The U.S. would lose the Cold War, face potential annihilation. He put down his spoon and stared into space.

He threw down some bills to pay for his uneaten lunch and walked the blocks around the courthouse, feeling the stiff wind of fall coming off the lake. What was going to happen to him? To his family? Yes, in the war, David had proudly called the U.S. flag 'the banner of the right,' as that Grand Old Flag song said. But he didn't believe the U.S. was *right* to have brought all these Germans over. Sure, the country needed their scientific knowledge, but the country had sold out its own versions of law and human decency by admitting criminals like Adler. Had it vetted the others and just missed Adler? Or turned a blind eye to their actions in the war? As he slogged up the courthouse steps, he decided that, right now, all he could do was make it through the afternoon. Later, he'd figure out his future, which was looking ever grimmer.

When the hearing resumed, Saunders called the president of Case Institute of Technology, lavished praise on his education and exalted position, and ran through with him what happened at the Adler confrontation. "What has been the aftermath of that act of public humiliation?"

Clearing his throat, the president said, "It's had some serious consequences. Professor Adler has been most upset, has threatened to leave us, and I have spent considerable time and university resources ensuring he stays. I had thought we might lose the joint program with the Lewis Labs, which is critical for the university to bring its science labs up to modern standards, but that now seems to be coming along nicely. That afternoon was horrible for me, just horrible." He jiggled his head and a shiver ran down his body.

"Did you believe the accusations?"

"Mr. Saunders, I am president of a fine university, and I have on my faculty an excellent professor in Dr. Adler, and many other fine faculty of German extraction. I have no evidence of any disloyalty to the United States on the part of any of these faculty members, and Adler, in particular, is a keystone in helping this country win the Cold War. That's what I care about. What he did in Germany during the war is past history, better forgotten."

"And why do you think Mr. Svehla made those accusations?"

"The only answer that comes to me is that he wants the U.S. to fail in this war."

"You mean, that he is a subversive."

"Yes."

"Your cross, Mr. Svehla."

David stood slowly and, arms at his side, did his best to appear non-threatening. "Sir, do you have any evidence, other than the opinion you stated, that I am a Communist or desirous of using force and violence to overthrow the U.S. government?"

"I saw what was written in the newspaper."

"Perhaps I should have said first-hand evidence, data you've gathered yourself?"

"No, I hardly know you."

"Thank you."

Saunders faced the board. "I had planned to bring in more witnesses to the Adler fiasco initiated by Mr. Svehla and more professors from Case to swear to Adler's importance to our victory in the Cold War. But I know you're all smart and busy men. We've heard what's important, and we know it's true. The defense rests."

David had nothing more to share. He and Saunders made their closing statements, really only pro forma. Afterward, the board members filed out to decide his fate, and he sat in his wooden seat, hands folded on the table. He'd given every bit of energy he'd had and it wasn't enough. He and Grace would lose the house, and what would she think of him? A loser who couldn't even defend *himself*. Hildie popped into his mind asking "How could you lose, Daddy? Good guys win." Davy sure wouldn't understand. "Didn't you find the other guy's weakness, like you told me to do?" Well, he'd tried.

After less than an hour of consideration, the board returned to the hearing room, looking solemn. With a grumbling voice, Evans stood, straightened his suit coat, and asked David to stand.

David had that familiar sense of the hairs on the back of his neck standing at attention. All eyes watched him rise before focusing back on Evans.

"Mr. Svehla, the board has voted four to one to uphold your dismissal. You are no longer an employee of the Cleveland Board of Education."

While Saunders shook hands with his team and schmoozed with the board, laughing and giving David sideways glances, David stuffed the remaining files into his briefcase, hefted it off the table, and strode out of the room.

CHAPTER 17

SEPTEMBER 1955

All the way home from the hearing, David stewed over how to tell Grace. He wanted to talk to the Grace who listened, who understood him, the one who believed the world was wrong in treating him like a pariah. The Grace he loved. Not the woman who was moving away from him, the one who was building a life apart from him, the one who couldn't see the sense in his actions. If only he could give her some good options, define an acceptable future for the family. But he wasn't sure he saw any. Still, putting the conversation off was no good. A phone call wouldn't do. He needed to be able to see her, see how she reacted to the news that he'd been canned for good.

He passed right by their street and set the car on the path east for Chardon. It'd be after dark by the time he got there. They'd all have finished dinner and not be expecting a visitor, but he couldn't waste time stopping to phone.

Hildie spotted him first and ran into his arms, backing him against the door with a thud. "Daddy, we didn't know you were coming."

"I wanted to see you, and I couldn't wait." He waved from the entry hall to Ben, Grace, and Davy, still sitting around the kitchen table with a game in progress. From the look of things, Hildie was winning. Ben waved back, no obvious emotion on his face. Frances nodded, picked up Ben's coffee cup, and headed to the pot on the stove. Davy had his fist under his chin and looked up with surprise. And Grace. She half-rose, anxiety showing in her creased forehead and tensed shoulders.

Hildie pulled on his hand. "Daddy, Daddy, Ben made me a horse jump. Want to see me take Minnie over the jump?"

"Not right now." He glanced down at her excited face. "It's too black out there. Minnie couldn't see."

"Oh . . ." Hildie slumped, still clinging to his hand. "You staying overnight?"

He ruffled her hair with his free hand. "Not tonight."

Davy snuck in front of Hildie, holding out a new Hardy Boys book. "I'm on page 174, Daddy. I read it all by myself."

David held out a hand to Grace, who had slid back into her seat. When she didn't stand, he picked up Davy's book, *The Secret of the Old Mill.* "Pretty big gears in that mill wheel. Might be one around here."

Ben grunted. "Yup. Near the cider press."

David glanced at a frozen Grace and patted Davy's shoulder. "Looks like I'll have some time in the next few weeks. Maybe we can go see it."

"You'll take me?"

"Yeah."

Davy whirled around. "Mommy, did you hear that? We're going to a mill."

Grace slowly stood, eyes fixed on David. "So, you lost?"

David herded the kids back into the warmth of the kitchen. "I lost, even though I fought like hel—heck. I think they had to dismiss me."

Grace covered her mouth with her hand. "What are we going to do?"

David wanted to take her in his arms and reassure her that everything would be all right, but he wasn't sure it would be and he wasn't going to lie.

Hildie prodded his side. "What do you mean you lost?"

David bit his lower lip and squatted down, pulling Hildie toward him. "You know people have been calling me a Communist, right?"

She nodded.

"Well, the school board was afraid those people were right, and we all don't want Communists in our schools."

"But you aren't a Communist."

"That's correct, but they decided they couldn't take a chance."

She stamped her foot. "That's not fair!"

He hugged her. "I know. But that's what happened."

Lorelei Brush

"You want me to tell them the truth?"

David grinned at her. "I bet you'd do that real well. But, no. We gotta figure out somethin' else."

"Hildie," Grace said, "it's time for you and Davy to get ready for bed. One of us will be in to read to you in a few minutes. Go on now."

Davy stopped partway toward the stairs and turned back. "It's okay, Daddy. Don't feel bad. We all lose sometimes."

David sucked in his breath. His eight-year-old consoling him. He blinked to stop incipient tears, watched the kids hassle each other about who got to be first into the bathroom, and then faced Grace. "Come on. Get your coat. We can talk outside."

She raised her eyebrows at Frances, who said from her position at the sink, "Don't worry about the children. You go talk." She pulled a kerosene lamp off an open shelf. "Here, take this with you."

A chill wind blew the dried leaves at their feet as David and Grace headed to the barn. Grace let the lantern swing as she walked, and David wondered whether Ben and Frances couldn't afford a flashlight. Maybe they just liked the old things. "It must be ten degrees colder here than in town." He zipped his army jacket and turned up the collar.

Grace was silent until he heaved the barn door shut behind them. Then she set the lantern on the floor, and in its glow, he could see her rigid shoulders and lined face.

"I'm not moving back to Cleveland Heights, David. I won't put the children through that. When everyone hears about all this, it'll be awful."

He reached for her. "Grace, you know I'm not a Communist." He ached for that time, right after the war, when she'd kissed him full on the lips and called him her "hero."

She pulled back, not allowing his hands to touch her. "That's not the point. Everyone will avoid us or give us the cold shoulder. How can we go to church? How can I send the children to school? Friends will shun us."

He dropped his hands and closed his eyes for a moment. "I'm sorry it's all turned out this way. I think we can tough it out. We won't be news for long. It's not fair, as Hildie says. But, well, I still have some clients, I still . . ." He couldn't go on with a rosy projection.

She crossed her arms over her chest and took two steps further into the gloom, facing away.

David picked up an old horse blanket, shook out the grit, and laid it on the dirt floor. "Come, sit down. Let's talk."

"I don't want to sit down. I'm too angry, angry with the situation, angry with you." She paced across the space, from horse stall to milk cans, pulling her coat closer. "Why did you have to go through with this? Why did *we*? Couldn't you have thought, ahead of time, of the consequences? You're so ready to fight, aching to push in where you're not wanted, willing to take silly risks. I'm tired of it all."

"Look, I'm as angry as you are. I'm pissed at the board for accepting innuendo without proof. It's wrong. It's not the law." He paused, sucking in his pride. "You're right. I like risks. And I'm probably too ready to fight. But I never meant to scare you. It never occurred to me we'd be run out of our home."

"I'm not scared, not now. I'm angry! You've torn up our lives. I lived in the same house from the time I was born until we married. It was a stable home, a good life for a family. Children need that stability. Our children need it."

"I'm sorry. I didn't want—"

"I know, I know. You didn't *intend* any of this. It's just your nature."

He sat down on the blanket, mulling over the weight of his guilt and his simmering anger at her lack of sympathy. Leaning back against the wall of Minnie's stall, he grimaced at the strong odor of manure. Grace paced. When she turned toward him, he patted the blanket. "Please, Grace, please come talk."

She sighed and joined him, settling down with both legs tucked to one side. "All right. I'm listening."

"I did well in the hearing. I asked good questions. I gave strong opening and closing arguments. I showed I can be a good trial lawyer. And I want to try. We've talked about it before. I know it's a risk for me, not having a secure paycheck. But it might bring a big reward."

"A reward? David, you might not even be allowed to practice law."

"That's true. But, hon, lawyers like concrete evidence, and there isn't any about me. They'll see that. I don't think I'll be disbarred."

"Maybe. But what about us, the children and me? I have the job at the church. The kids like the school here and have friends. I don't want to move us again, not on the off chance you'll find clients who aren't afraid to employ you. And I'm not going back to Cleveland Heights."

He stared into the dancing flame, hating the idea of giving up the house they thought they'd live in forever, hating being at odds with Grace. Maybe she was right, at least about where to live. Perhaps starting in a new place would be better, easier. Why not try Chardon? "How about we sell the East Scarborough house? Maybe we could rent here, see how it works out?"

She tore a piece of straw into tiny bits.

"I could sign up with the court in Chardon, get assigned cases where guys can't afford a lawyer, make a name for myself. Maybe Ben and Frances will recommend me to friends."

She ripped up more straw. "I suppose. Well, if anyone says they need a lawyer. And will hire *you*."

"Heck," he said, his own energy getting behind the idea of settling in Chardon, "you're related to half the people in this town."

She flicked at the bits of straw, chasing them off the blanket. "Oh, David. I don't know, and I'm too cold to debate it. I want to go inside. Maybe we don't belong together anymore."

"You don't believe that, do you? Please, stay. We've got to thrash this out."

She stood, hands on hips. "I don't want to. I don't think you can live in a sleepy town like this one. All I see is your continuing unhappiness and your taking it out on the children and me. What I see is a divorce in our future, and maybe we should just decide on that now."

"Grace, I don't want that." He scrambled to his feet and reached for her hands.

She pulled them away. "I've tried to be supportive, to believe in 'for better or for worse.' I've worked at seeing your point-of-view, why this whole Adler thing was so important you'd risk your job, our home, our happiness. What I see is a hugely selfish man, and I'm not sure I want to be with someone who doesn't care about the harm he's doing to his family."

"I do care . . . about *everyone* in the family. I try to be a good husband and a good parent. I think that means being honest and, sometimes, fighting for what I believe in."

"And where has that gotten us?"

"I hope it'll bring us together. Make us a stronger family. Solidify our beliefs in what the government should stand for, what we stand for."

"That's so like you. An intellectual belief system that somehow misses the feelings."

"I haven't ignored your feelings. I'm well aware of them. And I'm sorry you've had such a rough time. But I'm proud I stood up to the authorities."

"And are you proud that we're practically bankrupt and having to beg relatives to put a roof over our heads?" She started pacing again.

He rubbed his forehead. This was way harder than he'd anticipated. "Grace, look at me."

She stared at him, unflinching.

"I love you. I love our kids. I promise I'll try my best to be a success as a country lawyer. I'll work my tail off to get clients, take all the shit they shovel my way. I'll hate the humiliation, but I won't let that show. I'll make you proud."

She sighed. "I'm too angry to decide anything now. I'll think about it. That's all I can offer."

Back in Cleveland Heights, David sat alone at the kitchen table nursing a tepid cup of reheated coffee, sunk in this prison of his own making. Doors seemed to have slammed shut around him, and he wasn't sure he could be a country lawyer. Was he going to lose Grace in all this? God, was Adler worth it?

Grace. Not able to accept his offer to move. He rolled his cup from side to side and watched the grounds shift.

A knock on the glass of the back door roused him. Jacob lifted a hand in greeting. David dragged himself to the door. "I'm afraid I won't be very good company."

Len stood beside Jacob, hands tucked in his coat pockets. "Okay if we come in?"

"If you want."

The men shed their coats. Jacob pointed at the cup in David's hand. "Is there any more of that?"

"Oh, yeah, I think so."

David emptied the coffee pot's contents into a small saucepan and put it on the stove. He ordered himself to pay attention to his guests. He didn't have a lot of friends left. When their cups were poured and on the table, David sat down, resolved to listen.

"So," Jacob said, "it was bad, n'est-ce pas?"

David nodded. "Four to one against me."

"That is sad."

"Yes."

Len spoke quietly. "It was Marvin who voted for you."

"I guessed that."

"He said to tell you he was sorry it turned out as it did but that it was inevitable."

"Yeah."

"Not because he thinks you're guilty or should have been dismissed, but because people are scared. He's seeing their fear encroach on their legal judgments, not just in your case."

"Okay." He made his voice lift at the end of the word.

Len took a deep breath and leaned forward on the table. "He was impressed with your research and arguments. He thinks, with a little honing of your skills, you'll make a fine trial lawyer."

"Yes, um, thank him for the compliment." David pushed that recalcitrant lock of hair out of his eyes. So nice that Len had come to relay the message. Good that Glanz thought well of him. But how did this get him out of his present hole? "There's still the issue of my being disbarred."

Len shook his head. "You won't be. Too many lawyers don't like this McCarthy approach to justice."

"Thank God for that."

"I know it's little compensation for you right now. But there're a whole lot of attorneys in town who admire what you did, standing up for due process."

David blinked at impending tears. "That's good to hear. I've been feeling left out to dry."

Len stood and extended his hand. "Thank you. Thank you for standing up for justice."

David stood as well and shook the outstretched hand. "Thanks for coming, Len. And thank you and Marvin for the support."

David saw Len out and turned back to Jacob. "It was good of you to bring him by."

Jacob smiled. "Come, sit. I must talk to you."

David slid back into his chair. "What is it?" He didn't think he could take much more, even sympathy—especially sympathy.

Jacob put both hands on his knees and sat up tall. "David, I must thank you. You do not know it, but you helped me face my greatest fear. Perhaps it is because of the prayers we will say in these High Holy Days, but I have lost a great burden. You know it is that time in our year? Rosh Hashanah and Yom Kippur."

A wave of embarrassment swept over him. He'd been meeting with a group of Jews for months, and he'd forgotten their holidays. How selfish, when they'd worked so hard for his cause. "I'm afraid I haven't been paying attention."

"Ah, of course. You see, facing Adler has changed how I look at the world. He is bully, and I am strong since I stand before him. I know there is no need to forgive him. He is not sorry for what he did. Enfin, I must look into myself. I see now there is balance of strength and weakness.

Maybe I have forgiven myself for my weaknesses. Today, I do not live in hiding. My nightmares are less frequent. Rebecca, too, is sleeping better." He chuckled. "It is new life for us. Because of what you did."

Tears again prickled in David's eyes, and he worried he'd embarrass himself in front of his friend. "But *I* didn't do all that for you."

"Yes, David, you did—you made it possible. You convinced me to face Adler; you stayed by my side so I could not change my mind. It is your strength that made me strong." His eyes bored into David.

"Well, you're welcome." He was, for once, at a loss for words and embarrassed to boot.

"You have changed the way I look at America. It is good country. It allowed me to come, to be electrician, to have family. Now, I also see it is not perfect. What it has done to you is not possible to forgive. I am sorry you are hurt."

Jacob was right there, too. It did hurt. It hurt a lot. David sighed and gave Jacob a weak smile. "It's been a surprise, all this. Not the U.S. of my dreams either. Perhaps I'll be a better man, maybe a better lawyer for it, if I get the chance. You'll have to give me time on that one."

"I wonder, David, if the trial you have faced will allow you to forgive yourself?"

"Forgive myself?"

"I brought you a bar of chocolate. Perhaps you are ready for it now?"

Tears stung David's eyes as he stared at the large bar of Hershey's milk chocolate. Isaac. Had this whole exercise been about his killing that poor man? Had he done enough to make up for the life he had taken? He had certainly sacrificed over this Adler affair, sacrificed whole pieces of his life. "You're a very wise man."

Jacob rose, and David did, too, expecting to walk him to the door. Instead of exiting, Jacob took hold of David's arms. "In France, we do this to say thank you." He kissed David on each cheek, giving him four salutes.

With his hand on the doorknob, Jacob said, "Forgiveness frees us. It is what I wish for you, too."

David sank into the nearest chair, allowing the tears to crawl down his face. He pulled his handkerchief out, wiped his face, and blew his nose. He'd put the chocolate in his briefcase, see if he could bring himself to eat it.

Two days later, in mid-afternoon, David sat at his desk in the sunroom considering the advice of a neighbor who was a real estate agent. It looked like they'd make good money on the house. They'd bought it for $3,000 in late 1945; she'd estimated it would sell for $12,000. Should he put it on the market now or wait and see? Wait for what? The board to see the light and reinstate him?

He reached for the phone to call Grace and realized she'd be at work. But with his hand in the air, the phone rang and he picked it up.

"Mr. Svehla, it's Gladys Thompson." She was hyperventilating, gulping air between syllables. "I just heard from the police that Joe's getting out next week. You gotta do something. He's going to kill me."

An image of Gladys on the hall floor with blackened eyes, swollen face, and broken leg flashed into his head. David had succeeded in having Joe jailed for the attack on his wife, but the man must be getting out early. Without alcohol, he'd probably been a model prisoner. "Gladys, please, sit down, take a breath. You know panicking isn't healthy for you or the baby. Calm down now. Where is the baby?"

"Sleeping."

"Now, I want you to take a deep breath and let it out nice and slow." The rasping sound of a thin stream of air came through the phone line, followed by the hiss of exhalation. "That's the way. Do it again. You're doin' fine." He paused to allow time for another good breath. "You know, when I was in the army, they used to yell at us to breathe. There we were, facing an enemy who could strike at any moment, and we're being told to breathe. Seemed pretty dumb, but it did make a difference." He couldn't remember any officer saying this stuff, but he thought she needed something harmless to think about, and her breathing was softer and more regular now.

She laughed, a little huh-huh that seemed half-hearted. Still, she wasn't panting into the phone anymore.

What he'd said had worked. It hit him, like a slap to the head. He could do this, talk people through their crises, free them from their inertia. "Let's review where we are. The court has issued a restraining order, so he shouldn't come near you or the baby. Right?"

"Yes, but he ignored those before." Her voice got strained again, the pitch higher.

"Gladys," he said, needing to raise the big question, "we've talked about your filing for divorce. How do you feel about that now?"

"I love him, but I'm scared. I . . . I don't know. Maybe I won't be after a few months, if he stays off the booze. He's supposed to get help. The judge said so."

"But—here's the thing—can you trust that he'll stay sober?" David spoke calmly, spreading out his words so she'd have plenty of time to think about them.

"I . . . I don't know." She took several fast breaths and didn't speak for a long time. "I guess I'm just not ready for a divorce."

"Then let's work on keeping you safe. Can you move in with your parents or your sister for a few weeks until you see how he's doing?"

"I hate to bother them."

"I know, it feels kind of weak, almost like begging, and it's inconvenient, but we need you safe. And we don't want anything bad to happen to your daughter, right? You two deserve to be safe and happy."

She breathed more slowly for a minute or so. "I could call my sister, I suppose."

"That sounds good. Very good. You call her tonight, right after we hang up. Okay? And let me know what happens. Call me tomorrow. I'll be here."

She sighed. "You're very kind to me. Thank you. Thank you very much."

David took his own advice and inhaled deeply as he hung up the phone. He'd listened, suggested some actions, and got her agreement. He could do this kind of work. Give people a path forward. Now, he had to convince

Grace—and, frankly, himself—that he could make a living from it. He needed a good, solid plan.

On Saturday afternoon, David drove out to the farm on his regular weekly visit, feeling better about himself than he had in a long time—in fact, since right after the Adler confrontation. When he pulled into the drive, Ben came out of the barn, shovel in hand. He waved, so David strolled up the track to meet him.

"Tough week, eh?"

"Yeah, I hit bottom, I'm afraid."

"Happens sometimes. Shovel?" He held the tool out toward David.

"Ah, sure. Why not?"

Ben used gestures to show how David was to clean Minnie's stall and went to milk the cows. David contemplated this option of shoveling shit for his future, and a smile crawled across his face. Once was okay. As a daily event, forget it.

When Ben came by to check his work, David leaned on the stall door, wondering if now was a good time for his proposal. Ah, what the heck. "I've been thinkin' about you and Frances."

Ben raised his eyebrows.

"You've been so good to us. I can't thank you enough. But I watch you doing all this physical work. And I ache from helping for half an hour. How long will you be able to keep the farm going? What's your long-term plan?"

From the flash of anger that passed across Ben's face, it looked as though he wouldn't answer. But with a sigh the anger dissipated. "None of my kids want to farm. I guess I'm holding on because I love this place so much."

"I can understand that."

"Been bothered by several developers."

"And?"

"What do I know about real estate? Nothin.'"

With this opening, David sucked in his gut and stood tall. "I'd be pleased to help you deal with them, pleased to offer my services as negotiator and get you the best deal possible."

Ben screwed up his eyes and stared at David for a full minute.

"It'd be my thanks for your help to Grace and the kids."

"Well, where do we go, Frances and me? We don't know no other place."

"Where would you like to be?"

Ben's eyes drifted upward, unfocused. "Small house, room for a garden. The edge of town."

"We could do that, find you a house. Or maybe get one built."

"Let me talk to Frances. Fact is, she's wantin' to sell. Maybe, with your help . . ."

"You have it."

Ben nodded and disappeared with the milk pails.

David scraped his shoes on the edge of the stall door, evaluating the conversation. It was humbling, not being the teacher but a penitent. Asking favors of a man far less educated. But he'd done it and nothing bad happened.

Grace peered into the dim barn to call them for dinner and shook her head at him. "Come on in when you're cleaned up."

He smelled pork chops frying and spied the big corn pot when he entered the kitchen. Thick tomato slices lay in a circular pattern on an old, flowered plate, probably picked that afternoon.

"Daddy," Hildie said, looking up from setting the table, "when did you get here? You didn't come tell me."

"Ben set me to work mucking out Minnie's stall."

She glared at Ben, hands on hips. "That's my job."

He shrugged his shoulders.

David thought Ben was suppressing a grin as the older man wiped his mouth. David raised his hands at his daughter in a pantomime of retreat. "That's fine with me, sweetie. I won't do it again. That's a promise." Then he met Grace's eyes and saw a smile in them.

He walked over to the table, slung his coat around the back of his chair, and registered the dull thump of Jacob's candy bar as it hit the back of the chair. He'd forgotten he'd stuck it in a pocket, thinking it would be a treat for the kids. Grace set down a plate of steaming corn, and he stopped her with a kiss. "Can you sit down now? Listen for a minute?"

She nodded, her body stiffening. But, David noted, she didn't object. He sat down next to her, forearms on his knees. "I been doing a lot of thinking about the future and what you said about liking it here."

"Yes?"

Frances turned the heat off under the chops, and the kitchen grew quiet. Even Hildie and Davy seemed to understand that something big was in the air.

"Well, you see, Gladys called again—you remember her, right? I had to stop her husband beating her."

Grace nodded, slowly.

"I've done her some good. See, she was scared; her husband's getting out of jail. I calmed her down, got her to make a couple of decisions to be safe. I could do that kind of thing here. Help people in trouble. Make sure they get a fair shake."

Davy had his elbow planted on his book. "You mean we can stay? My friend Elijah will like that. And there aren't any bullies in my school."

David had to smile at that conclusion, after only a few days of class. Maybe Davy was right—or maybe he was getting better at fending them off.

Hildie, danced up to Ben and pulled his sleeve. "I could ride Minnie every day, right, Cousin Ben? And brush her? And clean her hooves and her stall?"

The older man nodded. "Let's hear from your mother about this."

All eyes turned to Grace, who smoothed her skirt and folded her hands on her lap. "You know moving here, starting over, won't be easy for you. There'll be people who won't accept you. Word travels, and Cleveland isn't that far away."

"I know. I'm not going to like being snubbed or cut out of things."

"No, you're not. How are you going to react?"

"I'm working on patience. And humility." He paused with a smile. "I'm sure I'll get mad from time to time. And I'm sure you'll let me know if I seem to forget myself."

"And for work? It's hard to come by out here."

He glanced up at Ben. It wasn't time to reveal their discussion. "On Monday, I'm gonna sign up at the courthouse here to be assigned to prisoners without counsel. Then, I'll introduce myself to the shop owners in town."

Ben interrupted. "I 'spect I know them all."

David looked up, surprised. "That's great. I'd like to meet local lawyers, too. Maybe find a partner, an office."

Grace seemed to be lost in thought, just nibbling at her lower lip. "I do hear stories from parishioners sometimes about their problems. Perhaps I can mention you."

"I . . . I think I can do this, with the family as partners." David smiled at them all.

Grace didn't smile in return. "What about Adler? Are you done with him?"

David sat back and looked at the expectant faces. "I've done what I can. I let people know what he did. You know, he's in something like my own position, hoping the recent to-do will blow over. Oh, some people'll shun him. Like me, he'll have to work through that."

"Can you live with him having a great job and fine house while we've been forced to sell ours and you have to search for a job?"

David sighed, still holding onto some jealousy. "I'll have to. Heck, if Jacob can let go of the man—and he says he has—then I should be able to, too."

She slid her hand down the side of his face. "All right, then. Let's do it. We'll live around here, try something different."

He wished they were alone so he could show his pleasure—and his relief—in the return of *his* Grace. He settled for a big smile and a tight hug.

As they sat down to eat, he looked over at his wife, his head tilted a fraction. "I got some good news about the house. We can make a profit if we sell."

Frances rested her eyes on Grace and then turned to David. "My parents' old house, the one at the corner of North Street and Woodin Road, has been vacant for a while. But it's a good price, not too high, and I know the family wants to sell."

"Grace? What do you think?"

She wiped her lips with her napkin, let her hands fall to her lap, and looked out the window. "Why don't we drive over there after dinner?"

"Can I go? Please?"

David laughed at Hildie, never wanting to be left out. "We'll all go. Make it a family outing."

CHAPTER 18

FEBRUARY 1982 – MARCH 1984

David stomped his feet on the outside mat before walking into the kitchen. The thaw had begun, and he didn't want to leave sloppy footprints across Grace's clean floor.

His graying yet still beautiful wife came into the kitchen from the laundry room carrying a stack of his shirts, all neatly ironed and folded. "The mail's here. There's an envelope with a Washington postmark you might want to take a look at. It's marked personal."

He raised his eyebrows. The last time he'd got a personal letter from the capital was twenty-seven years ago. Who'd write him now? About what?

Without taking off his coat, he strode to the buffet in the dining room and picked the white business envelope from the basket. No return address. He dug under the flap and ripped open the envelope.

Two paragraphs. Signed by *Bruce Williams*. His eyes flew to the substance.

Dear David:

I hope your law practice is doing well, though by now you might have retired as I have. I think of you from time to time with sadness that your good intentions in reporting Adler had to be crushed back in the '50's. We needed the help of those German scientists in the space race, and you were part of the fall-out from that decision. Well, times have changed. Recently, a friend of mine in the Department of Justice told me they'd opened a new Office of Special Investigations (OSI) to find Nazis who "persecuted individuals on the basis of race, religion, national origin, or political opinion" and are living in the United States. In general, if a judge agrees that their crimes fit this description, the accused can be stripped on his U.S. citizenship and deported. I thought immediately of you. The DoJ staff in OSI are very interested in having a conversation.

Adrenaline tore through him like a tsunami. "Times have changed" was an understatement. Just like Williams. Not a man to exaggerate.

I don't want to build expectations that are unrealistic. The Office can only win its case to deport a Nazi if it has clear documentary evidence (not hearsay) that the individual committed atrocities. I think you can help.

Yours truly,

Bruce Williams

P.S. Your oath not to speak of what you did holds for OSS actions. Since the liberation of Dora was an Allied responsibility, not an OSS mission, you may give details of that action.

Grace touched his arm. "What is it? You're still as a statue."

"An invitation to help deport Adler."

Her hand covered her mouth. "My God. Is he even alive?"

David growled. "Oh, yes. Livin' in the same house."

"You've been checking?"

"I've just looked him up in the phone book every couple of years."

"Is this going to be another public affair? Is this going to take up all your energy, like the last time?"

He pulled her into a hug. "You've been begging me to cut back on my legal work since I turned sixty-five. Maybe this is my excuse. Oh, don't worry. It won't be full-time. It won't consume me. We won't be run out of Chardon. I'll just send some information to Washington, maybe help with the legwork."

She pulled away. "Will you drag Jacob back into it? He's almost eighty now and frail."

"Grace, I'll ask him. It's his choice."

David unlocked his office door at 8:00 the next morning and, as expected, was the first to arrive. His partner, Ron, slept in whenever he could, reminding David of his son, Davy, as a teenager. That kid could sleep until mid-afternoon. Ron hadn't yet outgrown that urge, though he was over thirty, the "junior" partner in the practice. Janice, their administrative assistant, always breezed in on the dot of nine.

Jacob, too, was a man of habits. Even in retirement, he rose at 7:00, breakfasted at 8:00, and was on the road to some volunteer activity by 8:30. David lifted the receiver and dialed. "Jacob, got a surprise for you."

"David, it is surprise that you call me at all."

"Aw, it hasn't been that long." They laughed, an old joke between old friends. "I got a letter yesterday from my old OSS boss."

"What?"

"Turns out the Department of Justice is going after Nazis who persecuted Jews, and Adler's one of their targets. I'm gonna call the Special Operations folks and volunteer to help, and I wanted to talk to you first about being a part of this. What do you think?"

Jacob didn't speak for a minute. "What must I do?"

"I don't know for sure. I expect we'll be interviewed. They'll ask if we have hard evidence. If we know anyone else who was at Dora. Stuff like that."

"Will this be in public?"

"No, no. Just one, maybe two investigators. It'll be informal. We'll tell what happened. What we know about Adler. They might ask us to write it down. But the whole process is not open to public discussion."

"Rebecca will not like this."

"Because the nightmares may come back?"

"Oh, she does not worry for herself. I do not kick her any more. She worries for me, like you say in English a 'mother hen.' Will I return in my head to that time?"

"What do you think?"

"I must talk with Rebecca."

"Jacob, whatever you decide is fine with me. I won't press you."

David carried that promise in his head for several days, ordering himself not to call Jacob again. It was his to decide if he still wanted to shame Adler as much as he did back in the fifties. He'd said then he could let the whole episode go as part of his past. Perhaps he couldn't open it all these years later. Rebecca would probably advise him not to participate. David chafed, wanting a decision now. The stress roused him in the middle of the night.

On the Friday, three days after the initial call, Jacob rang him at home. "David, I have decision. I must do this. For me, for all those at Dora—and for you."

"Rebecca's okay with it?"

"She is not happy. But she is okay."

Tears pricked David's eyes. "Thanks, thanks again. I'll let you know what parts we'll play after I talk with the folks in Washington. And give my best to that wife of yours."

David shivered with excitement. He'd been putting off a call to Mac and the big one to OSI, wanting to be sure that Jacob, the one who could describe first-hand Adler's activities in Dora, was game. A short call to Mac made sure that old coot was a part of this crackdown, and a quick 411 call tracked down the phone number for this new DoJ office.

"I'd like to talk to someone about a man I understand you're investigating for his participation in genocide: Dr. Gerhardt Adler, a German rocket scientist."

"Let me connect you with one of our historians, Gretchen Bauer."

"Historian?" He thought he'd be talking to a lawyer.

"Yes, sir, she's a top-notch researcher. We need them to provide context. You know, people forget what Germany was like in the war. The judges we go before are often too young to have any experience of it. Our historians present a clear context for them. Also, Gretchen speaks fluent German, so it's easy for her to read the relevant documents."

"Well, okay."

A young woman answered. She sounded a lot like Hildie's classmates at Wellesley. "Good morning, sir. I've been meaning to talk with you, on the suggestion of Bruce Williams. It's great that you called."

And David told her his story of liberating Dora, chasing down Adler in Germany, and discovering him again in Cleveland Heights.

Gretchen took copious notes and stopped his story several times to catch up. He paused often, as he did for the court reporter when she seemed to be running behind. Once he'd run through his own activities, she had a host of questions. "Mr. Svehla, it sounds as though you can supply hearsay about Adler. Can you provide any hard evidence of Dr. Adler's actions?"

"Yes. First of all, Mac McKenzie, my sergeant at Dora, lives here in Cleveland and will corroborate what happened at our liberation of the camp. Second, my friend, Jacob Strauss, was a prisoner in Dora. He's also here in Cleveland and willing to talk with you. His limp, from an injury inflicted by Adler, provides hard evidence to the man's barbarity."

"Excellent. Now, do you know or have any information on whether Adler resisted orders to starve or beat prisoners? Was anyone threatening his family, forcing him to commit these atrocities?"

He could tell she needed to make sure Adler wasn't coerced, that he'd done these acts of his own volition. "Not that I know of. All the Dora paperwork was hidden before I got there. But our Allied forces may have found it later."

"That's okay. I think Jacob will be a great resource for us. We'll see what we can find."

David paced the room the length of the phone cord. Maybe this was it. Maybe this time they'd get the bastard. "You want us to fly to D.C.?"

"No need, sir. We'll come to you."

Two weeks later, two DoJ investigators arrived in Cleveland for the interviews. They scheduled David, Mac, and Jacob, and then Len Barenholtz from the temple group and Marvin Glanz from the school board.

Presumably, they also talked with Adler, though they didn't share their actions with David. He had a good talk with Mac about his interview and heard from Jacob about the others.

David reported it all to Grace, having learned his lesson well not to leave her out of important matters. She wasn't pleased that he was bringing up the affair again, but after almost fifty years of marriage, she accepted that this was something he needed to do.

His patience was severely strained. Would they be able to deport Adler? He started each day in his Chardon office or in the local court, but if his schedule showed a free afternoon, he drove back into Cleveland Heights and cruised down Fairmount Boulevard to see Adler's house. No more VW bug in the driveway. The family had graduated to a BMW. But he verified Adler still lived there—saw him weeding the garden. His hair had lost its color, and when he rose to dump his basket of weeds, David noted the hump in his upper back and the paunch that rounded the front of his pants. The Nazi was an old man. No martial stride. In fact, his halting steps made him pathetic.

That old anger at his dismissal and being called a Communist stuck in David's craw. Old man or no, Adler'd committed crimes against humanity and deserved to be punished. In the rush of knowing that Grace would hate his initiating a confrontation, he stopped the car and got out. "Herr Adler!"

The old man squinted, obviously having no idea who David was. "Yes?" A tentative word, not an invitation to engage in conversation, but David wasn't waiting for one.

"You may not remember me. David Svehla? We met in 1955, at the ceremony for your collaboration with the Lewis Flight Propulsion Laboratory."

Adler's face convulsed with anger. In pointing his finger at David, he thrust a handful of weeds at him. "You!"

David laughed at the clownish sight and felt his own anger melt. "Yup, I'm still here." And, slowly, with no more words, he strolled back to his car and drove away.

David dropped down on the newly-made bed and glanced up to see his wife's opened mouth. "Oh, sorry, I'll fix the spread later. I gotta tell you about today. Come sit for a minute?"

Grace took the chair across from him.

"Hon, I saw Adler this afternoon, out in his yard, and introduced myself."

"You did what?" Her hands shot up and cradled her head.

"Don't worry, please. No confrontation. You see, he was old. Decrepit."

A slow smile spread across Grace's face and into her eyes. "Are you actually feeling sorry for him?"

"A little. But, see, I couldn't yell at him. Couldn't muster the energy. He's not worth it."

A year later, David had still heard nothing about the Adler "case." He was raking the September leaves when Grace called to him that Jacob was on the phone.

"David, I received call today from the Department of Justice."

"Oh?"

"Adler has been convicted. They are going to deport him."

They'd done it. They had him. "Congratulations!"

"To you, too."

"Sleep well, my friend."

David grinned from ear to ear as he hung up the phone. "Grace? Grace? We did it! We got Adler."

She hugged him. "It's been a long time coming."

"Yeah, justice."

"I know I've pushed back on this at every turn, but please believe I'm glad for you."

"I do. God, it's over. All these years of waiting, of wondering if the people I meet still have me pegged as a Communist. I feel . . . vindicated." He pulled Grace into his chest. "You know, that whole episode was the making of me. The board hearing was the first time I knew I could be a good defense lawyer. Oh, I didn't like their decision or the feeling I'd been pushed out of Cleveland. But, you know, our move here has given me the chance I'd wanted. I've had a few big trials, put together a couple of great business deals, gotten to know the people in this town. I suppose I've grown up, too."

"Amen to that."

He chuckled. "I haven't made a national name for myself or a lot of money. But that's okay. I helped people keep their farms or, at least, benefit from their sales. I've settled divorces to let people get on with their lives. I've made a difference."

"I read that thank-you letter from Stella Staniszewski. You remember? She called you a hero."

"Oh, yeah." It was a little embarrassing. But he'd liked it.

"And?"

He kissed her. "I think I'd like a chocolate cake."

In mid-March 1984, David was lingering over his morning coffee to page through the *Plain Dealer*. In a small article buried in the front section, he spotted Adler's name. The paper briefly recounted his actions during the war, his time at Case, and his current status as an emeritus professor. And then one stark sentence said he had renounced his citizenship and flown with his wife to Germany.

David smiled. Perhaps he'd finally retire this June, in time for his seventy-second birthday.

HISTORICAL NOTE

The idea for this work of fiction came from six months of research into my father's OSS role in World War II. I thought I would be writing a spy thriller of his actions behind enemy lines as a Liaison Officer in the German Army, taking messages from one unit to another and surreptitiously reporting to the OSS. He'd told my brother and me endless stories about his heroics, reporting that he had the rank of Major in the German army, higher than his rank in the U.S. Army. One tale was about my name, which he claimed was his code name when he was deep in Germany. "Lorelei," he said, protected him in dangerous times, and he claimed it would also protect me. Imagine my surprise when I learned "Lorelei" was never used as a code name for an OSS operative, and my father was never behind enemy lines (let alone serving as a German officer). I could have been angry at his lies, but instead I felt relief. He wasn't the superhero of his stories, but a fallible human being.

In creating the scenes in this book, I researched the 1950s to find a way a man like my father might have satisfied his need for risk and his desire to be a hero. The resulting story bears no relationship to how he actually spent the 1950s: he never gave up his job teaching high school science, and his law work continued to serve the working poor and middle class of Cleveland. What I did find was an active fuels laboratory at Case Institute of Technology, a Case faculty with numerous German last names, and a busy Lewis Labs handling government contracts. These facts formed the basis of my plan to create a plausible sighting of a rocket scientist, though I have no specific evidence of any serving as professors. Adler and his work are figments of my author's imagination.

I also spent considerable time in the National Archives II, reviewing the OSS's wartime activities and especially those of the Target Forces. It is important to note that these reports do not include the discovery and liberation of any concentration camps. Rather, they focus on the specific targets (e.g., people, research facilities, and government buildings) that had been assigned to each Force. Dora was, in fact, liberated on April 11, 1945, by the U.S. Signal Corps, part of the 104th Infantry Division, Twelfth Army Group, which included a young photographer. A team of war crimes investigators followed the soldiers, and Allied scientists poured over the pictures, microfilms, and eventually the documents that were unearthed. I did not find evidence that OSS members were involved in the liberation, but because it made for a more intense story, I included them.

Operation Paperclip is well-documented, and for those interested in the details, I recommend Annie Jacobsen's *Operation Paperclip: The Secret Intelligence Program That Brought Nazi Scientists to America* (New York: Little Brown & Co., 2014). She estimates that 1,600 German scientists were brought to this country under the program.

The actions of Senator Joseph McCarthy and the House Un-American Activities Committee, along with congressional responses, have been amply covered as well. To delve into the details, I particularly recommend Ellen Schrecker's *Many Are the Crimes: McCarthyism in America* (Boston: Little Brown & Co., 1998). Over 200 public school teachers were dismissed from their positions because of accusations that they were Communists.

Finally, The Department of Justice established the Office of Special Investigations in 1979 to prosecute war criminals residing in the United States. They began with Nazis living in the U.S. and have expanded to include those from Bosnia, Serbia, Rwanda, and Darfur. With regard to the group of rocket scientists, only Arthur Rudolph, the deputy production manager at Mittlewerk, was returned to Germany.

Though I have done my best to accurately represent historical events, I may well have erred in some respects. All errors are my own.

ACKNOWLEDGMENTS

I am particularly thankful for all of the help I received from staff at the National Archives II in College Park, Maryland, for their everlasting patience in helping me find every possible reference to my father's OSS assignments in WWII. I ended up with a detailed calendar of his activities throughout the time he in was in the European Theater of Operations. I also must thank the archivists of Western Reserve University, who showed me pictures of Case Institute of Technology in the 1950s, including classrooms and staff, and talked through the curriculum. And I send great appreciation to members of the staff of the Maltz Museum of Jewish Heritage in Beachwood, Ohio, who were helpful in describing life in those years for their community.

To ensure that I appropriately described a teacher's dismissal hearing, I appealed to two friends who are lawyers: Randy Jonakait and Mary Pat Wilson. Thanks go to Randy for finding numerous relevant cases in Ohio and against teachers. My thanks to Mary Pat for providing background information on the differences between hearings and trials, and for reading and correcting relevant scenes.

I also wish to thank William Putt, a fraternity brother of my brother, for his information on life at Wright-Patterson Air Force Base in the 1950s. His father ran the program combining the work of German and American scientists at the base. Bill gave me several key facts, such as the lack of socializing between German and American scientists. Many thanks for searching childhood memories that had long been buried!

I had the opportunity to speak with a number of children of Holocaust survivors and one survivor through the assistance of a friend, Wendy Liebow. My thanks go to her for those connections, and also the connection to her father-in-law, who was the journalist covering the Nuremberg trials.

My deepest thanks go to my fellow writers who have read and reread drafts of this work. To Margaret Rodenberg, who has a canny ability to see the big picture and also respond to specifics that just aren't working. To Pragna Soni, who works at the Office of Special Investigations of the Department of Justice, for making sure I was correct in describing their work. And to Raima Larter, Susan Lynch, and Christine Jackson, many thanks for making it through every chapter and holding me to high standards of clarity, grammar, and good story telling. They tamed my tendency to say in many words what could be communicated in a few.

Finally, I'd like to thank my family: my father, who was the inspiration for the story; my brother, who believed to the very end that all Dad said was true; my nephew and niece, who have been curious about this tale and are waiting to see its final form; and my son, who is always ready to say "You go, Mom."

BOOK CLUB QUESTIONS

1. Though *Chasing the American Dream* is fiction, it is anchored by true government activities in the 1950s. Were you aware of the extent of McCarthy's actions, those of the House Un-American Activities Committee, and the degree of cover-up? What sorts of questions did these actions raise for you?

2. Prior to reading this book, were you aware of Operation Paperclip? In some ways, this reaction following World War II is similar to our reaction following 9/11/2001, when we passed the Patriot Act to suppress certain aspects of due process. Do you agree the government has been correct in these instances to respond as they did? How long should the restrictions go on?

3. There are certainly instances in which the U.S. government rightfully declares information to be top secret and not available to the public (e.g., names of potential terrorists, plans for anti-terrorism actions, negotiations with foreign powers, actions of spying). However, it is also legitimate for those of us living in a democracy to question how much is hidden and for how long. Where are the limits? What do you think should be hidden? What made public? When?

4. One central theme of this story is the pitting of a need for risk against the need for stability. The 50s were a time when people tended to put stability first. What is a healthy amount of risk-taking? Where are you on the range from "engage in risky activities whenever I can" to "love and embrace stability in all things?"

5. The two children in this story, Davy and Hildie, tend to embrace opposite poles of the risk/stability range, which may seem to reverse the stereotype of boys liking risky activities more than girls. Do we still impose those stereotypes on our children? How has the risk/stability range manifested itself in your family?

6. Another theme in the story is the idea of being able to forgive oneself for actions of which you are not proud. Did David's eventual ability to forgive himself seem realistic to you? Have you struggled with forgiveness or "letting go" as you think about your past?

7. In what ways do you see Grace as old-fashioned? Can you see your mother or grandmother believing and acting as she did? How well did she balance the family's needs with David's? How would you have responded to an obsession like his?

8. Looking back on World War II, we acknowledge the horrific injustice that occurred, and that Americans were slow to react to it, slow to admit Jewish refugees when the war ended. Looking to the future, where do you think our grandchildren will see our failures?

9. Who was your favorite character? Why?

10. This story emerged from my family history. Are there stories in your family history that you'd like to research? Any that might make a good novel?

ABOUT THE AUTHOR

After writing hundreds of government reports, Lorelei Brush has stepped into the glorious freedom of fiction. She loves to occupy a comfy coffee house chair and imagine her characters acting out each scene.

Chasing the American Dream is her second novel. It rolled from her pen following a six-month stint in the National Archives researching the role of her father in the Office of Strategic Services in World War II. He'd told his children exciting stories of his feats as a spy behind enemy lines, all of which turned out to be lies. She had to write about his quest to be a hero and how, when the war had not provided the opportunity, he might have used the 1950s to achieve his goal.

Her first novel, *Uncovering*, was set in northwest Pakistan. It was a work of love arising from her time among many gifted people committed to Islam as a religion of peace and helping others.

Along with two gentle cats, she lives outside of Washington, D.C. in a community of good neighbors, friends, and fellow writers. In her spare time, she reads novels, sings with a community chorus, hikes, and works out at the gym.